BAD SEED

BAD SEED

Jessica Eames

First published in Great Britain in 2019 by Trapeze
an imprint of The Orion Publishing Group Ltd
Carmelite House, 50 Victoria Embankment
London EC4Y 0DZ

An Hachette UK Company

1 3 5 7 9 10 8 6 4 2

A CIP catalogue record for this book is
available from the British Library.

ISBN (Mass Market Paperback) 978 1 4091 8976 3
ISBN (eBook) 978 1 4091 8977 0

Typeset by Born Group
Printed and bound in Great Britain by Clays Ltd, Elcograf S.p.A.

MIX
Paper from
responsible sources
FSC® C104740

www.orionbooks.co.uk

To Sophie Christopher

I wish you could be here to see this published.

Thank you for being a tiny ball of energy and constant writing champion, for your absolute, never-ending belief that I would be an author one day, and for always being the optimism to my pessimism. We used to read out our names in the acknowledgments of books with pride to one another, so I hope you would have loved seeing your name here.

I miss you and I will be forever glad I had you as a friend.

Prologue

I stare down at your coffin, at the sleek, dark, wooden box that hides your already decaying face, its shiny newness at odds with the rest of the graveyard. The minister's words wash over me as he tells us how much you will be missed, how much you meant to everyone here, how we must celebrate your life, all the more so after your tragic death.

Like mine, everyone's eyes are trained on your coffin, but they steal glances at me when they think I won't notice, watching me to get their cue on how to behave. If I am stoic and still then they will be, if I sob uncontrollably then it's OK for them to do so, too. I sniff and blink out a set of tears, feel them trace heat down my cheeks, taste the salt of them as they pool in the corners of my mouth. The eyes turn back to you.

You would have wanted this, I know. Wanted the classy coffin, its perfection hiding you at your worst, the crowd of friends and family to prove just how popular you were. The outdoor ceremony, heels sinking into grass underfoot, the breeze just cold enough to make us uncomfortable in our black funeral attire.

I did it for you, in honour of the relationship we once had, in honour of whatever love once existed between us. You should know that.

The minister finishes, closing his book and inviting me, along with the others who were closest to you, to be the first to throw dirt on your grave. I am not amongst those who say something about you, not one of those who stand there sobbing dramatically as they choke out their words. We discussed it, the family and I, and I said I couldn't bear to, that it would be too much, that you already knew what was in my heart so there was no need to speak it out loud. I couldn't have said what was in my heart, of course. Not in front of these people who still think you are deserving of their sympathy and love. I hope you know, though. Hope you know that I do not regret it.

After the ceremony I stand at the edge of your grave, looking down at the coffin now half covered by ground that will soon swallow you. People come up to me to murmur condolences, to lay a tentative hand on my shoulder, offer what they think are words of comfort as they mistake my stillness for grief. Those closest to me, the family in our inner circle, hover uncertainly for a few minutes more, but when I don't respond, when I let more tears streak down my face, they pick up on my desire to be alone and give in. They'll see me at the wake, they say, and leave.

I hold my back stiff until the voices fade into the wind, until all I can hear is the rustle of leaves, the faint chirping of birds, a far-off car horn. Until I know that you and I are alone. Then I smile.

All these years, you thought you'd got away with it, didn't you? You thought you'd take to your grave your secret. And I suppose you did, in one way.

I'm just glad I was the one to put you there.

PART ONE

—

Nicola

Chapter One

Blood for blood. You will pay for what you did.

Nicola's mind was blank as she stared at the words, typed in ordinary Times New Roman font, the text centred, taking up only the very top of an otherwise blank piece of A4 paper. It had been addressed to her in an envelope, also typed, alongside a letter from NatWest. Fiona, her sister-in-law, must have dropped them both off at some point when Nicola was out, given she didn't actually have her own postal address, here at the little annex in Fiona's garden where she'd lived since her husband's death nearly a year ago.

She reread the note, her lips parting to mouth the words. Her fingers gripped the page more tightly, the tips of them turning as white as the paper, as the reality of what she was seeing sunk in. The near-constant pain in her stomach intensified and the hot flush she'd experienced only moments before vanished, replaced by a cool dread that seeped through her, turning her blood so cold that it felt like tiny shards of ice were splintering her veins.

This couldn't be happening, it couldn't be real. There could only be one thing this note was referring to, and no one knew about that. No one. She'd been so careful.

She lowered the piece of paper, her hand shaking. The secret she'd kept buried, learned not to think about even when alone, whipped its way back through her, leaving her breathless.

She jumped violently at a knock on the door. 'Just a minute!' she called, her voice high and unnatural. She lurched across the kitchen, her bare feet sticking to the terracotta tiles, and tore the note up into tiny shreds, threw them in the kitchen bin, then dumped the rest of her tea in the bin on top of them just for good measure. Adrenaline was coursing through her, the need to do something tangible almost unbearable. But what? There was no return address, no way to know who sent the note. Maybe it was a prank, she thought to herself wildly, just a stupid joke someone was playing on her. But even inside her own head, that didn't sound convincing.

There was another, impatient knock at the door.

'In a second,' she snapped. She took a slow, deep breath, then opened the door, letting in a cool September breeze which whisked away the sweat that had formed on the back of her neck.

'I'm sorry,' she breathed, looking up into Phil's tanned face. Her boyfriend, for want of a more appropriate word for people their age. 'I just need to . . .' She trailed off, having completely forgotten what he was here for.

'Are you all right?' Phil asked in his low, gravelly voice. 'You look pale.'

'Yes I'm . . .' But she couldn't bring herself to say the word *fine*. Because she wasn't, was she? Not by a long shot. Not that she could tell him that, because if she did then she'd have to tell him about the note, and then he'd want to know what it was referring to, and she couldn't very well have that. God, the thought of what would have happened if Phil had arrived moments earlier – if she'd opened the envelope in front of him – sent anxiety clawing through her stomach.

She rested one hand on the doorframe to steady herself, and Phil stepped towards her, his eyebrows creasing into a frown over his deep brown eyes. She wanted to tell him to give her space, but a wave of intense dizziness swept through her, stealing her breath and making the garden behind him swirl into a mass of colours, green and brown merging with pinks and yellows. And red. Somewhere in there were bright red flowers, the colour of blood.

There was a ringing in her ears, then the ground underneath her gave way.

Nicola scowled at the pale wooden door in front of her, already regretting the decision to come even though she'd gone along with it when Phil insisted she get an appointment. Still, she was here now, had waited a good thirty minutes after her allocated time, so she squared her shoulders, knocked.

'Come in,' said a bored male voice.

She walked stiffly into the small room, wrinkling her nose at the warm air that smelled like antiseptic, bleach, and BO all mixed together. She focused in on the young man sat hunched over at his desk, tapping away on his keyboard, no doubt writing something about his last patient. She didn't know this one – her old GP had left, so they'd passed her on to this chap. He was *very* young, she noted as she perched on the plastic chair opposite him, placing her handbag in her lap. Was he even old enough to be a doctor?

He turned to face her, his glasses sitting crookedly on his nose. Attractive, she supposed, in a youthful, puppy-like sort of way. Strange to have someone his age at their little village surgery, just at the edge of Bath where the height of excitement was the Sunday market in the nearest town, where the majority of residents were over forty-five or under eighteen. Bristol was close enough, why not go there? It was bound to be more exciting for someone his age.

'What can I do for you, Nicola?' he asked, smiling blandly.

She patted her hair nervously, aware that she hadn't brushed it before she left the house, that she was due another hairdresser's appointment, streaks of grey now showing through the dyed red-brown. 'I, well, I've been having some . . . symptoms.'

'Aha,' said the man patiently, if a little distractedly. Dr Williams, she remembered. That was his name. 'What kind of symptoms?'

She'd already decided not to tell him about her little episode this morning, in case it led to any difficult questions, but in truth that wasn't the only thing bothering her. 'Well, various things, really, over the last couple of weeks. I've had a bit of a headache. A few stomach cramps, a fair number of hot flushes. I haven't been able to sleep very well because of it, in all honesty.' She couldn't help wondering from the way he hardly blinked, seeming to stare at a point on her forehead rather than at her, if he was really listening.

She shifted in her seat, crossing one leg over the other. The movement seemed to jolt him back. 'Aha,' he said mildly. 'And is there anything else?' He said it in a way that made it clear he did not think hot flushes and stomach cramps were enough of a problem to warrant taking up his time.

She narrowed her eyes at his tone. She might not have *wanted* to come, but that didn't mean she didn't deserve his attention. 'I've had a few bouts of nausea,' she said stiffly. 'Quite bad, actually,' she went on, his ambivalence making her more honest about it than if he'd been caring and interested. Unbidden, an image of the note flashed in her mind. *You will pay for what you did.* A burning heat trickled down the back of her neck. It crossed her mind then that maybe these symptoms, maybe the confusion, the sickness, the pain, that all of it was deserved. Maybe it was karma, the universe's way of making her pay.

No. That was ridiculous. There were certainly worse people out there than her. Terrorists, now you didn't see them coming down with bouts of nausea, did you? What she'd done was nothing in comparison. Besides, she didn't go in for all that superstitious crap, the universe certainly didn't care about her or what she may or may not have done.

Someone out there cared, though. She shivered, but Dr Williams didn't seem to notice, clicking at something on his computer screen.

'And how long has this been going on for?' he asked.

'I'm not sure exactly. Not too long. A month, maybe a bit longer.'

'Have you been putting on weight?'

'No. If anything I've been losing it.' Indeed her clothes felt like they were hanging off her recently, her once slim, toned figure now turning saggy and frail.

'And what about your periods?'

'What about them?' Quite frankly, she didn't see what it had to do with anything.

'Have they stopped?'

Ah. She thought she saw where this was going now. 'They've been a bit . . . irregular . . . lately, yes.' Then, before he could say anything, she added, 'I know what you're going to say. You're going to tell me it's the menopause, aren't you?'

He opened his hands in front of him, a conciliatory sort of gesture. 'Well, it does sound like that, yes. And it wouldn't be unusual at your age.' *Your age.* Honestly, you'd have thought she was ancient, the way he said it, rather than in her early fifties. 'Hot flushes and cramps are among the most common symptoms,' he added.

'Nausea?' she shot back at him.

9

'Perhaps less common,' he conceded. 'But there are a range of symptoms that can last several years, including the ones we've talked about, as well as things like night sweats and sleep problems. Then there are the more psychological side effects like mood changes, forgetfulness . . .' He droned on, going through the list like he'd memorised it from a textbook.

His face was too pale, Nicola decided, like he hadn't seen the sun in months, and his cheeks were sunken in, giving the impression that he himself needed a good night's sleep. As she studied his face, it began to distort in front of her, his cheeks sinking in further so that they displayed the bones underneath, his skin becoming almost translucent, ghost-like, his brown eyes widening and stretching underneath his glasses, like they were eating away at the flesh around them. No. This wasn't right, this couldn't be happening. She pressed her back against the chair away from him and squeezed her eyes shut. When she opened them he was normal again, and was looking at her expectantly.

She let her breath out on a whoosh. In her head. It was all in her head. Blood and death were just on her mind after this morning, that was all. And she was bound to be feeling a little off after collapsing on her own doorstep.

'Are you all right, Nicola?' Dr Williams asked, the question sounding more like a courtesy than genuine interest.

She swallowed, her mouth dry. 'Just feeling a little light-headed.'

He fumbled around behind his desk. 'Let's take your blood pressure, shall we, just to make sure?' He produced the pump and strapped it on her arm. After a moment he said, 'It's a little low, but nothing to worry about.' She half expected him to say that that, too, was a product of the menopause. Instead he glanced at his computer. 'Your husband died coming up to a year ago, is that right?'

Nicola jolted, the question so unexpected. It felt like something very heavy had settled on top of her, restricting her airflow. 'Yes,' she said shortly. *Though I don't see how that's any of your business,* she wanted to add.

'And it says here that you saw a doctor after he died because you had trouble sleeping? That you lost your appetite?'

She stared at him disbelievingly. How dare he insinuate that this was the same thing? What she'd been going through then had no bearing on how she felt now. 'I don't want to talk about that,' she snapped. The room felt too close, too hot all of a sudden, and it was all she could do to stay seated, not to get up and storm out. She couldn't think about Charlie, not now, especially not after this morning. Grief and guilt roared up inside her, still so indistinguishable from one another, even now.

'Of course. I don't mean to upset you. I'm just noticing some similarities between what you were suffering then, and what you're describing now.' He paused, as if letting that sink in, then said, a little more softly, 'I see that, at the time, you declined the option of antidepressants.'

'I'm not depressed,' Nicola said firmly.

'I'm not saying you are. But the menopause can heighten mood swings, and if you've already been suffering from a low mood, it can be a very . . . difficult . . . time to go through.' There he was, back to that again. She imagined she could tell him she'd fallen over and broke her ankle, and he'd put it down to the bloody menopause.

'I'm not depressed,' she stated again. There was a time, right after Charlie died, when she'd thought she might be. When she'd been unable to get up and face the day, face her new reality. When she couldn't stop wishing she could replay their last moments together, if only so she could do it differently, so she wouldn't now have this constant weight to carry around, everywhere she went.

'Well, I'd still like to give you the option of some pills to help you,' he said, with another bland smile. 'Sometimes, you see, our emotions can make us feel physical symptoms, such as nausea, and actually treating the underlying emotional problem, rather than the symptom itself, can be the most beneficial thing.' He tapped away on his keyboard, and the printer next to him spat out a prescription. She stared at it disbelievingly. Was this what doctors did these days, when they didn't know what to do with patients? Stick them on antidepressants? Her daughter, Sarah, had been on them for a while after Charlie's death, she knew. Had it been this easy for Sarah to get the pills?

Dr Williams waved the prescription in front of her until she took it. 'It's a mild dose, shouldn't have too many side effects. Not an antidepressant, per se, just something to help your mood, take the edge off any anxiety. Take them, see how you get on. And I'd like to see you again in a couple of months, to hear how you are.' He seemed to weigh something up, then said, 'It's not a weakness, you know. Feeling low. And it can come and go, seemingly erratically. It wouldn't be at all surprising if you've been feeling down again, given a change in your hormones and given the, well, fairly traumatic nature of your husband's death, even if it did happen a while ago now.'

Unbidden, she was forced back in time, forced to remember Charlie's face, ashen white, contorted with pain. She blinked furiously against the memory. She didn't want to have to think of it, not now, in this too bright room with this man-child watching her.

Dr Williams glanced over her head and she knew he was checking the clock. She took the cue and got to her feet, but he waved a hand at her. 'Wait.' He opened one of his desk drawers and rustled around, then produced a couple of leaflets. 'Here, have a read of these, too.'

How to Tell if You're Suffering from Depression and *The Menopause: What to Expect.* Nicola looked from the leaflets to Dr Williams and back again. She wanted to say something to him, to admonish him for treating his patients as children, to ask how on earth a leaflet would help, to tell him it sounded to her very much like he ought to go back to medical school. But instead all she came out with was a stiff, 'Thank you,' before she yanked the door open to let herself out. Really. She hadn't *expected* him to tell her it was anything serious, but she also hadn't expected to leave feeling more worried than when she went in. Because he hadn't really listened to her, had he? She'd wanted to be reassured, to have someone explain something she didn't know, not be told that it was probably all in her sodding head.

She didn't realise she was breathing more heavily than usual until she reached the waiting room. Phil was there, sat on one of the green plastic chairs between an old, frail woman and a sullen-looking teenage boy. She hastily stuffed the prescription in her handbag as he spotted her and stood up. He sauntered over, thumbs hooked in the belt loops of his jeans, showing just a hint of his well-toned stomach. He put a big, muscled arm around her when he reached her, pulling her to him. She liked that about Phil, liked that he always wanted physical contact, wanted to be stood right next to her whenever they were out in public. He was so unlike Charlie in that respect, who, she thought sadly, after Sarah was born, hadn't seemed to need her at all.

'Well?' he prompted as they left behind the sounds of coughing and impatient muttering.

'He thinks it's nothing,' Nicola said, forcing a casual tone. She didn't know exactly why she didn't tell Phil about the pills the doctor wanted her to take. Only that, well, she wasn't sure how well he'd take it, thought he may well be the type to see depression as an excuse, something that didn't really exist. Besides, they hadn't been seeing each other that long, she didn't want him thinking that she had too much baggage.

'That's good then,' he said as they stepped out of the surgery and into the fresh air. He turned her to face him when they reached his car, his big hands sliding down to her elbows. 'So I've been thinking,' he said, his lip quirked up into a half smile. 'And I think we should exchange keys. You know, make a statement. It would mean I wouldn't have to wait for you outside if you're ever late back from work or something.'

She noticed the assumption that he'd be waiting for her at her house, rather than her being round at his, but let it go. Still, she hesitated, not sure if she liked the idea that someone could invade her privacy like that whenever they wanted. The smile fell off his face and his hands tightened on her arms for a second before he dropped them to his sides. 'You don't think it's a good idea,' he stated, his voice monotone.

'No, no it's not that,' she said immediately. She forced a smile. 'Sorry, my head's still a little fuzzy after this morning, the doctor said I have low blood pressure, you know.'

'Oh.'

She reached out, took his hand. 'I think it's a great idea. Let's do it.'

Immediately, his face lightened. 'Great! Well, in that case, I think we should go and seal the deal over breakfast, what do you think?'

'Oh, well, I have—'

'Don't worry about getting to the shop for your shift – I rang Mary while you were in the doctor's, told her you'd be late.'

Nicola frowned. The idea of someone calling in sick for her grated. 'You did?' And then, 'You have Mary's number?'

'Nah, I called the shop. She said to just come in when you were feeling better.'

'Oh. Oh well, in that case . . .' She couldn't think of a way round it, not without upsetting him.

'Great.' Phil grinned. 'I've got to be on site with my guys this afternoon, but that gives us plenty of time to get some sugar into you and then get these keys cut. We can go to the garden centre for breakfast, and I think they'll do the keys there too.' Despite herself, she smiled a little at his boyish excitement about the idea. He reached round her to open the passenger door and she slid into the car silently. She made sure to keep her handbag clutched closely to her, where the prescription was hidden. She didn't want Phil to see. She didn't want *anyone* to find out about the pills for that matter – they'd wonder why she needed them, why now, why still.

Even so, she couldn't help feeling a tiny flicker of hope at the thought of them, despite the fact she hadn't wanted them. Was there a chance, perhaps, that they *could* work? A chance that they could take away the gnawing she was feeling right now, the way the acid was swirling in her stomach, tearing at the lining there?

Something heavy slid from her heart to her stomach. No. No pill could do that.

No pill could make her forget.

Chapter Two

It was exactly 7 p.m. when Sarah let herself in through the front door of the main house, using the key Fiona always left in a plant pot on the doorstep. Ben and Fiona had gone out on their weekly 'date night' so Nicola had been left to babysit their daughters, her nieces, a duty she knew was the only reason Fiona tolerated her living in the annex. Nicola felt her chest relax when she saw her own daughter. She knew it was wrong that she'd doubted she'd turn up. But in her defence, it was only in the last few months that Sarah had started speaking to her again.

When Charlie died Sarah had retreated into herself, shutting herself from everyone, especially Nicola. She'd grieved more than anyone else, and Nicola hadn't known how to help her, couldn't help thinking that it was hypocritical to even try to do so, all things considered. But Sarah was coping now, Nicola told herself, tried to make herself believe it. Sarah was finally finding her way through it all, and they were finding their way back to each other. They'd be OK, the two of them.

As long as Sarah never found out, that was.

Nicola tried to shake off that thought as Sarah shut the door behind her. It had been two days since she'd got that note through the post. Nothing else had happened, no one had made any move towards her. So she'd convinced herself that it was nothing, a hoax.

'Hi, Mum,' Sarah said in a slightly muffled voice. Nicola could tell just from that tone that something was wrong and actually, she welcomed the distraction of someone else's pain, as horrible as that might make her. She watched as Sarah shrugged off her leather jacket and bent down to take off her muddy boots, showing grass stains on her skinny blue jeans. And she knew then where Sarah had been, what was making her smile in a way that looked painful. Sarah might not think that Nicola knew her as well as Charlie had done, but she was wrong.

So she knew without asking that Sarah had come from Charlie's grave.

And she hated it. Hated the idea of her there, crying as she traced his name with her fingers, sobbing the way she'd done at his funeral when she'd spoken about her dad. Hated the thought of her sitting there, alone, damp seeping through her jeans as she knelt on the grass, growing cold in the September air.

Nicola crossed the distance between them. 'Hello, darling, lovely to see you.' She wondered whether to try and offer some words of comfort. Knowing her tells didn't mean she knew what to say, though – she was just as likely to make her more upset as she was to cheer her up. 'Lily and Emily are still up,' she said instead. 'They wanted to see you before they went to bed.'

A genuine smile spread across Sarah's face this time. 'Nice earrings,' she commented as she followed Nicola into the living room at the front of the house, which looked out onto the gravel driveway.

Nicola raised a hand to touch one of the sparkling studs. 'Oh, thanks, Phil got them for me.'

Sarah raised her eyebrows but didn't say anything. She didn't really have to – Nicola knew all too well what Sarah thought of Phil, though at least she wasn't vocalising it as much these days. Really, though, she was hardly going to take seriously Sarah's thoughts on any man she was dating – she knew Sarah considered it a betrayal that she'd even consider dating anyone after Charlie. Though Nicola had to admit, there were times when she almost felt the same way herself.

Lily and Emily were curled up together on the deep red sofa, watching *Peter Rabbit* for the millionth time. Emily grinned at Sarah, pushing her light brown hair, growing so fast these days, away from her face before sticking her thumb in her mouth again. Three-year-old Lily just continued to stare at the TV, one hand curled up in her wispy blonde hair. Sarah deliberately moved in front of the screen. 'Are you going to say hello, then?'

Without the distraction of a talking rabbit, both girls launched themselves at Sarah, who twirled them round in circles one at a time – enough space in here that she could do so without worrying about knocking anything. It gave Nicola a pang watching the three of them together like that, so much unreserved love there. It intensified when Lily, who was almost mistrustful of Nicola sometimes, wrapped her arms around Sarah's leg and gave her signature cartoon giggle. She looked so like Sarah had at that age.

'And as Sarah's here,' Nicola said above continued squeals of delight, 'that means I'm afraid it's bedtime.' Nicola ignored the protests from Emily and glanced at Sarah. 'Sorry, love, are you going to be—?'

Sarah waved a hand in the air. 'Go. I'll help myself to stuff in the kitchen.'

By the time Nicola had got both girls to bed, if not quite to sleep, Sarah was standing over the stove, stirring a risotto, a glass of wine in one hand. She was so much more at ease in Fiona's kitchen than Nicola would ever be. 'Hope you don't mind, I started on tea.' She glanced over her shoulder. 'Wine?'

Nicola shook her head, the movement feeling heavy. 'I think I'll just have tea.' She moved towards the cupboard but Sarah waved her away.

'I'll make it,' she said firmly. 'Sit down, you look tired.' Nicola tried and failed not to feel put out that she still looked tired after all the effort she'd made this evening, subtle make-up so that she'd look healthy and, yes, younger; menopause be damned. Sarah set those familiar grey-green eyes on her as she slid onto a chair and rested her elbows on the mahogany kitchen table. Really, who needed a mahogany kitchen table, for God's sake? But of course, it was only the best for Fiona.

'You went to see the doctor yesterday, didn't you?' Sarah asked. 'What did they say?'

Nicola wrinkled her nose. She shouldn't have told her about that. 'I did and it's nothing to worry about, so please don't.' When Sarah didn't immediately look away, Nicola sighed. 'It's just the menopause, love, that's all.' It wasn't all, not by a long shot, but there was no way she was admitting that.

Sarah seemed satisfied with that, turning to take the tea leaves out from one of the wooden cupboards, much nicer cupboards than Nicola had in the annex. Sarah had made them all switch to tea leaves recently because they were better for the environment, apparently – regular teabags had plastic in them, who knew?

'Oh, well, if that's it then that's OK then,' Sarah said mildly. Nicola resisted the urge to snort. She should wait until she was going through it before she brushed it off so lightly. 'So they didn't take bloods or anything?'

'No, no need for anything like that.'

'Well, that's good then, they're obviously not too worried.' Sarah brought a cup of tea over and nodded to the plain blue coaster on Nicola's right. Smiling slightly, Nicola moved it in front of her then took the tea. Even as a child, Sarah had been the tidy one – so similar to Charlie in that respect. She went back to her cooking, sweeping back long hair, naturally blonde even before the highlights she put in. Gorgeous hair she most certainly didn't get from Nicola.

'And there was nothing that made you particularly want to go to the doctor's? I mean, I know you've been feeling sick and all that, but there wasn't anything else?'

Nicola kept her face neutral. She was like this, Sarah, never very good at just letting things drop. 'No, nothing,' she said lightly. 'Just wanted a check-up, you know.' She knew that her face was calm, her cheeks unflushed as she spoke. She'd always been able to lie well, when she'd really wanted to. Had enough practice at it by now.

It was hard to tell whether Sarah believed her but, really, Nicola found she didn't care. It was the reason Sarah was here, after all, the reason she was back in Nicola's life again. She'd been more attentive, been around far more often since she'd found out, no doubt through Ben or Fiona, that Nicola wasn't feeling great. She'd been willing to come and cook for her, to take care of her. So secretly, Nicola could admit that she was a little thankful for the bouts of illness, would gladly take more of it if it meant keeping her daughter around. Not that she deserved to have her around, of course. Or at least, that's what other people would say, if they knew.

Nicola sipped her tea and grimaced a little. 'What's the matter?' Sarah said, too observant as always. She set plates on the table. Expensive plates, Nicola thought bitterly. Ones

Fiona had had made specially, with hand-drawn flowers on each of them. The type of plates Nicola would have had in her old life. 'Isn't it sweet enough? I can add more sugar?'

'No, no, it's fine, love.' She reached out and squeezed Sarah's hand. 'Just a bit hot, that's all.' It was actually a little *too* sweet, if she was honest, but she wouldn't tell her that. It still felt new, this relationship between them, the way they were adjusting to life without Charlie.

Sarah turned to take the risotto off the stove. 'I saw Mrs Norwood today,' she said in a would-be casual voice.

Nicola's head throbbed, a headache starting up even without the wine, and she resisted the urge to massage her temples. 'Oh?'

'Mmm-hmm. She said I should come by, see the house now she's done it up.'

So, Sarah had brought Charlie up anyway, even though Nicola hadn't asked. Sure, it was indirect, but Nicola knew that was what she was getting at by mentioning Mrs Norwood, who had bought the old Victorian-style house that she'd had to sell after Charlie had died. It had been glorious, that house, with a beautiful outdoor patio and a kitchen that would put even Fiona's mahogany table and fancy plates to shame. That wasn't why Sarah had loved it though, she knew. Sarah had been horrified when Nicola sold it, had hated to say goodbye to the house which held so many memories of her dad, even though Nicola had tried to explain that she just couldn't afford it, not with the bills she'd been left with, not on her measly income. Especially not because Charlie hadn't told her just how bad their finances were after he'd had to give up his job.

'You're still in touch with her then?' Nicola asked.

'Not really. I just bumped into her in Waitrose and she started chatting to me. I think she's lonely.' It was hard to tell, with Sarah's back to her, if she really was as unbothered about it as she sounded. Nicola couldn't think of a thing to say, in part because she couldn't believe her own daughter now shopped at Waitrose. 'Anyway,' Sarah continued as she brought over two plates of pea and asparagus risotto, 'I thought I'd take her up on it and go see it at some point.'

She wondered if Sarah was hinting, wanting her to come with her. But there was no way she was willing to go back to that house. She wasn't putting herself through that, even for Sarah. So she just settled with, 'That'll be nice.' Her next words came out almost unbidden, the suggestion overflowing before she could think better of it. 'On another note, I was just thinking that, maybe, if you'd like to, we could do something on the fifth.'

There was a pause, then, 'Dad's anniversary,' Sarah whispered.

'I thought . . . I thought maybe we could go to his grave together, get some of those pastries he liked from the bakery or something.' Her words were coming too quickly and she made herself take a breath, slow down. She didn't want Sarah to think she was nervous. 'Do something together to . . . remember him,' she finished lamely.

Sarah considered her, cocking her head. And then, to Nicola's enormous relief, the corners of her mouth crooked up into a slight smile. 'I'd like that,' she said.

They were still in the kitchen, finishing up an M&S lemon tart that Sarah had picked up, when Ben and Fiona got home. Usually when she was babysitting Nicola could hear the car pull into the driveway, could prepare herself, but sitting in the kitchen at the back of the house meant that she didn't notice they'd arrived until she heard their voices. She tensed automatically, her shoulders going stiff, even as she reminded herself that Fiona had asked her to be here.

Sarah glanced at her, a slight frown creasing her forehead, as if she could pick up on what Nicola was feeling. But the frown dropped away when Fiona came into the kitchen and Sarah smiled warmly. Nicola jumped to her feet, though regretted it when a wave of dizziness hit her. She'd caved and had just one glass of the New Zealand Sauvignon Sarah had opened, but surely one glass wasn't enough to make her feel this light-headed. No doubt that man-child doctor would claim it was another bloody menopausal symptom.

'How was your evening?' Nicola asked.

Fiona pushed back her chocolate curls and Nicola felt a little bolt of jealousy at how smooth her skin still looked, how you could really tell Fiona was nearly ten years younger than her. 'Oh, yes, good.' Fiona didn't even bother to fake an enthusiastic tone. 'How were the girls?'

Nicola prattled on about how good they'd been, but she was barely concentrating on what she was saying because Ben had come into the kitchen behind Fiona. He looked so similar to Charlie, in some respects. The same brown hair, same height, the way they both let their stubble grow out, just a little. But they'd been step-brothers, and it showed – Ben's eyes were the seaweed to Charlie's deep ocean-blue, his cheekbones more pronounced, nose smaller. He was leaner, too, even now, just creeping into his late forties. And yes, fine, he was attractive. It wasn't a crime to admit that to herself, now was it? Particularly tonight, in his jeans and white designer jumper.

Though she refused to meet his gaze, she could feel his eyes on her, burning her skin. Intense, watchful, just like when she'd first met him. She was glad in that moment that she'd made the effort to look nice, glad she still had the figure she still worked so hard to maintain, even if it was leaning more towards frail than toned these days. She hated the thought of him seeing her as she really was – exhausted, both physically and mentally.

Fiona slid into a chair next to Sarah and Sarah lifted her nearly empty glass. 'I'd offer you wine, but I drank it all.'

Fiona's lips twitched. 'That's all right, we had wine at the restaurant and if I have any more I'll suffer tomorrow.' She yawned, and Nicola thought it might be pointed, but she wasn't sure if that was just her being oversensitive. 'I'm knackered anyway, I'll probably go to bed in a minute.'

'Oh, well, in that case I'll head back,' Nicola said immediately, actually a little grateful for the excuse – as much as she loved her daughter, she wasn't sure she could last much longer.

'Want me to walk you back?' Ben asked casually, coming to stand behind Fiona with one hand on the back of her chair. Because of that, he didn't see the way Fiona's lips tightened, the fleeting look she gave Nicola.

'It's just across the garden,' Nicola said lightly, 'I think I'll manage.'

There was a moment of silence, then Sarah stretched and stood up. 'I'll head too, got an early start tomorrow.' She gave Fiona's shoulders a squeeze, then hugged Nicola. 'Love you, Mum.' She said it firmly, almost like she was reminding her, reminding everyone in the room, which made Nicola suspect she'd caught the look Fiona had given her a second ago.

'Love you, too.'

Nicola quickly said goodbye to Ben and Fiona then let herself out the back door in the kitchen, onto the patio area. Her annex was across the other side of the L-shaped garden, almost directly opposite where she was stood on the patio now. She crossed to the paved path, which led from the side of the big main house right to the front door of the annex, through the main part of the garden with a line of pear trees running down each side of the path. To the left of the annex was the other part of the garden, the wilder part, locked with a gate so that Lily and Emily couldn't get in there to play.

She walked down the path, breathing in the smell of the flowers, the cool night air settling her a little. It was dark now, especially as she left the glow of the kitchen behind her, so she couldn't make out the individual plants, not that she'd be able to name most of them anyway – Ben and Fiona were the gardeners, not her. The shapes of them distorted as she drew closer to her annex, the bushes getting bigger, the thin-stemmed flowers seeming to rise and twirl towards her, looming over her, like they were watching her every move. She hitched in a breath and stumbled, catching her jacket on one of the branches of the pear trees. She steadied herself and looked down to where she was still attached. The wood was pale and light in the darkness, strangely luminescent. She released her jacket from where it was snagged, but as she stepped back the slim branch reached towards her, becoming an old, gnarled finger that tried to grab her again.

Panicked, she jolted away, then charged the last few steps down the path, keeping her head down, trying to ignore the way the other pear trees were now doing the same, branches shifting into handless fingers that tried to grab her, to stop her. She was breathing far too heavily when she reached the front door, her hand shaking violently as she unlocked it. She glanced over her shoulder before she let herself in, but everything was normal, the garden quiet and still, the pear trees hidden in shadow, no sign of the menace they just showed her. She shook her head. Ridiculous. It was the wine, combined with her already worried state of mind – it was making her imagine things.

It was when she was taking off her earrings – the ones she'd worn because she knew she would see Ben – that she noticed a necklace – the one Charlie had given her just after she'd given birth to Sarah – was missing from her jewellery box. She hadn't worn it in years, not since that night, must be five and a half years ago now, when she'd worn it for Charlie on their anniversary. Worn only that as she walked into the bedroom to surprise him, to try and kindle a passion that they'd never really had, if she was being brutally honest with herself. He'd looked at her and dismissed her, said he was too tired. She pressed her lips together at the memory, the humiliation of it. But despite that, it was an expensive necklace, and beautiful – a gorgeous emerald, for the colour of Sarah's eyes. And unlike their anniversary, that was a memory she wanted to keep – the day Sarah was born, the joy of it, of her, despite everything. The necklace was a reminder of that and she didn't like the idea that she'd lost it.

She frowned. She must have just put it down somewhere and forgotten about it, that was all.

Chapter Three

Nicola finished stocking up the drinks fridge, putting a hand on the fridge door when she got up out of a crouch too fast, causing all the blood to rush from her head. 'You all right, chick?' asked Mary, the shop owner and Nicola's only colleague.

Nicola glanced over to where Mary was cashing up at the till. 'I'm fine, just got up a bit quickly.'

'Well, sit down a minute, we're done for the day now.' Knowing better than to argue with Mary, Nicola perched herself on the little stool she'd been using to reach the top shelf. She fiddled with the name badge Mary insisted they both wore, even though it was ridiculous – it was the only village shop, and everyone who stopped in knew who both she and Mary were. Would do even if she hadn't been working in the shop for the past two years, given she'd lived here for the last twenty-five, for God's sake.

'There,' Mary said, clicking the till shut. 'Now what do you say we have a bit of that leftover cake, shall we? It won't be good too much longer.' Mary was continually having a bit of the 'leftover' cake that she got one of the local ladies to bake, hence the reason she was a little on the large side. She smiled widely at Nicola and in that instant her face changed, just like the doctor's had. Her fleshy cheeks disintegrated, shrivelling and turning a nasty grey colour, like something was eating away at her face. Part of her mouth fell away so that her teeth were on show, yellowing and crooked. Nicola stared, trying to tell herself that it wasn't real, that it couldn't be real. But her breathing was coming quicker and quicker, her heart frantically trying to escape the confines of her chest. She wanted to close her eyes but she couldn't. She couldn't because of Mary's eyes, staring at her, wide and glassy as if from pain. Exactly like Charlie's eyes had been.

'And *then*,' Mary was saying, taking two big slices of the Victoria sponge from the glass-fronted cake display, 'Mrs Winterbourne, you know, the woman who lives on the corner beside the pub, told me that all those trips her husband had been taking into Bristol for those big meetings were actually for a different kind of meeting altogether, if you see what I'm . . . Are you sure you're all right, chick?' she asked again. 'You look very pale.'

'I'm fine,' Nicola managed, though her voice came out croaky. 'Just, you know, being hit a bit hard by the menopause at the moment.' She hated herself for saying it, for blaming every little thing on it, but the thought was in her head now after that bloody doctor. God, she just needed a good night's sleep, that was all. Needed just one not plagued by stomach cramps.

'Ah yes,' Mary said sympathetically. 'I remember it all too well, I had a dreadful time with it myself, hot flushes like you wouldn't believe, and at the most inconvenient times, I tell you. Sure, you just need some sugar, that always helped me.' She forced a paper plate with cake onto Nicola's lap, and Nicola nibbled at the corner of it. 'Now, how are you getting home? Is that fella of yours coming to get you again?'

'No, I was planning on walking actually.' She glanced at her phone automatically, thinking of the text she'd got from Phil earlier – he wasn't too pleased that she'd insisted on making her own way home today, seemed to like the mind-numbingly boring chore of picking her up and dropping her off, even though she lived close enough to walk and besides, had her own car, even if she wasn't the most confident of drivers. And it was hardly her fault that she wasn't – Charlie had always insisted on driving too.

'Ah look, don't be silly, you can't walk when you keep coming over all light-headed. I'll drive you home after we lock up.'

'But it's only—'

'No, I won't hear it,' Mary said. 'Now, where was I? Ah, I was telling you about Mrs Winterbourne, wasn't I? And that's not even the half of it, let me tell you.' On and on she went as they closed the shop and drove home, prattling on about the various village gossip, the secrets that she always seemed to be the first to uncover.

Mary not only insisted on driving her, but also got out the car when they pulled up outside the house and walked her all the way through the gate at the side of the main house and along the paved path across the garden. They'd had rain the last few days and it showed in the garden, the grass a deeper green and a bit overgrown, the way Nicola liked it best. She knew Lily and Emily liked it better this way too, liked it when it was more on the wild side so they could pretend there were faeries there, hiding in the overgrowth. It was why Fiona had to lock the gate to the other part of the garden with the more exotic plants, the ones more difficult to grow – Lily and Emily would be in there otherwise, trampling everything.

It was sunny and warm today, and the garden seemed peaceful, the flowers drifting slightly in the light breeze, the pinks and purples warm and inviting, like they were welcoming Mary. None of the menace Nicola sometimes felt from it when she was alone, like the garden knew she was a trespasser on Fiona's property, like it knew that she didn't belong here.

Nicola opened the annex door and, seeing no choice, let Mary in behind her, who was still chattering away though Nicola had lost the thread of the conversation. They walked straight into the kitchen, and Nicola dumped her keys and purse on the windowsill.

She didn't notice something was wrong right away. It was only when she looked around, trying to decide if she was hungry enough to bother making dinner, that she saw. The fridge magnets. The alphabet ones which been a present from Sarah to both her and Charlie years ago, when Sarah was still a teenager.

She couldn't quite believe what she was looking at. Her body was frozen but her mind was reeling, refusing to accept that someone had done this. That someone had deliberately rearranged the fridge magnets so that they spelt out a message. Just one word.

Scared

No question mark as there wasn't a question mark magnet, but she felt the question was implied. The word was in the middle of the fridge, the other magnets scattered around it. Nicola felt tears burn the back of her eyes and blinked furiously.

But this had to mean someone had been in her home. Someone who knew she'd be out. Someone who wanted her to be frightened. Her heart sped up into a warning drum.

Mary had gone quiet. Nicola didn't know when she'd stopped talking, hadn't noticed the lull in noise. Mary didn't seem to notice anything was wrong, hadn't picked up on the anxiety now shredding the lining of Nicola's stomach. She did follow the direction of Nicola's gaze, though, and wandered over to the fridge, blocking Nicola's view of it.

'Ah, now isn't this sweet?' Mary took the drawing Emily had done for Nicola at school down from where it was stuck to the bottom of the fridge door.

'What? Oh. Oh yes, my niece did that for me and she'd be very upset if she didn't see it whenever she comes round here.' Nicola laughed, a high-pitched, manic noise. Mary turned to look at her, clearly sensing at last that something was wrong. As she shifted, Nicola saw the magnets had been moved again, no longer in distinct words but spaced out oddly. Nicola stared. 'Did you . . .?' But she broke off, mouth open around unformed words. She couldn't ask if Mary had moved the magnets around without explaining why she wanted to know.

'Did I what, chick?'

'Nothing,' she said quickly. 'Nothing, don't worry.' She pushed a hand through her hair. 'Ah, actually, this is going to sound stupid but I'm having a moment – do you remember if I unlocked the door to let us in? Or was it locked? I just . . .' She trailed off, not really knowing how to explain how much she needed to know for sure that she *had* unlocked it.

Mary chortled, but it was a kind sound. 'Sure, I have those moments all the time. But you definitely unlocked it, so nothing to worry about.'

Nothing to worry about. If only.

Still, she let out a slow breath. 'Thanks.' So maybe she'd imagined the whole thing. Like Mary's face earlier, like the pear tree branches the other night. Just a trick of her tired mind, just because she was on edge, her brain too deprived of proper sleep, of time without headaches, to function properly.

'It'll be the change,' Mary said. 'I was like it when I was going through it, terribly forgetful all the time. Horrible while it lasts but it does get a bit better, I promise.' Nicola just nodded. 'Anyway, I'll be off, leave you in peace to have a nice sit down, eh? And I'll pop in, say hello to Fiona on the way out.' And try to get the gossip on her and Ben no doubt, Nicola thought.

It took all of two minutes after Mary left to give into the temptation and call Phil, asking him to come over. And yes it was pathetic and downright cowardly to want to hide behind a big strong man just because she was worried, but quite frankly she didn't care. She *could* deal with it on her own, she knew that, had proven it to herself in the past, so why should she have to do it now? Besides, this was sensible. If there was someone out there who wanted to scare her, perhaps scare her into blurting it all out, then having a second person around meant they were less likely to come at her. And Phil would be pleased. He liked to feel needed.

After she spoke to him, she made herself look around the annex. Nothing else out of place, not that she could tell. As she acknowledged this, she became more and more convinced that she must have just imagined it. Though she wasn't sure how comforting that was, in all truth. Because people's faces distorting in front of her, seeing words that weren't there – it wasn't exactly a sign of something *good*, now was it?

Chapter Four

Sarah was curled up in the old, worn armchair across from Nicola in the little annex sitting room, her whole body covered by one of Nicola's overly large, unattractive cardigans, bare feet sticking out to show electric blue toenails. Nicola was trying to focus on what she was saying, but her mind was so damn foggy she couldn't even remember how long Sarah had been there, let alone what they'd been talking about. It was those pills that idiot doctor had given her, she was sure of it. Stupidly, she'd only thought to read the side effects today and sure enough, there in small print was the fact that, in less than one per cent of cases, they could worsen sleep problems and induce nausea. She'd thrown them out immediately, but the effects were still lingering.

There was a tapping sound at the window and Nicola jumped violently, spilling some of the lukewarm tea she was holding over herself. She stared at the window, but with the blind closed she obviously couldn't see anything. She waited but there was no other sound. It must just have been one of the tree branches in the wind.

'Mum?' Nicola jerked her head and saw Sarah looking at her in way that suggested it wasn't the first time she'd tried to get her attention. 'What's up? Why are you so jumpy?'

'Nothing. Sorry, love, just thought I'd heard something.'

'You've been weird all evening. Seriously, what's wrong?'

She could just brush it off again. But actually, because she was so damn tired, because the constant dull ache in her head made it difficult to keep pretending, she didn't lie. Not completely, anyway. 'I think . . .' She glanced to the window and back again. 'I think someone might be following me.'

'What?' Sarah sat up straighter. 'What do you mean? You mean someone's stalking you?'

'No, I . . . Well, yes, I suppose.'

'Mum! This is serious! Why didn't you tell me before? Who is it? What are they doing?'

She bit her lip. Maybe she shouldn't have said anything, given the panicked way Sarah was looking at her right now. 'I . . . I'm not sure.'

'What do you mean you're not sure?'

'Well, I haven't *seen* anyone, not exactly.'

'So how do you know someone is following you, then?'

She grimaced. 'Maybe following wasn't quite the right word. I just . . . it seemed like someone had been in the house the other day, moved things around, and then something went missing and . . .' And the note. The main thing, the only move she could be sure someone had made. But there was no way to tell Sarah about it, no way to tell anyone. Not until she figured out if it meant what she thought it did and, even then, she wouldn't confess until she absolutely had to. She wasn't ready to face the consequences yet.

'What went missing?'

'A necklace, from my jewellery box. The one your dad gave me, you know, the emerald one.'

'I know the one,' Sarah said quietly, a little sadly. She knew too what the necklace represented, knew her dad had been thinking of her when he bought it. She slouched back down in the chair, the tension apparently draining from

34

her. 'But, Mum, that doesn't really sound like someone's *stalking* you. You'll probably find the necklace, and can you be absolutely sure that someone was in the house? What things were moved around?'

Scared. The word, brightly coloured in fridge-magnet lettering, flashed in her mind. The one she couldn't be sure she hadn't imagined. 'No, no you're right. I'm being silly. Just tired and reading too many thrillers at night, that's all. It's making me doolally.' And it's not like anything really bad had happened to her, had it? Not yet, anyway. She felt a cold prickle run down her back, but resisted the urge to shiver.

This time, when there was a loud bang, Sarah started as well. 'What was that?'

Nicola frowned. 'I think it was the door to the main house?' It must have been slammed hard, if they heard it all the way across the garden.

They heard Fiona's high-pitched voice next, her words muffled but the tone clear. Nicola felt a tiny twinge of satisfaction, which she tried to quell. She shouldn't want them to be arguing again, knew it was wrong on so many levels. But she had a front row seat now to watch Fiona, with her perfect house and perfect children, the house with an interior that looked like it was out of a catalogue. Even knowing Fiona's life wasn't perfect – far from it – Nicola still resented her for all those things that she used to have herself, before her life came crashing down around her.

Ben's voice now, the garden swallowing the words so that by the time it reached the annex all they could hear was an angry rumble. 'Can you always hear them like this?' Sarah asked.

'Sometimes. They're not usually this loud.'

'I don't like it, all this arguing. They've been off lately, don't you think?'

'Hmmm, maybe.' Nicola knew very well that Sarah was right, but that didn't mean she wanted to get drawn into a conversation about it.

'It's sad. I always used to think of them as the perfect couple, you know?' The perfect couple, so unlike she and Charlie, Nicola thought sadly. Nicola used to think they were hiding that from Sarah. After all, it was never shouting with Charlie, their fights were much more subtle, long silences and disapproving looks – only with Nicola, none of that was ever directed at Sarah. But despite that, Sarah had still picked up on the cracks. 'And on that note . . .' Sarah yawned, stretched. 'I better go. Nika's had a rough day at work and I promised I'd be back in time for a glass of wine before bed.' Nika – Sarah's flatmate, Nicola remembered.

She insisted on walking Sarah out, and as she opened the front door, they were hit by the sound of Ben's voice, loud and angry enough to cover the distance this time, the garden changing tack and amplifying it, like it wanted them to hear him. 'Oh, don't fucking start that again.'

The two of them exchanged a look. 'Are the girls home?' Sarah asked.

'I presume so.'

Sarah set her mouth in a hard line as she shrugged on her leather jacket. She'd always been like this – very strict standards for what was right and what was wrong – too strict, really, in Nicola's opinion. After all, no one could be perfect all the time, they were all entitled to little slip-ups every now and then.

It was dark outside, and though Nicola told herself to stop overreacting, she couldn't stop herself flinching at the rustling noises amongst the plants, her mind turning the innocent explorations of little creatures into something much more sinister. Ben and Fiona's voices hummed through the wind. Nicola tried not to listen, but when they reached the end of the paved path, coming up to the main house, it became impossible not to.

'Don't *touch* me, Ben. I've told you I don't want to talk to you when you're like this.'

'Oh, come on, don't be such a—'

'Such a *what*, Ben? Such a what?'

'You're being—'

'I said don't touch me!'

There was a sound of something smashing, glass on a hard surface. The sound of Fiona screaming, high and shrill. Of Ben swearing.

Then it went quiet. Why did it go quiet? Nicola was frozen at the end of the path, staring at the kitchen window. But the blinds were shut, the curtains pulled across them, so although she could see a dim glow of the light inside, it was impossible to make out any shapes.

'Maybe we should pop in, check everything's OK.' Sarah's voice, hesitant as it was, made her jump. She stepped out of reach of the pear tree closest to her and onto the patio, just in case.

'Do you think?' Nicola whispered. 'Maybe we should just leave it, let them sort it themselves?'

'No, I want to check Fiona's OK,' Sarah said firmly, and though she was whispering, too, it didn't sound quiet enough to Nicola. They were right next to the back door now, surely Ben and Fiona must be able to hear them.

It was because of that, because she thought they must know they were there already, that she murmured her agreement, trying to ignore the way her skin was thrumming, nerves all too ready to jump into action.

'Good.' Then, so quietly Nicola wasn't sure if she was supposed to be able to hear, Sarah muttered, 'Besides, who knows what Ben is capable of when he's in a mood like this.'

Nicola opened her mouth, the words to contradict her already forming. But she stopped. Because, besides the fact that she knew she shouldn't be automatically jumping to his defence, she supposed Sarah was right in some respects – you never really knew what anyone was capable of.

The two of them walked in silence to the back door of the house. It was nothing, Nicola told herself. Stupid to be jumping to conclusions, to be picturing the worst. It was just a fight, like the countless others she was sure they'd had.

Sarah knocked, and when no one answered, she opened the back door into the kitchen. Nicola slipped in behind her.

Sarah reacted first to the scene. 'What the fuck?'

Her sharp voice made Fiona flinch. Fiona, who was sat at the kitchen table, one hand holding a paper towel to her left cheek. Nicola focused on her and only her in that first moment. Focused in on the blood, seeping through the white paper, a smear of it on her chin where she hadn't mopped it up yet.

'It's nothing, it's not what it looks like,' said Ben, perhaps a little too quickly from his position by the counter. Nicola wasn't sure exactly what it did look like, though. For the first time, she noticed the smashed glass on the tiles, shattered into tiny pieces that reflected the glow from the too-bright lights overhead. God, surely this wasn't deliberate, was it?

'We heard shouting,' Nicola said dumbly, her words feeling thick and sticky in her mouth.

Fiona grimaced, glancing at Ben for the first time since they'd walked in on them. No, not glancing. Glaring. Then she met Nicola's questioning gaze. 'We just had an argument, that's all.' The *and it's none of your business* was quite clearly implied.

'That doesn't look like just an argument,' Sarah said, stepping further into the room.

'It was an accident,' said Fiona sharply.

Sarah raised her eyebrows, clearly about to comment, but before she could say anything to make things worse, Nicola looked to Ben, who was standing on the other side of the fragments of glass. 'What happened?' she asked.

He pulled one hand through his hair so that it stuck up in odd angles. 'I just . . . The glass slipped. I've had a bit to drink so I . . . I didn't mean to throw it. God, I didn't mean for it to *hit* her.' Nicola noticed the correction at the end so couldn't help wondering whether it truly had slipped, whether it was even possible for a glass to slip out of someone's hand and smash like that, with the pieces closer to her than him. Ben was staring at Fiona now, his face a little pale. 'I didn't mean to, Fee.'

'I know.' But Fiona looked resolutely down at the table.

'We heard a scream,' Sarah stated.

'You'd scream too,' Fiona said, 'if there was a glass coming towards you.' Nicola wondered if that was true – Sarah wasn't exactly the screaming in fear type. 'Look, I'm sorry if we worried you, but it really is fine. It's worse than it looks.' She brought the paper towel away from her face, and though it was a little red, Nicola couldn't see any visible wound. No gashing hole, no sign that she'd been hit hard.

Sarah walked up to Fiona, gave her shoulder a squeeze, and Fiona smiled, perhaps a little grimly, up at her. Nicola felt a sharp bolt of resentment, though she worked to keep her face impassive. It was so easy, their relationship. As it should be, she reminded herself – Fiona was Sarah's aunt, even if they weren't related by blood. But that didn't stop her from feeling bitter, that Fiona seemed to genuinely love Sarah yet had made her dislike of Nicola no secret. Didn't stop her, in her dark moments, from wishing Sarah would side with her, hoping that she would refuse to be warm towards Fiona in a show of solidarity.

Almost to try and combat those thoughts, she shuffled across the kitchen to stand with Sarah, behind Fiona. The three of them in a line, allied against Ben. Ben seemed to shrink back against the counter, his tall frame collapsing in on itself.

'So it was really just an accident?' Nicola needed to hear them say it again. She didn't want to have another reason to lie awake at night. Didn't want to have to wonder if Ben was turning violent.

'It was,' Fiona said firmly, and she actually gave Nicola a fleeting smile, a slight softening of her mouth. Ben nodded vigorously but said nothing more, like he didn't want to risk saying the wrong thing under the force of their combined gazes.

'So what's wrong then?' Sarah asked after an uncomfortable silence. 'Why were you arguing?'

'It's nothing,' Fiona said, patting Sarah's hand where it still rested upon her shoulder. 'Usual couple stuff, you know.' As she spoke, a tiny pinprick of blood reformed on her cheek. Nicola watched its progress down the side of her face, all the way to the top of her lip before Fiona noticed and wiped it away. The sight of it left a metal tang in her mouth.

Something must have shown in her expression because Sarah's gaze rested on her, her stormy eyes assessing. So full of expression, those eyes. Just like her father. No. She wasn't to think like that, Sarah wasn't like him, not in the ways that mattered. 'You OK, Mum?'

Nicola thought she heard Fiona mutter something under her breath, but she could have been wrong, it could just be her mind playing tricks on her again. She felt Ben's attention on her now too, his eyes full of concern, and wished she'd made a bit of effort with her hair, was wearing something other than this shapeless blue dress. She would have, if she'd known she'd be seeing anyone other than Sarah.

'I'm fine,' she managed. She was aware of how wrong it was, that Ben and Sarah were worried about her when Fiona was the one bleeding, and embarrassment clouded by a little smugness wormed through her.

Sarah nodded, turned her attention back to Fiona. 'Well, if you're sure it's nothing?' Fiona inclined her head wearily. 'Then I'll head off.'

'Yes,' Nicola said quickly. 'Yes, we'll leave you to it then.' She cringed a little at how that came out, like she was encouraging them to keep arguing, but no one else seemed to notice. She half turned towards the back door, now desperate to be away from the scene, but stopped at the sound of Fiona's wooden chair screeching across the tiles.

'Wait,' Fiona said, and she crossed the kitchen, seemingly unconcerned that her bare feet might meet sharp glass along the way. 'I think this is yours?' And she held up Nicola's emerald necklace. The thin gold chain glinted as it swung from Fiona's hand. Sarah gave her an almost exasperated smile, rolled her eyes as if to say *I told you so*.

'Where did you find it?' Nicola asked.

'It was in Ben's underwear drawer,' Fiona said shortly.

Nicola frowned at Ben, who held up his hands, palms facing her. 'I didn't know it was there, I swear.' But a tinge of red travelled up his neck. 'I must have just tided it away without realising.'

'Oh, and it just found its way in between your boxers, did it?' Fiona asked scathingly, still holding the necklace out to Nicola, as if it was something contaminated. Nicola stepped towards her gingerly, even though she still had her pumps on, and took it, the chain warm as she threaded it through her fingers.

'I told you, I didn't even know it was hers.' This time, when Nicola glanced at Ben, he wouldn't meet her gaze. She wondered if that were true, if he truly hadn't recognised it. The fact that Fiona knew it was hers – the fact that Charlie had given it to her, had made such a big deal of her – made her doubt it. Ben had been very aware, back then, of the intricacies of her and Charlie's relationship.

She was close enough to him now that she caught a whiff of the alcohol he'd apparently been drinking. He didn't *seem* drunk, but then he'd always been able to hide that, much better than Charlie had ever been able to. She remembered more than one night drinking with the two of them, before Fiona had even come on the scene, when Charlie would pass out from drink long before Ben showed any effect, leaving Ben and Nicola to stay up, talking nonsense.

'Did you leave it here?' Fiona demanded.

Nicola frowned. 'I suppose I must have.' She didn't remember doing so, but wasn't that the point of losing something, that you didn't remember where you last put it? And there was no reason for Ben to take it, surely. Forgetfulness, just another part of the menopause, that's what Mary, what the doctor said. 'Yes, I'm sure I left it here,' she said more firmly, and Fiona's expression smoothed out a little.

'Mummy?' Lily's small cartoon voice made everyone in the room jump. She must have been so quiet, tiptoeing down the stairs and to the doorway, for none of them to notice her.

Ben moved towards her before she could step fully into the kitchen and risk her fragile little feet on the glass. He scooped her up onto his hip where she twirled a hand into her wispy blonde hair, surveying the room with her suspicious eyes. Nicola swore Lily's gaze rested on her a fraction longer than the others like she knew, somehow, that this was her fault, that she was the reason her parents weren't happy.

'What's wrong, Lils?' Ben asked softly. And there it was, the side of him Nicola knew was always there, even if she saw less of it these days. He was so good with his daughters, so genuinely caring. It made her heart ache, watching him with Lily, Lily who reminded her so much of Sarah, clinging to Charlie that way. 'Come on, let's get you back to bed.'

Lily looked over Ben's shoulder to Fiona, who nodded and forced a smile. 'Go with Daddy, my darling – I'll be up in a minute.' Nicola, Fiona and Sarah said nothing as Ben carried Lily back up the stairs, chatting to her about something or other, his voice light, easy, no trace of the tension he must be feeling. Nicola envied that ability.

'Before you go,' Fiona said, stopping Nicola on her way out for a second time, 'there's a bunch of flowers for you on our doorstop. They got delivered here,' she added unnecessarily, given the annex didn't have its own postal address.

'Oh, that's nice.' Nicola tried to sound bright, to combat the mood of the room. She wondered who they were from. Phil, maybe, reminding her that he was still there, still thinking of her. She should remember that, too, rather than worrying about what she looked like in front of Ben.

Nicola followed Fiona and Sarah to the front door, Sarah making promises to come around more often, spend some more time with the girls. When they reached it, Fiona thrust the flowers into Nicola's hands. White roses. Phil never listened, she'd told him she hated white flowers before, she was sure of it. She hadn't told him why, of course, that the colour reminded her too much of Charlie's skin right before he drew his last breath. She didn't need the reminder of that. She saw it every time she closed her damn eyes, despite her best efforts.

She shook the thought away and opened the little white card attached to the flowers. Almost immediately, too much blood rushed straight to her head, so that for a second the hallway spun. Sarah and Fiona were still talking, but the hum of their voices made no sense to her. Because all her attention was on the card. On the cursive writing, typed up in one of those fancy fonts. Just one word.

Soon.

Chapter Five

Phil had not sent her the flowers. She'd been clinging to that hope, that he'd just meant he would see her soon. But he hadn't and she knew of no one else who would want to send her flowers with that message. She'd tried and failed to track down where the flowers were from – the card had no branding on, the flowers in simple plastic that could be from anywhere.

You will pay for what you did.

Soon.

Those words had gone round and round her head over the last twenty-four hours until it felt like they were tattooed to the inside of her skull. She hadn't been able to sleep and the churning in her stomach was only getting worse.

The flowers were definitely real, like the note, not a trick of her tired mind. Someone she knew, who knew where she lived, had sent them to her. Someone was watching her, to see what effect they were having on her. Waiting for her to break and confess everything. Because surely that must be the endgame here?

Fiona had been her first thought. Fiona, who had never liked her, who didn't trust her no matter what she said. She hadn't wanted Nicola in the annex, she'd made no secret of that. But maybe that wasn't just because she didn't trust Nicola around Ben, maybe that's because she knew. There was no way to be sure, though, not without asking – and she wouldn't risk that.

Relief coursed through her at a knock on the door. She'd asked Phil to stay round again tonight, unable to be alone for any length of time. Phil had made it rather obvious that he was glad about that – he'd been doting on her the last few days, stepping up to the role of 'man of the house' in a way that might have been a little overbearing, had she not had such need for it right now.

But it wasn't Phil who stood behind the door.

'What are you doing here?'

'And hello to you, too.' Ben stepped into the kitchen without waiting for an invitation. His hair was damp, little droplets of misty rain clinging to it.

'What's wrong?'

'Wrong? Nothing. Why?'

She gave in and shut the door. 'Just wondering what's up with the impromptu house call.' She worked hard to keep her voice casual, not to let the ball of anxiety inside her make its presence known.

'Aren't I allowed to pop in to say hello to my neighbour?'

A sour taste rose to her mouth at that. Neighbour. More like charity case, forced to live in their little annex because she had nowhere else to go, because she hadn't thought far enough ahead to foresee what would happen when Charlie wasn't there anymore. Not that she'd say any of that to Ben, knew it would sound ungrateful. 'Where's Fiona?' she said instead.

'She's on her way back from her shift at the hospital, picking the girls up on her way.' He said it easily enough, but Nicola didn't miss his quick, almost involuntary glance to the door, and she knew he was fully aware that Fiona would be none too happy with him being here.

She leaned back against the counter. The silence between them bubbled. 'Ben . . .' His gaze bore into hers. 'What really happened last night? With Fiona?'

He shook his head, bemused. 'Nothing. We told you that. I don't know why everyone is so worked up about this – we argued, I dropped a glass. Really no big deal.' Nicola wondered who the 'everyone' in that sentence was. When she said nothing, he blew out an impatient breath. 'Look, do you really think I'd throw something at her? If I wanted to hit her, I'd do a better job than that.' It was clearly a joke, but it fell flat, like a ball thudding to the ground with no bounce. He grimaced. 'Sorry. Bad taste, I didn't mean that.'

Nicola sighed. 'Why are you here, Ben?'

'You know why.' His voice was different now, low, more intense. And despite herself she felt the prickles run along her forearms, felt his words add a current to the air between them. It was just because she couldn't have him, she told herself firmly. Just because they couldn't have each other. That was the only reason she was thinking that the stubble along his jawline was sexy, was hyper aware of the smell of him as he stepped towards her. 'Nicola.' His mouth crooked into a half smile, one that was so familiar. 'It's driving me mad, knowing you're right here and not being able to do anything about it.'

God, the way he was looking at her, like she was desirable, rather than something old, frail, broken. The temptation to give in to that was almost unbearable. 'You should go,' she whispered. 'Charlie will be here any minute.'

He frowned and said 'Charlie?' at the same time as she said 'Phil'. She shook her head. 'Phil. I meant Phil will be here any minute.'

'Is that what you're worried about? Charlie? Because he's not here anymore, Nicola.'

'I'm aware of that,' she snapped. 'Your wife is, though.'

He laughed. 'Right, like you and Fiona get on.' She wondered briefly if they would have done, if Ben hadn't made his discontent so obvious. At the beginning, when Ben and Fiona first met – they'd been friendly to each other then, hadn't they? She was sure that it was only in the last year, maybe really only in the last few months, that things had got worse, that Ben had started to watch her with those intense green eyes. Only now that Charlie wasn't here anymore.

'That's beside the point,' Nicola insisted. He just stood there, too close, looking at her indulgently. 'You have to stop this, Ben.' She tried to back away, but the kitchen counter left her nowhere to go. She put a hand on his chest instead, gave a gentle shove. He didn't move. 'Please,' she whispered.

His answer was just to place his hands on her arms, move in closer. She felt the skin there flare under his touch and hated herself for it, hated her body for betraying her that way. 'Please, what?' He didn't give her the chance to answer, his lips were on hers before she could draw breath. She was responding before she could think better of it, her hands reaching up to grip his forearms, her body leaning towards the warmth of his. Then she remembered. And she pulled back.

Ben's eyes were bright and she wondered if hers were the same. She felt her stomach tighten, not from pain this time. But when he moved in again, she jerked her head back. 'No,' she said, and was relieved to hear her voice was firm. 'I told you, you have to stop this.'

His lips twisted into a wry smile. 'Oh, come on, stop playing hard to get, I know you want to as much as I do.'

She managed to twist partially out of his grip, one of his hands falling away. 'I said no, Ben.'

She saw it, the tightening of his lips, the narrowing of his eyes to show lines that for once betrayed his age. Knew he was about to say something, to argue. He'd never been one to take no for an answer, too used to his crooked smile, the charm he could turn on in an instant, getting him his own way. But he never got the chance to push it.

They sprang apart when the door opened, and Nicola's heart jolted when she saw Sarah standing in the doorway. More importantly, right behind her stood Phil, his eyes on her, his fists tightened at his sides, like he'd seen, like he knew exactly what was going on.

'Phil and I saw each other in the driveway,' Sarah said, brightly. 'So we walked in together.'

Nicola unstuck her now clammy palms from the counter behind her. 'Right,' she said, trying to match Sarah's tone, deliberately not looking at Ben. 'Well, it's lovely to see you both.' Phil came to stand next to her, putting a possessive arm around her. He bent down to drop a chaste kiss on her head. Nicola smiled up at him, even if his grip on her shoulder was a little too tight to be comfortable. He didn't return her gaze, only glared at Ben who returned the look with equal venom.

'Ben,' Phil growled in greeting, his hand tightening on Nicola's shoulder as he spoke. Ben gave a sharp jerk of his head in return.

'So how's your day been, Mum?' asked Sarah, in an admirable attempt to override the not-so-subtle tension in the room.

'Oh, the usual, you know.' She felt too hot, pressed next to Phil's side, but she didn't dare move in case he misread it. Ben was still there, hovering. For God's sake, why hadn't he made an excuse and left yet? The kitchen was too small to fit all of them in. Did no one else feel it?

'And how are you feeling?' Sarah asked, helping herself to a drink.

'Oh, fine, love,' she said automatically. 'Thanks.'

Sarah cocked her head. 'Really? You look flushed.'

Nicola felt her cheeks grow even warmer. She wondered if that was a deliberate move on Sarah's part, a subtle way of telling her off. 'Oh, it's nothing, just feeling a bit peaky.' It wasn't a lie, to be fair, but then that was her new normal these days.

'Well, then why aren't you sitting down?' demanded Sarah. 'Here, come on.' She took her elbow and led her towards the sitting room. Only Phil didn't immediately let go of her shoulder, so there was a moment where she was caught between them, a teddy bear being fought over. Sarah and Phil's eyes met over Nicola's head and some sort of silent communication must have happened because Phil released her.

Nicola didn't protest when Sarah made her sit down on the sofa and covered her with the cardigan that was forever lying around. Phil sat down next to her, putting one hand on her knee, above the cardigan where everyone could see.

'Well, I'll—' Nicola looked up to see Ben standing in the doorway, blocking her view to the kitchen.

But Sarah had started speaking at the same time, cutting him off. 'I think I should ring the doctor, check whether it's normal for you to still be feeling ill, or if you need to go in again.'

Phil frowned. 'You said the doctor wasn't worried, didn't you, Nicola?' Nicola felt her chest loosen just a little – thank God he'd spoken at last, much better than the moody silence.

'Well, yes, he . . .' She trailed off at the hard, determined look in Sarah's eye. 'But if it'll make you feel better, love, then that's fine, of course. I'd appreciate it.' She gave Sarah a tired smile, even as she felt Phil tense beside her. She knew he hated it when she sided with Sarah over him, even though he should know that she'd always pick Sarah over him when it came down to it.

'I'll ring the NHS helpline, I think,' Sarah said. 'My phone's out of battery, though. Can I borrow someone else's? Ben?' She swivelled to face him.

Ben looked a little alarmed at being brought into it, but shrugged and said, 'Sure.' He fished it out of the back pocket of his jeans.

'Thanks. What's the passcode?' Ben took the phone, entered it in for her. 'Great. I'll be back in a minute.' She squeezed past Ben in the doorway, forcing him further into the living room, and Nicola heard the front door open and shut. Wise of her, to take it outside when all three of them would no doubt be listening intently otherwise. But Nicola wished she *had* stayed indoors so they could do just that and avoid the horrible awkwardness that was now creeping through the room like fog.

Phil edged closer to Nicola on the sofa, and Nicola saw Ben trace the movement with his eyes. 'I'll put the TV on, shall I?' Nicola said, with an attempt at a smile, deliberately not looking at either of them for longer than a split second.

Even with the noise of some soap or other, she was sure the whoosh of relief she let out when Sarah re-entered the house was audible. 'Well?' called Nicola, desperate both for the distraction and for Sarah to give Ben his phone back so he could leave.

Sarah's damp hair was evidence that it was still raining. 'They think it's nothing to be overly concerned about – that you should concentrate on having lots of fluids and getting some rest.' Nicola nodded. 'And sugar,' Sarah added. 'Sugar will help if you're feeling faint.' She spun back around, probably off to immediately dig out some sugar from the kitchen. This time Ben followed her, after a mumbled, 'I'll see you later,' to Nicola. He'd never actually stand up to

Phil in person, Nicola knew, never try to stake his claim obviously. No, Ben preferred to do things quietly, unseen by anyone, avoid the confrontation. She supposed he and Charlie shared that trait at least.

Phil edged even closer to Nicola once they were both out the room and she was suddenly hyper aware of the way he took up so much room on the sofa. His breath was hot, tickling her ear as he leaned in to mutter, 'What was Ben doing here?'

She fought to keep her voice normal, though matched his low tone. 'Oh, he just popped in to say hello, you know.'

'I don't like it.'

She wouldn't wince. She wouldn't betray any sign that something was wrong. But she was sure, right then, that he'd arrived too late to see anything, because otherwise there was no way he'd be this calm. But, God, so close. She couldn't let it happen again, she didn't need something else in her life to fall apart. 'He's just being neighbourly, I think, checking up on me because I've not been feeling great.'

He grunted, glanced to the kitchen, then dropped his voice even lower. 'I saw him, the other day,' he said slowly, 'rifling through your things.'

Her pulse jumped. 'What? When?'

'Just the other day,' he repeated vaguely. It wasn't the first time, unfortunately, they'd all ended up in the same house together.

'What do you mean, rifling?' she hissed.

'In your bedroom. I thought he was just looking for something, but . . .' He finally eased back, though didn't let go of his grip on her knee. 'I just . . . Just be careful with him, OK?'

'Ben wouldn't do anything to hurt me,' she said automatically, even as there was a trickle of doubt creeping through.

'Are you sure?' Phil asked lightly. And then, before she could answer, 'I'm just worried about you, Nicola. I'm just looking out for you, that's all.' He squeezed her knee firmly, as if to reiterate that point.

Nicola couldn't reply because Sarah reappeared with a packet of biscuits. She didn't want to draw Sarah into this. But . . . Rifling. The necklace. Ben had been adamant he didn't know it was there, but was there a chance he'd taken it deliberately? And if he'd taken the necklace, then . . . No. She stopped herself going down that route. Surely he couldn't have been the one who sent the note, the flowers?

You will pay for what you did.

Was there a chance that Ben knew? But surely he would have said something, if he did. Surely he wouldn't still want her. Unless . . . Unless kissing her, trying to seduce her – unless it was all part of a game, one for which she hadn't figured out the rules.

Chapter Six

A day or two passed in a smoky haze, the constant nausea only getting worse through lack of sleep. She *couldn't* sleep, though – not just because of the cramps, the hot flushes, but because of the nightmares that plagued her every time she closed her eyes.

You will pay for what you did.

Every time she tried to sleep, her mind just conjured up images of what else they might do to her. This person she knew, who was close to her. Fiona, Ben, maybe even Phil – she'd wondered briefly if he'd known Charlie, if he'd asked her out because of it. But her Internet searches had shown up nothing of the sort. Besides, she'd been married to Charlie for twenty-five years – surely she would have discovered every single one of his friends during the course of that. Not that Charlie had *had* many friends. He'd always been one to enjoy his own company, hadn't ever been too bothered about what people thought of him. It was one of the things that had drawn her to him, in the beginning.

'Nicola!'

She tried to ignore him as she crossed the garden, the sound of his voice making her stomach churn. *Rifling through your things.* She hadn't asked him if what Phil had said was true, couldn't think how to bring it up – and besides, like he'd take anything Phil said seriously.

It was wet today, and cold, colder than it should be in September. The garden was angry about the weather too. The greens were muted against the grey sky and to her right the gated part of the garden seemed wilder than usual, vines creeping up the edge of the gate, the big pink flowers poking their heads out of the mass of plants at the back near the hedge, defiant against the changing season. They seemed to watch her, those flower heads, staring right at her as if waiting for her to make her move.

'Nicola!' It was only when Ben was practically on top of her, just outside her door, that she gave in and turned.

'Didn't you hear me?' Ben asked, a little breathlessly. She didn't answer, glancing left to the pond in the corner of the garden instead of at him. The china hedgehog Emily had picked out at the garden centre over a year ago was still sitting there, positioned by Emily herself, close enough so it could take a drink, if it wanted to. 'You done at the shop, then?' Ben asked.

'Yep.' She waited.

'Nicola,' he said, his voice low, soothing. 'We need to talk about what happened.'

'Nothing happened,' she said sharply. She unlocked the door and stepped into the annex, Ben right behind her, the height of him making her feel small, insignificant. Powerless.

She felt rather than heard him go to speak, but put a hand up to stop him. Because her attention was on the kitchen. Big, muddy footprints, everywhere. All across the tiled floor, up the white walls, even on the ceiling. They swirled around her, those footprints, walking towards her, closing in on her.

'Nics?' The sound of Ben's voice made her jolt. She'd backed right away to the door again, she realised, her back pressed against it. She had no idea what her expression looked like, but it couldn't be good, given the way Ben was looking at her.

'I . . .' She looked down at the floor again and took a breath. There was only one footprint there. Only one. Like someone had noticed they'd left it, taken off their shoes to leave no more.

'What are you—?'

'Look at that,' she said, pointing, staring at it, her heart starting up a warning drum.

'Yeah, it's a footprint, so what? Just mop it up.'

'It's not *my* footprint.'

'I can see that. Doesn't really matter, though, does—'

She spun to face him and her expression must have been alarming, because he actually jerked back. 'It is not my footprint, Ben,' she hissed. 'Someone has been in the house.' Oh God. The reality of that barrelled into her. Someone had been in the house, this time she was sure of it. Ben could see it, too, it was real.

'What do you mean, Nics?' He spoke slowly.

'It's not Phil's,' she said, trembling now. 'He wasn't here last night.'

Ben's brow was furrowed, like he was trying to keep up with her train of thought. 'OK . . .' he said slowly. 'So you think, what, someone broke in? But the door was locked, right?'

'I . . .' He was right. There was no sign of forced entry.

'And I've been working from home most of the afternoon.' She didn't respond. Because that meant he could have come here, if he'd wanted to. And even if wasn't him, he hadn't been here this morning – that was plenty of time for someone who was watching the house to get in, get out. 'Who has a key?' Ben asked, and his voice was overly soothing, like trying to calm a wild animal. He didn't get it. God, he didn't bloody get it – first Sarah, now him. No one understood.

She tried to think logically, focused on his question. 'You,' she whispered. But if Ben had been here, left evidence, then why would he come up to her later like this? 'Fiona, Sarah . . .' But that wasn't a woman's footprint. 'And Phil,' she finished. 'I gave Phil a key the other day.' Her eyes met Ben's and Ben tightened his lips. Well, too bad if he didn't like it, she had bigger things to deal with right now.

'Well, there you go then,' he said. 'If you gave Phil a key, then I'd guess he's come round while you've been out.'

She nodded slowly. It could well be, the more reasonable part of her brain told her. Of course he could have come in, noticed he was leaving a mess and taken off his shoes. And it would be just like him not to bother to clean up after himself. Why he'd want to come in when she wasn't here was beyond her, but maybe he'd hoped to surprise her. Or walk in on her, she thought wryly. But still, she didn't move any further into the house.

'Do you want me to take a look round?' Ben asked.

She closed her eyes briefly, saw the word 'soon' like it was etched to the inside of her eyelids. And she hated herself a bit for being so pathetic when she said, 'Yes. Do you mind?'

'Not at all.' He gave her a smile as he stepped past. A cheeky, cocky smile – one that reminded her of what he'd been like when she'd first met him, all those years ago. One that reminded her of why she'd been tempted in the first place.

It didn't take him long to do a sweep of the place and come back to where she was still standing rigid by the doorway. 'It's all fine, Nics. Doesn't look like anything's out of place, nothing obvious missing. And I checked, there's no one hiding in the wardrobe or under the bed.' He flashed her a grin which she didn't return. He wasn't taking it seriously, wasn't taking *her* seriously. And why would he? To him, she was just being ridiculous, overly dramatic. She wondered then if she should tell him, come out with it once and for all. It was what this person wanted, wasn't it? The words were almost there but they stuck inside her, her mouth frozen when she tried to let them out. Because, of course, she couldn't tell him, especially not him. He'd be one of those with the most reason to hate her for it. If he didn't already know, if he wasn't the one doing this to her.

But if he *didn't* know and she told, it wouldn't just be her life she'd be ruining. She'd upset so many more people, fracture all their lives. No, she was doing the selfless thing, not telling.

'There's a photo smashed, though, in the living room,' Ben added.

'What?'

'A photo,' he said again, for the first time a hint of impatience creeping in his voice, like she was being deliberately difficult. 'I guess you knocked it over or something, so you want to be careful you don't tread on the glass, maybe hoover it up. Anyway, look, I came to talk to you because . . .'

She ignored him, walking straight past him through the kitchen and into the living room, the cheap beige carpet scratching against her pumps. Ben gave a disgruntled sigh behind her. 'I told you, it's just one photo.'

Again she said nothing. It was just inside the living room, on the floor by the tiny Ikea bookshelf that Ben had put up when she first moved in. There were other photos there, of her and Sarah, one of her and Phil, one he'd insisted she display, even though she thought she looked terrible in it.

She bent down and picked up the photo, brushing aside the broken glass of the frame. It was of her, Charlie and Sarah, on holiday in Cornwall when Sarah was about ten. It was one of the only photos she had up of the three of them, one of the only ones with Charlie in. They were all smiling, looking at the camera, Sarah grinning with slightly crooked teeth, before her braces. If you looked closely you could see the chocolate stain on Charlie's top from where Sarah had spilled ice cream on him while he'd given her a piggyback.

She remembered it so clearly. Charlie had been on form. It had been a surprise, that holiday – Charlie had found the cottage, sorted the whole thing out, then sprung it on them one August morning, to Sarah's squeals of delight. Nicola was sure the holiday hadn't been completely dreamlike – was sure she and Charlie must have had one of their silent arguments – but she didn't remember that when she looked at the photo. No, all she remembered was how attentive Charlie had been that week – to both her and Sarah. She hadn't felt like an outsider to his and Sarah's duo, as she so often had, even when Sarah was little.

The perfect family, that's what they looked like in that shot. The perfect family on a perfect day.

'Did you smash it?' she asked Ben, still staring down at Charlie's face.

'No.' He sounded offended. 'Why on earth would I do that?'

She didn't answer, couldn't really think of a logical reason why he would. It was a photo of his brother, after all. Step-brother, but still, they'd got on, their parents had got together when they were still young enough to accept each other. That was the reason Ben was in her life, after all, for better or worse – he'd chosen to stay in their little town to be close to Charlie.

She thought again of Phil, who had access to her house anytime he wanted now. He might have wanted it gone, this very public memory of Charlie. They had an unspoken agreement never to talk about Charlie, just as they never talked about his ex-wife. But she knew he got jealous of Ben, even if he didn't know the extent of their relationship. Could he also be jealous of a dead man?

Ben was speaking again now, wanting her to pay attention to him, but his words washed over her, no more than a humming in her ears. It was deliberate, picking this photo, just this photo. She hadn't done it herself, whatever anyone else might think. And it wouldn't have happened just by falling on the carpet. Someone had destroyed it, had left it for her to find. To make a point that they knew – knew that she, Charlie and Sarah had by no means been the perfect family. Far from it.

Chapter Seven

It was the burning that woke her, angry flames caressing her skin. It took a moment for her to realise that it wasn't just the usual hot flushes, or not just that. Phil's toned, naked body was pressed up next to her, the heat pouring out of him and into her. Her hair was damp from sweat. Great. She may feel like shit but she didn't want Phil to see her looking like it when he woke up.

She sat up slowly so as not to disturb him, but even that was too much for her body. Her stomach reacted, churning, sending bile to the back of her throat that sizzled there. She was going to be sick.

In one quick motion she threw back the duvet and ran to the tiny bathroom, just making it in time. There was nothing much in her stomach to come up, but that didn't stop her from heaving. She grimaced at the taste of it. When she was done she stayed sitting on the floor, the cool tiles comforting against her burning skin.

'Nicola? Are you OK?' Phil tried the door handle, presuming it would be OK for him to just walk on in, and she was glad she'd thought to lock it.

'I'm fine,' she rasped. 'Out in a sec.' She clambered to her feet, stared at herself in the water-stained mirror. She looked just as she felt, her skin grey, hair dull, her age showing more now than it ever had. At this rate neither Phil nor Ben would want her, she thought wryly, even as something sharp closed over her heart at the thought of being left alone, unwanted.

Menopause, yeah, right. But of course it wasn't just that. The stress of everything was getting to her, taking its toll, leaving her body unable to cope. She raised a hand to smooth her hair and frowned as it shook. This wasn't normal. Even if no one else believed her, she was sure this wasn't normal.

She needed to tell Sarah. She'd come to that conclusion last night, when she couldn't sleep. She couldn't let this go on anymore. She couldn't take it, the invasions of her home, the knowledge that someone close to her knew her secret and was holding it over her. So she had to tell, and she had to start with Sarah – she owed her that. Maybe she'd even understand, once she'd explained it all. But she couldn't have a conversation with her when she looked like she was about to fall apart – she'd take some time to get herself together first.

When she opened the bathroom door, Phil was still hovering outside, completely unfazed by his nakedness. It was one of the things she'd found so sexy about him, but right now she wished he'd put some clothes on, get out of her way.

'Look, Phil, I'm actually not feeling that great.'

'Yeah. You don't look too good, if I'm honest.'

Well, that was just charming, now wasn't it? 'So I really need to shower and have some time alone, if that's OK?'

'Kicking me out, are you?' No trace of a smile there.

Yes. 'No. No of course not. I just . . . Please, I promise I'll call you later, OK?'

He just turned back to the bedroom, clearly in a huff. She followed and watched him pull his clothes back on, her head now pounding. Standing for too long was making her nauseous again so she sunk onto the bed. 'Phil?' she asked tentatively once he was dressed. A grunt in response. 'Did you come by the house yesterday?'

'Well, yeah, obviously as I'm here now . . .' The way he looked at her was becoming all too familiar these days.

'No. Before that, I mean. Did you let yourself in?'

'Would it be a problem if I had?'

She hesitated, unsure as to what kind of answer that was. Was he admitting to it? 'No, I . . .'

'Look, I have to go, anyway.' He was cutting her off, making the decision to leave his and not hers.

'Right, OK.' She wasn't going to argue, not when being alone was exactly what she wanted. More to clear the air than because she genuinely wanted to know, she asked, 'And are you off to do anything nice then?'

'And if I am?'

For God's sake, she got that he was pissed off, but he was now being deliberately obtuse. 'Well, I—'

'Just leave it, Nicola,' he snapped, far too annoyed, she thought, than the circumstance warranted. 'I'm allowed my secrets, just like you have yours.'

'What's that supposed to mean?'

He just gave her a level look, and she found she couldn't keep the eye contact. He could just be playing to her guilt, making her think he had something secret so that she got jealous, wondered where he was going. It would be like him, she was beginning to realise. Or else . . . *Scared?* Could Phil think there was something going on with Ben? Had he wanted to make her worried, so that she'd stop it? If so, she'd played right into his hands. What was the first thing she'd done when she got scared by it all? – call him, because she couldn't stand to be alone. Could that be what this was about – his knowledge that there might be something more than friendship between her and Ben, and instead of asking her about it, he wanted to make her frightened enough to stop herself?

She was still staring at him, little electric currents firing up in her brain, when he turned his back on her with a muttered, 'I'll call you later.' The front door slammed moments after.

She made herself send a quick text to Mary, telling her she wouldn't be in today, even though she knew it was the coward's way out – texting rather than calling. She was sure she'd only been sat down for a minute when the doorbell rang, but when she checked the time it had been over half an hour. Her mind felt hazy, like she was trying to pull it along through thick, sticky mud. And the throbbing in her head was worse, much worse. Flu. Maybe she was getting the flu, on top of everything else – that would be sod's law.

Mary stood the other side of the door, her wide frame obscuring Nicola's view of the garden. 'Hi, chick. I just brought you some soup, thought I'd check up on you on my way to the shop.'

Nicola took the thermos flask Mary offered and stepped aside to let her in, even as she resented her showing up like this – surely the point of having a sick day was that you didn't have to see your boss. She'd no doubt the soup would be horrible – Mary had never been much of a cook. Though she supposed she should be grateful that there were still people looking out for her. She wondered if she'd lose all of them, as soon as it was out. Because once she told Sarah, she doubted it would stay hidden for long. People wouldn't understand, she knew, they'd wonder how she could have kept something like that a secret. And wasn't it horrible that it was fear, rather than guilt, that twisted her stomach at the thought? What kind of person did that make her? she wondered.

'You look awful,' Mary stated. And Nicola realised then that she hadn't just come to be nice – she'd wanted to see if she really was ill.

Nicola's breath scratched her dry throat on the way out. 'Thanks. That's been the general consensus this morning.'

'Hmmm. You been to the doctor?'

'I will if it's still this bad tomorrow.' And when she went she'd ask for a different doctor, see if someone else would take her seriously. She wondered how long she had to talk to Mary for before she could send her on her way.

'Well, I'll be on my way in just a tick,' Mary said, as if she could read her mind – or perhaps her face. 'But look, chick, there's another reason I had to see you, and I hope you won't be offended by me asking.' A warning tingle ran down Nicola's spine. 'Now, I have to do month end today – I'm a bit late as it is, given it's already the second - but I was checking yesterday and the receipts just don't match up right.'

'OK,' Nicola said slowly.

'And so I just wanted to check, and I promise I won't get mad, chick, but I need to know – did you borrow some cash out the register again?' Nicola felt her neck flush, even as resentment curdled in her already weak stomach. One time. She'd borrowed money one time, just before it all had all gone downhill, fast, with Charlie. He'd stopped working completely by then and she'd been left to support them both – she'd *thought* they still had money in savings, something Charlie hadn't been honest with her about, but she hadn't wanted to dip in to those non-existent savings to pay for her hairdresser's appointment, so she'd just borrowed fifty pounds – that was all, just fifty pounds. She'd had every intention of returning it before Mary noticed – which would have worked just fine if Mary wasn't so damn observant with her money. Still, she *had* given it back, hadn't she? And Mary had said she'd understood, that that would be the end of it.

'No,' Nicola said firmly. 'I promise I didn't.' She turned away so she didn't have to look at Mary's expression of disbelief. She picked up the soup, took it to the fridge for something to do, took her time while Mary stood in silence behind her back.

When she turned to face her, Mary was a few paces away, by the windowsill where Nicola kept her keys. She refused to make eye contact, her gaze flicking to Nicola's and then away quickly, hands clasped behind her back. Why the hell was she acting so damn shifty? Did she just think Nicola was lying? Her head spun again, more violently this time, and she rested one hand on the fridge, breathing deeply, in through her nose, out through her mouth, to stop the wave of nausea from overwhelming her.

'Are you all right?' Mary asked, frowning now.

'No. I'm really not,' Nicola said honestly, not caring in that moment what Mary thought of her.

'You need to go back to bed, I shouldn't be bothering you like this, I'll go, leave you in peace.' She made a funny sort of spasm movement, that could be an attempt at a kiss on the cheek before she thought better of it, then let herself out with a hasty, 'You feel better now, I'll see you soon.'

Why was everyone in her life acting so damn strange all of a sudden? Or maybe they weren't. Maybe it was her reading into every tiny thing, waiting for everything to come crashing down on her. She watched Mary cross the garden through the two clear panes on the annex door. It was a sunny, crisp day from the looks of things, not that she had the strength to venture out. Despite the sun there were a few red-brown leaves collecting on the grass under the trees in the garden, the first ones she'd seen. She swore the flowers were also losing their shine, colours muting to green and brown, the garden seeming to accept that it wouldn't be the centre of attention anymore, that it would soon be somewhere people only rushed through, to get to their warm houses. It was so damn sad, this clear evidence that summer was now over, gone. Giving in to her leaden legs, she sank into a wooden kitchen chair and rested her head on her elbows on the table. And finally, she let her burning eyes, her tight, painful throat, have their way. She let it all out as she cried.

Chapter Eight

She was getting worse. She'd taken some paracetamol, crawled into bed and managed an hour of restless sleep, but it hadn't helped. Her head throbbed, her muscles ached. And this damn nausea just wouldn't subside. She'd Googled her symptoms, but she was pretty sure you couldn't get malaria in England, so it must just be the flu. The flu, stress, and the sodding menopause all at once.

The blue curtains in her bedroom were still pulled shut from that morning, and the room was too dark, stuffy. She managed to get to her feet and walked round the bed to the windows to open them. The blaze of sunlight hit her eyes, causing sharp, angry pinpricks of pain. She winced, squeezing them shut until it subsided.

When she opened them, she saw Fiona was out in the gated part of garden, tending to those flowers that refused to be tamed, the part of the garden Nicola was too nervous to go to, in case she did something to upset the plants. Fiona was wearing those red gardening gloves that made her hands look double their size. As Nicola watched those hands detached themselves, overly large, red, spider-hands, pulling at weeds and patting down dirt on their own accord. The sight made her sick. This, she thought to herself, was why the doctors wouldn't take her seriously when she told them she was ill, would ask why she'd thrown away her pills.

Fiona seemed to sense her watching and glanced over to her, but looked away quickly when they made eye contact. Nicola flinched. Everything made her flinch these days. Her palms were clammy and she wiped the dampness on her flannel pyjama bottoms though it didn't seem to help. Fiona. She'd thought it could be her before. Fiona didn't like her, had probably always suspected her of moving in on her husband, and Ben hadn't exactly been helping that. Could she be the one doing this to her, trying to get her away from her husband, to punish her?

She became very aware of the beating of her heart, its irregular, too-fast rhythm, when Sarah came down the paved path, through the line of pear trees, then let herself through the gate to join Fiona in the garden. She watched as Fiona smiled, brushed back her hair and left a smear of dirt on her cheek. Another reason Sarah and Fiona had bonded – since Charlie had died, Sarah had needed distractions, and one of those was gardening, a new hobby that she'd shown no interest in when she'd been growing up. Nicola wished she'd had any knowledge at all of gardens, just so she'd be able to spend more time with her daughter, but she had none. She was useless to her, in that respect.

Now, she thought as she watched her daughter. It was a sign, Sarah being right there, that she should tell her now. Each thud of her heart seemed to send the word vibrating round her body, a warning drum, like she might not get another chance. *Now, now, now.*

With a grand surge of energy, she dragged herself unsteadily to the kitchen. She was wobbly but she made it. Had almost convinced herself that she was really going to do it, that she really would tell Sarah, when the front door burst open, unwelcome light invading her home, piercing her already sensitive eyes.

Charlie? For a moment he was right there, a familiar sad, disappointed smile on his face. Back from the grave to haunt her. But then she blinked and it was just Ben. She trembled as he came towards her, her vision too fuzzy to make out the intricate details of his face.

'Nicola? You look pale.' His words were slurred, and it took a moment to realise that it wasn't him slurring but her, her mind distorting his voice.

'I . . .' But she didn't get it out, because the next moment the grubby kitchen tiles were heading straight for her. Ben's arm was around her, pulling her up, before she could hit them.

'Whoa there. Now, I'm not above women swooning in my arms, but this is a bit much.' She was looking up at his face, so she saw the smile fade, saw his expression twist into concern. And was so pathetically grateful that someone cared.

'Where's Sarah?' she managed.

'Sarah? She's gone, I think, saw her walking out to her car. Why? Nicola, what's wrong?'

But she didn't get the chance to tell him, because everything went dark.

She was paralysed. Fear shot through her at the realisation that she couldn't move, couldn't call out. Then a lash of pain ripped through her stomach, snapping her fully awake and out of it. She was lying on her bed, but every part of her body felt as though it was lying on burning, jagged rock.

Something was very wrong. The room was blotchy, and she could hear voices but she didn't know where they were coming from. She thought she could hear Charlie, which couldn't be right.

'Nicola? Nicola are you OK? Are you awake?' When her vision came back into focus she saw Ben holding out a mug to her. 'You need to drink something,' he was saying. And really, she was in no position to argue. Her head was still spinning and she couldn't remember when she last drank anything, which surely wasn't helping.

Ben cupped the back of her neck, helped her to drink the warm brown liquid. It tasted horrible and immediately sent her into a coughing fit. Ben backed away, eyebrows furrowing around his lovely eyes. 'Stay here,' he said, and his words were too harsh for her painful head. She shook her head. 'I'm serious, Nicola, I'll be back in a minute, OK?'

But where did he expect her to go? She had nowhere *to* go.

She remembered once she was alone again. Sarah. Before she'd blacked out she was going to tell Sarah. She reached for her phone, but it went straight to voicemail. 'Sarah.' Her voice was slurred, hissing on the 's'. 'Sarah, I need to tell you something.' But it wasn't something she could say over the phone, no way.

Ben appeared again. How long had he been there? He was watching her like he'd been listening to her, like he'd been waiting for her to finish. Had he even left? She couldn't think, her head hurt too much, so much that she wanted to scream now with the pain of it, only she couldn't get her voice to work. And something else now, unlike the stomach cramps or sickness. Something ugly creeping through her, stinging her nerves. Fear.

Fiona. Fiona was there, too. She was looking at her with concern in her eyes. For some reason that concern seemed hilarious and she burst out laughing, and when Ben and Fiona only looked horrified that made her laugh all the harder. Until the laugh turned into sobs, and the sobs into a hacking cough that made her taste blood.

'I'm not a bloody doctor, Ben, I just do the admin, you know that.' Fiona's words. Anxious, nerves bubbling away there. 'You should have checked on her earlier. Sarah asked you to.'

71

'*We* should have checked on her, you mean. Besides, I didn't want to disturb her, I thought you'd . . .' But the words were too quiet now, muttered, or maybe she was drifting out of consciousness again.

'Has anyone called a doctor?' Oh, Phil was there too now, apparently. How long had he been here? She didn't remember him coming in, and this room really wasn't big enough for the four of them, Ben and Fiona should really leave. She tried to find the words to tell them that, but she couldn't make her mouth move.

'I've called the ambulance.' *Ambulance.* The word echoed through her brain. She knew what it meant, knew it was bad.

'Sarah,' she mumbled. The one person she wanted, and she was nowhere to be seen. That wasn't fair. She didn't want it to be too late.

'Sssshh.' Ironic, that it should be Fiona comforting her in that moment, that the men who were more hers just stood idly by. 'We've called her, she'll meet us at the hospital.'

'Did you manage to get through to her?' Ben, in an attempt at a whisper.

'Not yet. We will do, though.' Fiona's voice was equally unquiet.

I'm not deaf! Nicola wanted to shout. *I'm not an invalid, I can hear you!* But of course, she didn't shout, because she wasn't sure she actually *could* shout.

Charlie had reappeared. He was there for her, she knew it. Maybe he was there to punish her, in her last moments, but she didn't think so. He looked too peaceful, too sad for that. And they'd loved each other, deep down, hadn't they?

'Hold on,' Ben was saying, but she shook her head, just a fraction. He didn't know, he couldn't see Charlie. But *she* knew. In those last few moments, she felt the realisation hit home.

You will pay for what you did.

She hadn't understood, hadn't taken it seriously enough. Hadn't realised they'd meant she would pay the ultimate price.

She became aware that her cheeks were sticky, tears streaking their way down them, so hot they were practically fizzing. She didn't want to go, not when she hadn't put things right. But she was so tired and in so much pain. And besides, Charlie looked OK, didn't he?

Ben, Phil and Fiona were all still there, and they seemed to be edging closer, looking down at her with grim faces. She didn't want to see that, no, not now. So she closed her eyes.

'Hold on,' Fiona was murmuring, and someone was stroking her hair. 'You're OK, the paramedics will be here soon, they'll give you something for the pain.'

'Hold on,' someone else repeated, and it echoed strangely around the room.

Hold on, hold on, hold on.

'Can't,' she mumbled, though she wasn't sure if she'd managed to get the word out properly, it sounded distorted even to her.

'What was that?'

'Did she say something?'

'Nicola?'

She was very aware of her heart in these last moments, of the way it seemed to speed up, like it was trying desperately to keep her alive even as the rest of her body failed her. She opened her eyes one last time, saw their faces looking down at her. Relief there, on all three of them. They'd know soon enough that the relief was unfounded. There was so much that she should say, but it would take too long. Too late now, to explain everything. So she shook her head sadly instead, looked to Charlie.

'It's in the eyes, you know,' she whispered, and Charlie nodded. 'All in the eyes.'

PART TWO

—

Sarah

Chapter Nine

The building in front of me is bland, all brick and white-rimmed square windows, indistinguishable from an ugly block of council flats or a small school. Even the sign is pathetic, the word POLICE in faded green lettering. It doesn't exactly impose the right sense of fear, of confidence that the people inside know what they're doing. Even so, my mouth is dry as I look at it, as I try to remember what I want to say. Try to decide whether I'm actually going to do this, just march on in there and make demands.

But I have to. It's been driving me mad, waiting. I need to do something. Something other than sitting alone in my flat, dealing with a constant stream of people invading my privacy, wanting to tell me how sorry they are, that they're here for me, that they understand. Every time it happens I want to tell them to fuck off. Tell them they couldn't possibly understand and that pretending they do is just making things worse. I haven't given in to that desire, of course. Yet.

Over the last couple of days, the moments of my mother's death have been playing on a loop in my mind. I can imagine her there, groaning in pain, thrashing in her bed. I know, from what Fiona has told me, that she asked for me. That they tried to keep her breathing until the ambulance came, but that her heart gave out minutes before it arrived. I can see her eyes, wide and glassy, the way they were when I was taken to her in the morgue.

Thinking of her like that now is the drive I need to start me walking up the steps to the entrance, my shoes clicking on the concrete, wet from another night of rain. I chose these black heels deliberately, to go with the dress, to make me look a together woman who means business. It's something I've learned through working at the council, where many of my superiors are men. They take me more seriously like this, even though all it's actually doing is marking me out as different, as feminine.

The smell of the waiting room hits me first, reminding me of my old school changing rooms, all damp clothes and stale sweat and unwashed socks. I wrinkle my nose against it as I do a quick scan, my gaze passing over the old man slumped in a corner and the teenage girl chewing gum, then resting on the woman at reception. I stride over to her and she smiles in a way that seems inappropriate, given her job. She's wearing a police uniform but her grey bob and round face make her look like she'd be better suited to working in a nursery.

'I want to speak to someone about my mother's death,' I say as firmly as I can manage.

'OK, dear,' she says. 'Who's the officer that you've been speaking to?'

'There isn't one yet.'

'So you want to report a crime, is that it?'

I take a slow breath, though immediately regret it when I inhale the ugly smell of the room. This is it, the whole reason I'm here, the reason I felt different waking up today because I knew I would do it. The nerves in my fingertips thrum but there's a moment, just before I speak, where I'm not sure I actually want to say the words out loud, not with this woman looking at me in her sickeningly patient way.

'No,' I say on an exhale. 'My mother died two days ago. I want to know what you're doing about it.'

'Right,' says the woman, frowning. So maybe, despite my carefully chosen outfit, I'm not doing that well at coming across like a sane person after all. *You wouldn't be sane either,* I want to hiss at the woman. *You wouldn't be so calm if you hadn't been able to sleep for two days, if you'd been through what I've been through.* 'I'm just not really sure what you—' She's cut off before she can finish.

'I'll take this, Gwen.' I spin to see a policeman, dressed in the same uniform as Grey Bob here. I hadn't even noticed him. He gestures for me to follow him and, after a brief pause, I do so.

'I'm PC Franks,' he says in a friendly tone of voice.

'Sarah Gregory.'

He leads me down a corridor, then stops outside one of the doors and opens it. 'In here,' he says, unnecessarily, and waits for me to step in ahead of him.

There is nothing in the small room except four chairs, two each side of a plastic table, which looks to be bolted to the floor. It's dark, the only window is high up and the glass is obscured, like they don't want people seeing in or out. Not exactly a warm, welcoming place, but somewhere deliberately designed to make someone nervous. Designed to make *me* nervous, I imagine. And despite the fact that I was the one to walk in here, despite the fact that I'm the one demanding their help, I feel my body respond the way it's supposed to, forearms prickling, mouth drying out, just a little.

The man smiles. 'Sorry about the decor,' he says jovially. 'Not too many places to have a private conversation around here.' I try not to wince at the realisation that he must have read what I was thinking from my expression. He takes the seat opposite me and leans forward, clasping his hands on the table. 'Now, I only caught the end of your conversation at reception. You wanted to report something about your mother's death, is that right?'

I make myself focus my attention solely on him. Now is not the time to lose it. I stare at his greying beard, his thinning hair, his too-red cheeks, as I speak. Anything I can to distract me from what I'm really feeling.

'No. Well, yes, maybe.' I narrow my eyes at his raised eyebrows and my next words are sharp. 'My mother died two days ago. At home, in her bed, before the ambulance arrived.'

'I'm sorry, that's—'

But I cut him off with a wave. I've had enough 'sorrys to last me a lifetime. 'The doctors said at the time that it was likely natural causes, a heart failure, but we're waiting for the autopsy results.'

At this, the policeman frowns. 'Well, err, if it's a natural death then there's not really much we can—'

'No, you don't understand,' I say, and without meaning to I'm leaning forward across the table too. 'It wasn't natural, it can't have been. My mum, she never showed any sign of heart issues, and she was young, only fifty-three. She has – had – been ill a bit recently, but it was nothing serious, she was still going to work and everything.'

I know before he's even opened his mouth that the words I've been going over and over all morning just don't sound convincing when said out loud, but I plough on. I have to make him believe me. 'And there's this,' I say, unzipping my handbag and sliding out my phone. He looks down at it, but I don't let him even open his mouth to get the first word out. 'She left me a message. On the night she died.' I press my lips together, psyching myself up to hear it again. Then, without asking him, I press play.

My mother's voice rings out, the little room giving her hoarse, slurred words an almost echoing quality. I know the message off by heart but still it makes me grimace, makes me dig my nails into the palms of my hands as I fight to keep emotion at bay.

'Sarah, I need to tell you something. I don't think I've got much time left and I don't want to go without you knowing. It's been driving me crazy, keeping it from you, you have to understand. Please, Sarah, I need to tell you and I need to do it in person. Please come, as soon as you can.'

I hang up and look at the policeman. 'She died less than thirty minutes after this was recorded,' I whisper. 'Please. All I'm asking is that you ring the coroner, ask for the results of the autopsy. They said it could be weeks before they release the full results to next of kin – to me – but I need to know sooner than that. I *need* to. Please,' I repeat. 'Her name was Nicola. Nicola Gregory. She was the only parent I had left.'

His eyebrows pull together, nearly meeting in the middle. 'Nicola Gregory?' His voice is thoughtful, musing, and I know immediately that I'm missing something. I can't figure out from his expression if that's a good or bad thing. 'Look,' he says, 'I don't know what I'll be able to do, but I'll do my best. Just . . . Give me a moment, OK? I'll be back in two minutes.'

With that he leaves me alone in this small, dark room. I reach my hand up to pull the necklace out from under my high-necked dress, running the gold chain through my fingers. It's the necklace my dad gave me for my twenty-first birthday and I've barely taken it off since then. I make myself breathe slowly. In for three, out for three. Because although I put myself here, there's something awful about being left in a room like this, alone with my own thoughts, my mother's final plea still ringing in my ears.

And I'm forced to sit with that for longer than two fucking minutes. I try to count my heartbeats. I lose track, but I think it's closer to ten minutes by the time the door opens again. I stand automatically.

It's not the same man who enters this time. Instead it's two people. A short, balding man with a sheen of sweat on his forehead, who is wearing a very bland expression to go with his bland shirt and bland green tie, and a tall woman, her short black hair hanging sleek and straight around her face. She's not dressed in a police uniform either, but in an unbuttoned blazer, blue blouse and loose-fitting black trousers.

She steps towards me, the space around her vibrating with energy, the balding man in her wake. 'Ms Gregory?' I nod, though it's a stupid question – of course it's me, given how I've been waiting in a room all by myself. She holds out her hand. I grasp it, and her handshake is satisfyingly firm. 'I'm DC Murphy. This is DS Ashby.' She waves a hand in his direction and he gives me a nod, a bland smile. He shakes my hand too, his is a little clammy. I resist the urge to wipe my palm on my dress. 'PC Franks filled us in,' says the woman.

Interesting, that she's his junior and yet is the one to introduce them. She gestures for me to sit and I do so only when the two of them do the same. When she looks at me, I know immediately what she's going to say. Know because her brown eyes seem to go soft, because she hesitates in that moment between opening her mouth and speaking. 'Ms Gregory,' she continues, 'you've actually beaten us to it. You were on my list of people to call today, I'm afraid.'

I say nothing – I don't need to, they already know why I'm here, what I think. Murphy's gaze is unnervingly direct on mine. 'You came here because you believe there was something suspicious in the way your mother died, am I right?' I nod, waiting for her to get to the point. 'Well, I can confirm that we've already spoken with the coroner.'

I reach up to clutch my necklace again, my throat tight. 'We're still waiting for a more comprehensive report, and the pathologist still has some tests to do, which is why you won't have heard anything yet, but as it stands the results seem pretty clear on one thing.' *Go on!* I want to shout at her. *Tell me!* She clears her throat, glances at the other detective. 'I'm afraid it looks like your mother died from poisoning, Ms Gregory.'

And there it is. *Poisoning.* For a moment everything stops, the word causing a ringing inside my own head, eclipsing everything else.

The two of them are watching me, waiting for my reaction, but I close my eyes to block them out. All I feel in those first few seconds is an intense relief coursing through me. They don't think I'm mad, they don't think I made it up. They're going to do something about it now. The other emotions will come, I know, when I'm alone. But for now, in this dark room, I feel as though I suddenly have space to breathe.

I open my eyes. 'So what exactly are you saying?' I ask, my voice croaky. 'What does this mean?' I let go of my necklace, drop my hand to my lap. It's an unnecessary question. I know what it means. And it's clear they both know that *I* know from the way they are watching me – the man's head tilted, the corners of the woman's mouth turned down in sympathy. But I need to hear them say it.

It's the man who speaks. His voice patient, but too even, given the gravity of the situation. 'Well, Ms Gregory, it means we'll be opening a murder investigation.'

Chapter Ten

Detective Constable Murphy glances at Ashby the moment she shuts the door on Sarah Gregory behind them. Sarah has agreed to wait a little longer, to be formally interviewed about her mother's death, but Murphy and Ashby need a moment to get their thoughts together, to make sure they're on the same track, before they do that.

They weren't expecting this. It was only late yesterday evening that they got the confirmation that Nicola Gregory's death was indeed suspicious, the pathologist having called in, uncertain and a little apologetic. Murphy understands why she'd taken that tone, why she'd been unwilling to call attention to her findings. The PCs checked it out as per protocol when Nicola Gregory's death was first called in, but had seen nothing to be concerned about, no need for the police to get involved. So when the pathologist had proven them wrong on that front, the whole team had been given a good bollocking. Needless to say, everyone is still a little on edge. And the victim's daughter showing up saying she's known all along it wasn't a natural death isn't exactly helping things.

Murphy waits a beat for Ashby to speak, but when he says nothing asks, 'What do you think?'

Ashby runs a hand across his clean-shaven jawline, leans against the wall of the corridor. 'Hard to tell just from that. What makes her so sure her mother was murdered, that's what I want to know.'

'Well, she was,' Murphy points out, to which Ashby simply raises his eyebrows in a condescending sort of way. Murphy grits her teeth, tries to get in a subtle shoulder roll. He's like this with her, Ashby, always judging every little thing she says, even if she just means it as an offhand comment. Little digs to remind her that he's senior to her. Even if he's only *just* senior to her. She wonders if it's because she's a woman, or if she's reading too much into that. She doesn't know him that well yet, given he's based out in this little town and she's only on loan from Bristol.

'The message, though,' Murphy carries on. 'You've got to admit that looks a little suspicious.' Ashby gives a noncommittal grunt. Unable to take the resulting silence she adds, 'Besides, people do this, don't they? Look for something to blame it on? Or someone? They want to believe there's a reason for death.'

Another infuriating eyebrow raise. 'People do what, exactly – jump to the conclusion that a loved one was murdered? I'd say it's more traumatic to think someone was murdered rather than accepting they died of natural causes, wouldn't you?'

Given that he doesn't actually want an answer to that, Murphy just says, 'We don't know she actually was murdered. She could have taken the poison herself – accidentally or on purpose.'

'True,' Ashby concedes.

Murphy sighs, resists the urge to play with her hair. It's a bad habit, marks her out as nervous, makes her look younger than she is. And she spends bloody ages straightening it each morning, she doesn't want to mess it up. 'So what now, do we go back in, ask her about it?'

Ashby glances along the corridor towards their office, and she knows he's thinking of DI James, their boss. He'd told them to deal with Sarah Gregory, to get a feel for her, get rid of her if necessary, but hadn't explicitly said to formally interview her. Surely it's a given, but Murphy knows Ashby won't want to do anything that could give the DI an opportunity to shout at him, given the fucked-up start to this.

'Yeah,' Ashby says eventually. 'Let's just give her a few moments, give her the chance to get a bit worried, then we'll go in. I know James wants me to lead the team on this.' Murphy's not sure why he says that last part out loud, why he needs to voice it to her, given she already knows it. It's like he's trying to reiterate that he's in charge and it grates on her.

Despite that, a jolt of excitement, like an electric shock, lances through Murphy's chest. This is the first time she's been allowed to interview someone on a murder investigation. The first time she's even been *involved* in a murder investigation this closely, though she isn't sure if Ashby knows that. She certainly isn't going to call attention to it if he doesn't – she doesn't want him running to DI James and insisting he come in on the interview instead of her. She wants to be there, she's *ready* for this. Has been ready for so damn long, but there's never been the chance – in a city like Bristol there are too many DSs for anyone to bother involving her in anything this exciting, that's why she agreed to come out here in the first place. Looks like she's lucked out, as wrong as it is to describe murder as lucky.

She tries to keep her cool as she asks, 'You want to get her worried? Do you really think she'd come in, try to get us to treat it as murder, if she was guilty?'

Ashby glances at her, his expression a little vacant, like he's forgotten what he said only seconds ago. 'No,' he says eventually. 'I don't, but we shouldn't rule anything out. We've got to treat everyone as a suspect until proven otherwise. And besides, she might have other secrets, or know something about someone else that will come in handy – and those things are more likely to slip out if she's worried. '

Murphy nods, but privately she's thinking that Sarah Gregory doesn't seem like the kind of person to fall for that. She came here, talking about the murder of her mother, and was nothing other than calm, maybe a little cold. Demanding, yes, and that's understandable given they're talking about the death of her parent. But she has a handle on her emotions, that one.

Ashby is frowning now. 'Gregory,' he says musingly, and Murphy waits. 'Gregory. I feel like I know the name from somewhere.' Murphy resists the urge to point out that there are a hell of a lot of Gregorys in the world. In a city like Bristol she's sure no one would think anything of a surname, finds it hard to believe that Ashby recognises it. But then, she knows Ashby has worked here for the entirety of his career, and in a town this size maybe it's more believable that you'd recognise a name. 'Can you look into it? Check if there's been another incident with any Gregorys in the last few years around here?'

'Of course,' she says.

'Great.' Ashby checks his basic, clearly bought for function only, watch. 'Let's go speak to our first suspect.'

SARAH ELIZABETH GREGORY
EXTRACT FROM RECORDED INTERVIEW

Date: 04/10/2018
Duration: 28 minutes
Conducted by Officers DC MURPHY and DS ASHBY

DC This interview is being tape-recorded. I am Detective
Constable Murphy of the Avon and Somerset Police. This
interview is being conducted at Frome Police Station in interview room 1. What's your full name?

SG Sarah Elizabeth Gregory.

DC And could you confirm your date of birth for us?

SG 17.11.1995

DC Also present is . . .

DS Detective Sergeant Ashby.

DC Great. The date is Thursday 4 October and by my watch it's
11.08 in the morning. Ms Gregory, I know I've already said this,
but I need to point out that this is an out-of-custody interview.

SG Right, you said. And it's Sarah.

DC Sarah. So this means you're not under arrest, and are free to
leave at any time.

SG Well yes, I should hope so. I'm the one who told you my
mother was murdered. I thought you wanted to talk to me to
find out what happened to her?

DC That's exactly right yes. This is just a formality. And I'm sorry, Sarah, as another formality, I need to reiterate that you understand that you're entitled to free legal advice? So if you'd like a solicitor present then we can arrange that?

SG Why would I need a solicitor?

DC I suppose that's something only you can know. It's completely up to you. Now, before we ask you any more questions we just need to let you know that you do not have to say anything. But it may harm your defence if you do not mention when questioned something which you later rely on in court. And anything you do say may be given in evidence.

SG I suppose that's another formality, is it?

DC That's exactly right, yes.

SG OK, fine.

DS OK, thanks Detective Murphy. We'll get started then. I'd like to reiterate that we're very sorry about your mother's death, and we will be doing everything in our power to find out how she died.

SG [Inaudible]

DS I'm sorry, Sarah, could you repeat that? You need to speak up for the voice recorder.

SG I said I hope that's true.

DS I can assure you it is. Now, you came here today to tell us you thought there was something suspicious in the way your mother died.

SG That's right.

DS Can you tell us how exactly you concluded that it wasn't a natural death?

SG It's like I said before, the paramedics initially put it down to heart failure, but we have no history of heart problems in our family and my mum was young – only fifty-three – so there's no way it just gave out one day. I just . . . I knew she couldn't have just died like that. And then there's the message she left on my phone.

DS Right, the voicemail you played us, which stated that she had something she needed to tell you.

SG Yes, exactly.

DS And do you have any idea what it was that she wanted to tell you?

SG I honestly don't. I've been turning it round and round in my mind and I keep coming up blank. But it's a pretty big coincidence, isn't it? That she wanted to tell me something and then the same day she dies? It's like she knew that something was about to happen to her.

DS It's interesting, certainly. But couldn't she have wanted to tell you something because she felt herself getting ill? Why are you so sure that someone else did this to her?

SG I've already told you this – my mother was healthy up until recently, so when she died I just knew something was wrong. I never said I knew it was poison – I just wanted someone to look into it, when everyone was accepting she died of heart failure, for God's sake.

DS Isn't there the possibility though that this could have been an accident?

SG What, that someone accidentally poisoned her? That comes down to the same thing, doesn't it? Someone killed her.

DS Or she could have accidentally poisoned herself.

SG What? That's insane. She was an intelligent women, there's no way she'd just eat something poisonous or whatever and not realise it. Besides, surely then she'd have gone to get help as soon as she realised?

DS All right. The other thing we have to consider here is that this might have been a deliberate move, on your mother's part.

SG What's that supposed to mean?

DS Well, did your mother ever seem inclined to want to hurt herself?

SG Hurt herself? No she . . . Wait, are you saying you think my mother did it to herself? That she committed suicide? Because that's ridiculous. She would never have done that. She was happy, she was in a relationship and everything. She didn't want to leave all that behind, I know that.

DC I'm sorry, Sarah. DS Ashby didn't mean to upset you. We understand how traumatic this must be.

SG Have either of you ever had a parent murdered?

DC I can't say that we have, no.

SG Well then. I don't think you can understand how traumatic this is, do you?

DC Sarah, you said your mother was healthy up until recently – by that do you mean she wasn't actually in perfect health lately?

SG Well, she'd been feeling a bit run down, yes. But it wasn't anything bad – she was just going through the menopause, that's all. And that's another thing – she went to the doctor about it. Would she really have gone to the doctor if she'd been planning on killing herself?

DC Ms Gregory – Sarah – like I said, DS Ashby didn't mean anything by it. We have to consider all avenues, as I'm sure you'll understand. Moving on, though, can you think of anyone who might have wanted to hurt your mother?

SG I don't know. She didn't have any obvious enemies or anything, if that's what you mean. She was an incredible woman – it makes no sense, why someone would have wanted to do this to her.

DC You said she was in a relationship?

SG Yes that's right. Phil is his name. Phillip Daley. But they've only – or were only – going out for about six months.

DC What about your relationship with your mother? Were you close?

SG Yeah, we were. I'm not saying we always saw eye-to-eye growing up, but she was my mother, you know? And I'm her only child. I was making sure I spent lots of time with her recently – I saw her a couple of times a week, at least. That's why I'm so sure this wasn't her doing – she would have told me if she was . . . struggling.

DC And were you there when she died?

SG No. I wish I had been. I wish I'd had the chance to . . . say goodbye, at least. Sorry, I . . .

DC That's OK, take your time.

SG Fiona – my aunt – called me to tell me what was happening, but I didn't get the message in time, just like I didn't see the message from my mum until it was too late.

DC All right. When was the last time you saw your mother?

SG Three days ago. I went round to her place – she was feeling a bit run down, but I called the doctor, they said it was nothing to worry about. And then . . . Well, I saw her through the window the day she . . . the day she died. I didn't go in the house, just popped round to give Fiona some seeds for the garden I said I'd pick up. I was late for work otherwise I would have. I wish I had gone in. Maybe I would have noticed something was wrong in time. Maybe I could have stopped it.

Chapter Eleven

When I get to work the next day, everyone is staring. The morons try to pretend they're not, gazes flicking away the moment I meet them, back to computer screens, but their hands are dead still on keyboards, eyeballs unmoving. They know, of course. Even if it hadn't been in the local news, it's a small town and people talk. They know my mother was murdered.

I head for my desk, next to the window that looks out at the bus station, pretending I don't notice that I'm the centre of attention. I'm halfway there when my boss, Henry, blunders out his little office and does a double take, despite the fact I told him I'd be coming back in today. 'Sarah!' He beams at me, his red face already shiny despite the fact it's only 9 a.m. 'How *are* you?'

'I'm fine. Thanks.' My voice is clipped, but I don't have it in me to be concerned how Henry will take that. 'Happy to be back.' He says nothing, though he glances a little frantically around the office, as if hoping someone else will jump in. 'I'm just going to sit down, get on with my job, if that's OK.' I need to. Need the distraction it will give me.

'Right. Yes, yes, of course.' He runs a hand over his balding head. 'Well, I'll let you get on with it then. And if you need anything, anything at all, you just let me know, OK? We're all really . . . Well, awful thing to happen, just awful.'

'Thanks, Henry.' I wonder how many times I'll have to thank someone today for their words, their concern. All so fake, isn't it – I have nothing to thank them for. But it's part of the dance I have to go through, even if it makes me want to fucking scream.

Lizzy, the small redhead girl who sits next to me on our row of sardine desks, gives me a hesitant smile as I sit down. She already has her headphones plugged in and is typing away. As far as colleagues go, I like Lizzy, precisely because of this. She leaves me alone, I leave her alone, and we both tick along nicely. It helps that she started after me, so although she's a little older, she doesn't have that inferiority complex so many of them seem to have. It was the same at school, though rather than the other girls being jealous that I got good marks so easily, now my colleagues don't like that I'm working my way up through the levels so quickly, don't like that I have ambition and that I don't bother to hide it. Those of them who have been here long enough think it's just because my dad used to work here that I've managed to do well, which is utter bullshit.

I shove my handbag under my desk and frown. Someone has been sitting here while I've been away. The computer screen is wonky, all my pens are mixed up and there's a ring of dried brown liquid on the white plastic desk next to the keyboard. People are just so fucking inconsiderate. I straighten the monitor, then head to the kitchen to get something to clean the desk with. I feel the whole bloody office trailing me with their eyes. I imagine they're waiting for me to break down in floods of tears or something. It would probably make them feel better if I did just that – I have a feeling they see me as a bit of an ice queen, so some emotional turmoil would make them feel on more even footing. But that is just another reason not to do that, to keep it together. I won't give them the satisfaction – they should be trying to make me feel better on my terms, not trying to alleviate their own discomfort.

When I get back to my desk, I wipe it down and sort out the pens. Lizzy raises her eyebrows at me and I grimace. She nods and returns to her typing. I start to wade through the backlog of emails from a local resident trying to get planning permission, but my office phone rings almost immediately. I answer it without thinking, then immediately regret that decision when I hear who it is at the other end.

'Sarah my darling, I thought I might get you here.'

'Hi, Fiona.'

'I'm so sorry to ring you at work,' she says hurriedly. *Then don't*, I want to say. But it's Fiona, and unlike my colleagues I believe she genuinely wants to help. 'I just . . . Ben and I have been trying to get hold of you, but you won't answer your phone. We're worried about you.' Fiona is worried, I'm sure. Ben, I doubt. He's probably thinking about him and *his* loss more than me.

'I know,' I say on a sigh. 'I'm sorry. I haven't wanted to speak to anyone, to be honest.'

'I understand that, really I do, but we need to stick together. We're family, you know.'

I glance at Lizzy. She still has her earphones plugged in, but still, I hardly want to talk about this here. Work was supposed to be a safe place, somewhere I could try to put it all aside, try to get away from this and Fiona is ruining it, no matter what her intention is. 'I know,' I say again, 'but you need to give me a bit of time, OK?'

'But I need to—' She stops abruptly. Then, 'Hang on, there's someone pulling in to the drive.' I can tell she's trying to say it lightly but it doesn't quite work.

'Someone?'

'Well, it's the police, actually. There's a police car parking on the drive.' She says it almost disbelievingly. I feel my shoulders tense. So the police have gone there already. Does that mean they've found something? Does it mean they suspect Ben and Fiona? Or does it just mean they want to check out the scene of the crime? Fuck, I hate this. I hate not knowing what they're doing, what they're thinking.

'God, Sarah, you don't think something has happened to Ben, do you?' Fiona's voice is breathy.

'What? No, why would you . . .' It dawns on me then. She doesn't know. She didn't read the evening news, the police haven't told her yet. How the hell she's managed to avoid someone blurting it out to her I don't know, but she doesn't yet know my mother was murdered. She has no clue what the police are doing there. That would explain why she'd call me at work, why she'd still insist that we all need to get through it together. That might change once she knows what's going on, knows that my mother was poisoned in her own home.

Shit, maybe I should tell her. I haven't wanted to, obviously, haven't wanted to speak to anyone about it after I told the police. But she'll feel terrible, when it comes from them and not from me. 'Fiona . . .' But I can't do it, can't just blurt it out over the phone, not with half the bloody office listening.

Luckily, she doesn't seem to be paying attention to me anyway. 'Sarah my darling, I'm so sorry – they're at the door now and I really need to see what it's about. God, I really hope he hasn't done anything stupid, he's been in such a state the last few days and I . . . Anyway, that's not for you to worry about, I'm sure it's all fine. I'll call you back, OK?' She hangs up without waiting for a response.

I grab my handbag and stand up abruptly. That phone call has proved something. There's no point staying here, no point pretending I'll be able to do anything other than think about my mother, about the investigation. I head to Henry's office and let myself in without knocking. He jumps, the back of his hand flying into a glass of water at his side, which he just manages to save before it goes everywhere.

'I'm going to go out, get some air. I'm sorry, I know I just got here but—'

He waves a hand in the air, pastes an overly sympathetic smile onto his face. It comes off as smarmy. 'It's fine, Sarah. Whatever you need.'

'I'll try and come back later if I'm feeling up to it.'

'Of course, of course. And are you doing anything nice for the weekend?' He flushes, like he's realised his mistake immediately.

I wonder whether to lie just to avoid making him uncomfortable. But lying would take up too much energy right now. 'It's the anniversary of my dad's death.' I don't tell him anymore and he doesn't ask, his face going even redder, if that's possible.

'Well, I'll see you when you're back, then but there's no rush – you take your time.'

'Thank you.' I shut the door and leave him staring after me. *Take your time.* I know he really means it. The problem is, I'm not sure if he means it for the right reasons. I worry him, despite the fact I'm excellent at my job, that my good work reflects well on him. Henry has worked for the council for twenty years, and I know he doesn't like the possibility that I'll keep working my way up, that maybe I'll be after his job one day in the not-so-distant future.

I head to my car the moment I'm outside. My dad used to cycle to work, setting an example to the rest of the council given that we're supposed to be reducing the traffic in the town centre. But I live too far to walk if I'm running late in the mornings, and I bloody hate cycling. Besides, I'm not like him. Not as good as him.

I slip my iPhone out of my pocket and find the number that Detective Murphy gave me, her direct line for me to call if I think of anything important. She answers on the third ring and though perhaps I should feel pleased by that, it actually worries me. Why isn't she in there talking to Fiona? 'Hello, DC Murphy speaking.' Her voice is efficient, not like the calm, soothing one she used with me at the police station.

'Hello, Detective Murphy, this is Sarah Gregory.' I use my work phone voice, the one I use to deal with annoyed residents or contractors. 'I'm sorry to bother you, but I was wondering if there are any updates on my mother's case.'

'Hello, Sarah.' Is it me, or is her voice now just a bit too cautious? 'Thanks for calling,' she says in a way that makes it clear she is not thanking me at all, 'but I'm afraid there have been no new developments since yesterday. As I said, we will keep you updated as and when we have anything concrete.'

Lies. She's lying to me, she's got to be.

'That's it?' I snap, then bite the side of my tongue to remind myself to talk more calmly. Getting angry won't get me anywhere.

'If there was any news I'd tell you, I promise.' Her voice is soothing again now, so maybe she can tell I'm on the edge, hanging by a thread.

I tap my index finger on the steering wheel, take a sharp breath. 'Have you spoken to the coroner?'

'Excuse me?'

'In more detail, have you spoken to him?'

'Well, like we said yesterday, she's confirmed that the cause of death was poison, but we're still trying to work out exactly which poison was used.' She sighs, and I imagine she's resigning herself to talking to me. As well she should. I am a *victim* in this, for fuck's sake. 'There are lots of poisons that have similar effects and look the same, so it may take a bit of time, but once we narrow it down that should make it easier to find out exactly what happened to your mother.' Who exactly did it, is what she really means.

I pause, unsure as to whether to push it further. But maybe that's not best right now – I don't want to piss her off, I need her on my side . . . So instead I ask, 'Did . . . Did the coroner say whether it would have made a difference, if she'd got to a hospital earlier? Would she still have died?' I realise I'm gripping the steering wheel tightly as I wait for the answer, and let go.

'We can't be sure of that, I'm sorry.' Her voice gentles with this – she's a barrel of contradictions, this woman, and it unnerves me that I can't get a read on her – people are usually much easier for me to get a handle on. It's part of the reason I don't connect with many of them – I see straight through them. 'You mustn't blame yourself, though,' Murphy says. 'It very likely wouldn't have made a difference, if indeed whoever was poisoning her was trying to kill her. It's their fault, Sarah, and theirs alone.'

'I know that,' I say stiffly, the effort of keeping emotion out of my voice almost painful. 'But you don't get it. I might not be responsible but I feel responsible.' The truth of that vibrates through me. Guilt snakes uncomfortably through my stomach. 'She was ill,' I say quietly. 'I told you that. She was just a little ill, in the weeks before she died, and I brushed it off. She thought it was the menopause

and I accepted that. And now . . . Now it seems like . . .'
I take a breath. 'I didn't notice something was wrong and I
should have. So I need to know what you're doing to find
who did this to her.'

'Sarah, we really are sorry for your loss, and the Family
Liaison Officer will be in touch with you very soon to—'

'I don't want to speak to them. I want to speak to you.'
I knew they'd do this, try and cast me aside.

'Well, I can promise you that we're doing everything we
can. I can't tell you the ins and outs of a murder investigation, and can't keep you abreast of everything we are
doing – I hope you can understand that. But I will keep
you updated on any big developments.' I hear something
in the background her end – a muttering. 'Oh, actually,
Sarah, there is one thing you could do to help,' she says,
her words coming quicker, like she's worried I'll hang up
before she can ask. Or like she has somewhere else to be.
'It would be really great if you'd let us look at your phone.'

I frown. It makes sense for them to ask I suppose, but
I hadn't expected them to do so this soon. 'What? Why?'

'Just to see if there are any messages from your mum, or
about your mum that might be useful.'

'There aren't,' I say bluntly. 'I would have shown you
if there were, like the voicemail. And don't you have my
mum's phone? Wouldn't you be able to tell from that if
anyone had been sending her anything weird?'

'We are looking at her phone, yes, but it would also be
useful to look at yours, see if there is anything there that
doesn't mean anything to you, but might mean something
to us. I promise it won't take long – a day, perhaps.'

I hesitate. I haven't been without a mobile phone for
longer than a few hours since I was about ten. But I can't
exactly refuse them, not when they're using it to try and

solve my mother's murder. So I agree, telling her I'll drop it by later, and we hang up.

Then I just sit there, clutching my phone. The blood is pounding in my ears and my chest feels tight, so tight I'm surprised it isn't crushing my heart. Maybe it is. Maybe that's how I'm able to keep it together, how I'm able to go through all this – because my heart is crushed, useless.

The bakery my dad loved is just across from my work. I have to see it every time I'm in the office, though I've learned to mostly keep my head down, ignore it. But today, because my emotional barriers are straining already, I allow myself a glance at it, and an image flashes into my mind, of my dad, my mother and I all sitting on one of those tables outside. I must only have been about seven, and it's one of my clearest memories from that time, though there was nothing particularly special about it. It was summer because I was wearing shorts and a T-shirt – in the days when I refused to wear dresses – and Dad's arms were golden brown. I'm laughing so hard in my memory, and Mum is smiling too, because Dad is saying something stupid, foam from his cappuccino on his top lip, icing sugar on his chin, pretending not to notice they're there so I can make fun of him. I remember how special he made me feel – not just then, but always. He was so quiet, most of the time – like me, he didn't need other people around him to make him happy. But he always wanted to be around me, constantly finding ways to make me smile, and I was the only one who could cheer him up, too.

The back of my eyes burn and I blink away the wetness. I haven't come to terms with it yet. There have been moments, a handful of them and always only fleeting, where I seem to forget, forget about the fact that the people who were my entire world growing up are now gone, that a huge part of what made me *me* has been snatched from me. So maybe, someday, those moments will grow longer, maybe I'll be able to make sense of it all and will be able to figure out who I am without them.

But for now I have to focus on getting through it, one second, one minute, one hour at a time. So right now I'll just worry about what the police are doing. And when that's over, when they have the bastard who did this to me – who ripped my identity from me – when they have him locked away, then maybe I can move on.

Chapter Twelve

Murphy hangs up the phone on Sarah Gregory then gets out of the little navy blue Corsa to join Ashby outside Fiona Gregory's house. She's not quite sure what to make of Sarah. It's not that she's never encountered this before – the pushy father, brother, partner. But when she's had to deal with it in the past it's always been about something less serious – burglary, ABH. She can understand the feeling of helplessness that Sarah must be going through given the gravity of what's happened, identify with her determination for sure. She's just not sure she likes the girl.

Ashby grunts at Murphy as she joins him on the drive, staring up at the detached, two-storey countryhouse, out in this little village on the outskirts of town. He holds out a packet of soft mints, offering her one. She takes that as a good sign, a peace offering, and accepts one. He'd been angry with her after the interview with Sarah yesterday, told her she'd butted in, took over when he'd explicitly told her not to. But the thing is, when the DI had looked back at the tape, he was pleased with the dynamic, thought it had been deliberate. Thought Sarah warmed better to Murphy because she's a woman. Murphy rather thinks that Sarah warmed better to her because she isn't a smarmy idiot like Ashby rather than because of her sex, but she's refrained from voicing that opinion.

'Suppose we better get on with it,' Ashby says. She doesn't ask why he sounds so unenthusiastic – although the DI sent them to have a look, they lost the chance to access a clean crime scene when they didn't notice it was a suspicious death right away so it's unlikely they'll find anything ground-breaking.

Ashby leads her through the gate to the left of the house and down the paved path towards the annex where Nicola lived. No need for them to knock at the front door – the bronze team have already done that, told Fiona Gregory why they're here and secured the annex. They also found out that Fiona is here with her two daughters but that Benjamin Gregory, the husband, is out.

Murphy glances around the garden as she walks. She knows very little about gardening, given she's usually based out in Bristol sharing a flat with someone she met off SpareRoom, but she finds it hard not to be awed by what she's seeing. She hadn't given much thought to the set-up of the house or garden before they arrived, but if she had she would have expected a perfectly mown lawn, a swing set or trampoline for the kids or something. There's none of that, though. Instead it seems like something that belongs on the cover of *Town and Country* magazine – from the neat line of pear trees running down each side of the path to the pond in the corner, surrounded by lilies and other green plants she doesn't recognise, that little section alone no doubt making the perfect home for frogs and insects. And then there's the rest of the L-shape, out to the left, cordoned off by a gate for some reason. The wilder part, purples, pinks and yellows all jumping out at her, even this late in the year. Plants that seem very much to be doing their own thing, refusing to grow where they're supposed to. She finds she likes that, the idea that the garden might have its own mind, rebelling ever so slightly against its owner's wishes.

'Sarah say anything useful?' Ashby asks, raising a hand to PC Franks who's standing outside the annex.

'No,' Murphy sighs. 'I thought she might be calling to tell us she realised what her Mum phoned her about or something.'

'Now wouldn't that make life easier?'

'Coincidental, though,' she pushes, 'that she wants to tell the daughter something right before she dies.'

It isn't a question but Ashby answers it like it is. 'Not really. People want to own up to all kinds of shit when they die, right? Clear their conscience in time for the pearly gates and all that.'

'You saving up your secrets till your deathbed, then?' It's out of her mouth before she can think better of it, but he surprises her by answering.

'Me? I've nothing to hide, an open book and all that. I'm sure you've figured that out by now.' He delivers it so deadpan that Murphy laughs. She actually laughs, and though he doesn't join in, his expression definitely softens.

They reach Franks who seems to be standing guard outside the flat, the CSIs just finishing up their sweep of the inside. Franks' gaze lingers on her and she looks away. She always feels like she stands out here. It doesn't help that she's tall, and not exactly slim, but it's mainly because literally every other person in the department that she's seen so far here is white, something far less noticeable in Bristol.

'Anyone find anything?' Ashby asks.

Franks shakes his head. 'They've tested the whole house, focused on the kitchen. No sign of poison. No sign of anything, really.' He rubs one hand across his neck. 'Though I suppose they could have cleared up any trace of anything? They've had enough time, right?'

Murphy's lips twitch despite herself. She can empathise with that – the eagerness, the desperation to prove yourself. She cocks her head. 'They?' Franks is just as tall as her, taller maybe, but he still seems to be looking *up* at her when he answers.

'Whoever killed her?' He clears his throat. 'I'm sorry, if we'd got here sooner—'

'Not your fault,' Ashby assures him. Murphy glances at him, surprised again. She'd have thought he'd be all ready to blame someone else. Ashby looks at her with that slight eyebrow raise, like he knows what she's thinking, then sighs. 'It's not *our* fault, I should say. They called the ambulance, not the police. There's no way we could have known there was anything suspicious until the report came in.' Which, Murphy thinks, doesn't change the fact that Franks is right – there's been plenty of time to get rid of any evidence.

Still, she knows what the DI would tell her, what Ashby would likely tell her, if they could hear her thoughts. She shouldn't dismiss it out of hand. There's always a chance they'll find a stray set of fingerprints or something, a suspect that shows up on the database. Though poison doesn't feel like a random killing. No, this was someone Nicola Gregory knew well, someone who wanted her death to be painful. Someone who wanted to punish her.

'I'm going to take a look around here,' says Ashby. She's about to ask what she's supposed to do then, when he beats her to it. 'You all right to go and talk to the wife?'

She jolts in surprise. 'Yes, of course.'

Franks looks between the two of them. 'Umm, she's not letting us in, won't let us search the house. She hasn't wanted to talk to us at all, since offering us a drink.'

'That's why I'm sending Murphy and not going myself – she might do better talking to another woman.'

Murphy fights to keep her expression neutral. Yes, she wishes Ashby would let her do something because he thinks she'd be good at it, rather than because of her damn sex, but she's hardly going to argue when it means she gets the chance to talk to someone close to the victim. She leaves Ashby to the annex and heads back across the garden, though this time it seems like the branches of the pear trees are reaching out to stop her, like they know where she's going and want to protect Fiona from the intrusion. From her. She snorts quietly as she heads through the side gate and to the front door, pushing the thought aside as she rings the doorbell. More polite this way, rather than going to the back door.

She flashes her best smile at the woman who answers the door. She has slippers on, brown, curly hair tied up in a loose bun on top of her hair, a faint layer of foundation and black eyeliner that is smudged a little around the corners. 'Fiona Gregory?' Murphy holds out her hand, tries not to let the nerves show in her voice. 'I'm Detective Murphy. I was wondering if you'd mind answering a few questions?'

'I've already spoken to one of you.'

'I know,' Murphy says, keeping her smile in place. 'And I'm sorry about that. This won't take long, I promise. Can I come in?'

'I'd really rather you didn't.' She steps outside the house onto the front porch as if to emphasise the point. 'My daughters are inside and they're very upset at the moment, and my husband isn't here.' None of these seem like justifiable excuses to Murphy, but she doesn't press. Not now, anyway – she doesn't want to make an enemy of this woman when they're only just starting on the investigation. She wonders why she is so adamant about it, though. Why it's so important that they don't see the inside of the house.

'All right. Fiona, do you mind telling me how long Nicola had been living in your annex for?'

'About a year. She moved in after her husband died – she couldn't afford her own place, so we offered to help her out.'

'OK, thanks. You were with Nicola on the night she died, is that right?'

Fiona's expression instantly turns wary. Damn. Maybe she's playing this wrong, going for the direct approach. 'Yes,' Fiona says evenly. 'I was the one to call the ambulance.'

'Oh?' Murphy smiles again, but it seems to have no effect. 'How long did it take for the ambulance to arrive, roughly?'

Fiona frowns in thought, her wary expression dropping, and Murphy feels a spark of satisfaction. 'I'm not sure. About half an hour?'

'And how long was she . . . ill for, before you called the ambulance? Roughly, of course.'

Fiona pulls a hand through her hair, making the bun even messier, a few curls falling loose around her face. 'I don't know. I mean, she'd been ill for a bit, you know. Well, I say ill, but really she was just going through the menopause and it seemed to be hitting her harder than some other people, and to be honest she was making rather a big deal of it all and—' She cuts herself off. 'I'm sorry. It still hasn't actually sunk in. What I mean is, it *seemed* like she was making a big deal of it. To me, anyway, given I'm also . . . Well. But of course, now it seems like she wasn't. I feel awful about that now.' She glances over Murphy's shoulder and then back again. 'You said, they said it was poison? That killed her?'

'That's right, yes.'

'So . . . so the fact that she was ill, that was because of the poison, too?'

Murphy opens her hands in what she hopes is a conciliatory sort of gesture. 'We can't be absolutely sure at this stage, we're still collecting all the facts, but yes, it seems likely.' Fiona nods slowly, her face paling. She certainly *seems* sincere in her shock. 'So you said you were the one to call the ambulance?' Murphy prompts.

'Yes.' She blows out a breath. 'Yes. Ben – my husband – came to get me when he saw that she was so unwell, and I walked in, saw her in bed. So was so pale and clearly delirious. She . . . Well, she clearly wasn't well, so I called the ambulance straight away. I work at Bristol hospital so . . .' Fiona trails off.

'You're a nurse?' Not a doctor. Murphy is fairly sure that if she were a doctor, she would have said so outright – it's something people are usually pretty proud of.

'No, I just do admin, but I spend enough time around sick people to know when it looks bad.' She smiles, a little sadly, and Murphy nods.

'I live in Bristol,' she says, conversationally.

'Oh?' Fiona doesn't sound in the slightest bit interested, but still asks, 'Where?'

'Out near St Paul's?'

'Oh. I don't know that area well, I'm afraid. I mainly just see the roads and the hospital.'

'Well, you're not missing much.' She raises her hand to her hair, realises what she's doing, and drops it again. 'Fiona,' Murphy says, sensing using her first name is the right call in this instance, 'I know this is a difficult time and must come as a bit of a shock to you.' Fiona nods mutely. 'But we really want to find out who did this to Nicola, and I'm sure you do, too. Can you think of anything, anything at all, even if it doesn't seem significant to you, that might help us at this stage?'

'I just . . . I really don't know. This is all a bit much, you know?' Murphy doesn't answer, just smiles encouragingly. 'What kind of thing are you looking for?'

'Well, did anything happen to Nicola in the last few weeks? Do you know of anyone who might have wanted to hurt her? Did you see anything suspicious going on in the annex?' She doesn't point out that, despite the big garden, Nicola was living practically on top of Fiona and her husband. That they perhaps should have noticed something was amiss.

'I don't know,' she says again, but more slowly, thoughtful this time. 'You know she had a new boyfriend? Phil,' she adds, without waiting for an answer. 'I'm not saying he would want to hurt her, he doted on her, actually. But I don't know, he was new on the scene, I suppose. And he . . .'

'Go on,' says Murphy, her fingertips tingling with anticipation.

'It's probably nothing, but he seemed like he was a little controlling at times. Look, I'll be honest, I tried to stay out of the way as much as possible. You know how it is,' she adds quickly, as if she thinks she's said something wrong. 'I didn't want to interfere with someone else's life, even if she did happen to be living right next to me.'

'Sure, it's hard living this close to someone. In what way would you say Phil was controlling?'

'Oh, little things, you know. Maybe I'm reading too much into it. He insisted on driving her everywhere, things like that. I'm sure it was just me not knowing the whole situation.' She seems eager to contradict herself, to reassure Murphy that she's not pointing the finger at anyone, and Murphy knows not to push it right now. But still, it's a start.

'All right Fiona, that's really helpful.' She notices how Fiona seems worried by this sentiment, not relieved. 'Is there anything else you can think of?'

'No, I . . . Well, I don't know. It's such a little thing, but last week – God, it was only last week – Nicola got these flowers. They got delivered to my front door because the annex doesn't have its own postal address – Ben and I didn't like the idea of someone walking through our garden, trampling on all the flowers, you know.' Like Murphy's team are doing right now, no doubt. 'But anyway, she didn't seem pleased at all by it, not like I would have been if someone had sent me a lovely bouquet like that. She seemed kind of spooked, actually.'

'Spooked?'

'I think so, yes. Not that I thought much of it at the time, but looking back . . .'

'Do you know if she kept the flowers?'

'I don't, sorry. It might be nothing. She was acting a bit oddly in general the last few weeks. Like I said, we all just thought she was struggling to come to terms with, well, with the menopause.' She flushes.

'All right,' Murphy says, making a mental note to make sure they've double-checked the rubbish. 'Thanks so much for your time, Fiona. I know it can't be easy, having people intruding like this.' She wants to offer Fiona a card, tell her to call her if she thinks of anything, but she realises she hasn't got any damn cards with her. So stupid. So she has to settle with, 'Give us a call at the station if you think of anything?'

'I will do.' Murphy turns to walk away, but stops when Fiona calls out behind her. 'Have you spoken to Sarah? Nicola's daughter?'

Is it odd that Fiona wouldn't already know that? Maybe not, Murphy considers. She doesn't know what kind of relationship they have, after all. 'We have, yes.' She doesn't add that Sarah was the one to come to them, doesn't want to call attention to it if Fiona doesn't already know.

'How did she . . . Is she OK?' Genuine concern there, for sure.

'I think you'd be better talking to Sarah directly about that,' she says, as gently as she can.

Fiona nods. 'It's just so awful. For Sarah. Tomorrow's the anniversary of her father's death, did you know that?'

'I didn't, no,' Murphy says carefully. And it's the kind of thing she should have known. The death of another Gregory. Could that be where Ashby knew the name from?

'I just . . .' Fiona's eyes are shining now, and Murphy has the distinct impression she's only just keeping it together. Maybe that's why she wouldn't let them in the house – she wasn't sure she could handle it alone. Murphy finds she hopes that's the case, though she knows she shouldn't think like that. But she does – she hopes that this woman has nothing to do with Nicola's murder. 'Sarah was so cut up, when her dad died. She beat herself up for not being able to save him, and now I know she'll be thinking the same thing about Nicola.'

Perhaps that explains somewhat Sarah's chilly demeanour, her insistence that she be kept up to date with what's going on. 'Save her dad?' Murphy asks, hating that she's on the back foot here, that she didn't just look into the name Gregory the moment Ashby mentioned it, rather than brushing it off, waiting for a more quiet moment.

'Silly, for her to think like that, but you can't argue with grief, now can you? Of course she couldn't have done anything to save him.'

She's going to have to ask. Christ, she's actually going to have to ask her something she should already know. 'And why's that? How did he die, I mean?'

Fiona grimaces. 'Leukaemia. He died of leukaemia.'

Chapter Thirteen

It's raining when I get to the church, but I don't bother with an umbrella as I lock my car behind me, flowers hanging loosely in one hand by my side. It's more a drizzle than a downpour and I like the feel of it on my face, even as I shiver slightly, my leather jacket not really warm enough on an early October morning. But the rain is cleansing, somehow, so I don't zip my jacket up all the way.

They've found space for my mother here, too, so she can lie next to Dad, but of course she's not here yet because I'm still waiting for the police to do their fucking job. Endless waiting, it seems like, until I'll be free of this, be allowed to return to some semblance of normality and get on with my life.

There is one other person here in the graveyard, an old man, but I ignore him, keep my eyes downcast as I walk onto the grass, the soft ground giving way underneath me. I reach my dad's gravestone, speckled grey and white so that it looks like granite. My mother chose it. I would've picked something different, brighter, like the orange and black diagonally down from his, something that reflected his sunny personality. I imagine I'll get to pick the gravestone this time around, not that it's any comfort.

I glance at the black slab to my right where she'll be buried, when the time comes. Her name is etched there, marking the spot for her. I know it's supposed to be so we can start grieving, can come here to lay flowers for her, but I don't like it. She's not here yet, so what's the point of it?

I deliberately look away, crouching down in front of Dad's grave. I trace the 'C' of his name with my index finger. The stone isn't too cold today and that's comforting, like it still possesses some of the warmth he had in life, a quiet warmth which was all the more special because it wasn't obvious to just anyone. 'Hi, Dad,' I whisper. 'How are you?' It's stupid, of course, the worst possible question, but it's a habit I've got into, so that I can convince myself that a part of him is still out there. I shift uncomfortably, too aware of the other man here, fumbling about with his flowers as he walks crookedly to wherever his loved one rests.

I close my eyes, only that's worse because I'm immediately back there, in the moments before his death. The hospital room, with its white, empty walls. My mother, tears streaming down her face on the opposite side of the bed. And Dad. In that horrible hospital gown, which didn't hide his skeletal form, translucent skin. The blue eyes that I'd so often wished I'd inherited, instead of the green I got stuck with, were glazed, and his face still seemed twisted in pain, despite the fact the doctors had assured us that he wouldn't feel it anymore. He'd fought so hard to stay with me, and it showed, in the few grey hairs that still clung to his head, the protruding knuckles on his bony hands.

He was still breathing. I remember that so clearly. The doctor told us that he was dead but his chest was still moving. It was just the breath still left in him, the doctor said. Not that I would accept it. Not until all signs of life were gone.

A year. One year ago today I lost him, but it doesn't seem to get any easier. Initially, yes, the pain of it faded from a sharpness that made it difficult to breathe into something duller. But that dull throbbing was constant, until it merged into anger at how *wrong* it was, that I should lose him that way. And it still hits me, every time I come here, the realisation that he's gone, that I'm missing a part of me that I'll never get back.

Only now it's worse, because everyone is watching me as I go through all the same motions again, waiting to see if I will be strong enough to survive it this time. 'Is she there with you?' I whisper. 'Does it work like that?' I don't think it does, of course. I don't imagine my parents are really together, holding hands on some other plane, watching me.

'I'm OK, you know,' I murmur, just in case I'm wrong. 'Or I will be, soon, I hope.' Silly, isn't it, this need to re-assure people who aren't here anymore that we're fine, that they shouldn't worry. I sigh. I have to do it enough with every single person I find myself with, I shouldn't have to do it here too.

My legs are starting to cramp so I grab the metal flower container and stand, emptying the old dregs of water. I haven't been in a couple of weeks, so of course no one else has been to lay flowers. Will it be the same for my mother? I wonder. Lots of people tend to visit at first – there's always an array of fresh flowers, right in the aftermath. You can tell just by looking around the graveyard which people have passed away recently. But everyone forgets, after a time. They move on, and the dead are forgotten.

I swallow the burning lump in my throat and fill up the metal vase. I glance around me as I walk back to his grave. The old man has gone now. I wonder who he came to see, that his visit should be so fleeting.

I slide the little pair of scissors out of my jacket pocket – the ones reserved for this purpose only – and cut the ends off the flower stems then arrange them in the vase, shoving each one individually through the metal holes at the top.

Because my legs can't sustain the crouch for much longer, I give in and fall back on my bum, not caring that the wetness of the grass seeps in through my jeans. I sit there, wrapping my arms around me, hot tears mingling with the cool rain on my face.

'I still miss you, you know,' I murmur. 'I still wish there was something I could've done to save you.' I bite my lip hard enough to taste blood and swallow it. I'm getting good at it now, holding my emotions in. When I whisper my next words, my voice is surprisingly even. 'I still feel guilty.' And it's only here, alone in the damp graveyard, that I can say it out loud. Because if I tell anyone, they will jump to defend me, tell me that cancer is cruel and I can't possibly blame myself. And I know all that. Logically, I know it. But that doesn't stop me feeling like it's somehow my fault, like I should've been able to do something to save him, if only everyone had been honest with me about it all sooner.

I'm not sure how long I sit there in silence, but it's long enough that I start to shiver more violently, that the rain has seeped not just through my jeans but down my neck and through the sleeves of my jacket so that my top underneath is damp. I get to my feet, my movements slow and clumsy, my gaze still fixed on his grave.

LOVING FATHER AND HUSBAND

So impersonal, so generic. I hate that. Empty, meaningless words that do nothing to tell the world what kind of person he was. He deserved better.

I pick up the second bunch of flowers and fumble to take off the plastic, then lay them on the slab that will soon be my mother's grave. No metal vase for her, not yet, so they lie on top, white on black. Her name is there but there's nothing else yet, not until I decide what I want. I clench my fingers at my sides, the tips of them icy against my palms. I don't know what to say to her, so soon after her death. It was always like this, I suppose, so much easier to talk to Dad than her – he was the one I talked to about everything, from problems at school and which university to pick to money and career worries. I'm sure I used to try to talk to her, too, but she was always too distracted and I learned not to, then I never needed to because I had him. So I say nothing now either, though I have to grit my teeth against the need to scream.

I'd hoped it would have passed by now, this anger, but it's still there, pulsing under my skin. Why haven't the police found something yet? I feel jittery, on edge with the waiting, like I've drunk too much coffee but all the time, my nerves never letting up. Angry tears threaten my eyes again, the heat of them at odds with the cold encasing me. Before someone can turn the corner by the church and see me screaming my head off, I turn away stiffly from my mum and dad, my back aching with the effort of being held so straight.

It's as I'm walking down the gravel pathway that leads away from the church, through the crumbling part of the graveyard that no one uses anymore, that I see him. Ben. Clutching a bunch of purple and pink flowers to his side. His eyes meet mine and he lurches forward, like a puppet. It's all I can do not to jerk back.

'Sarah.' He says my name like a lifeline, though I can't possibly think why. 'You're here.' His gaze is far too intense on mine – I've never liked it, that intensity.

I frown – the way he says it, it's like he timed it deliberately to try and see me. He'd know, of course, that I'd come today. I glance down at the flowers in his hand. One bunch only. Who are they for? His brother? Or my mother? My money's on the latter, and it fills me with disgust that he can be so hypocritical like that. Coming to lay flowers for her, on the anniversary of her husband's death. Her husband, who also happened to be his older brother, who looked out for him his whole life, even when Ben didn't need or deserve it. But then, Ben never did get the boundaries as far as my mother was concerned.

He's looking at me almost longingly, waiting for me to acknowledge him. His eyes are red-rimmed, his face taut. He looks like he hasn't showered in a few days, and his shirt isn't ironed. I want to cringe back from him, looking like that. He doesn't have the right to be in this much pain – that should be for me alone.

'Sarah, I . . . I don't know what to say.'

I roll my shoulders, try to get rid of what's bubbling inside me. I wonder how long I can keep crushing down all this emotion until it takes me over. 'There's not much you can say. Or do.'

'I need to do *something*. Your mum would have wanted me to be here for you. To look after you.'

He might be right about that. Doesn't change how I feel though. 'How? How are you supposed to "look after" me?'

He flinches, but there's something else in his expression, too, a slight flash in his eyes, and I know he's bitter about my scathing tone. He tries to hide it, that side of him, tries to pretend he's nothing but caring and charm. But I've seen it, every now and then – the way he'd react around my mother sometimes, the way he'd glare when he thought no one was looking when my dad said something he didn't agree with, something that meant Ben didn't get his own way. 'I just thought, it might be good for us. To be together, to talk about it. We don't have to do this alone.'

He's not alone, though, is he? He has Fiona, who he seems to have forgotten about, yet again. Something hard is pressing down on my heart, and I know I need to get out of here. I didn't want this, I wasn't prepared to see him, to see anyone. I was supposed to be able to do that on my own terms, when I was ready. 'She was murdered, Ben.' My voice cracks around the word. '*Murdered*. Don't you get that? That's not something you can just brush aside with cups of tea and reminiscing about good memories of her.'

'I know that, I—'

'I don't think you do.' He's certainly not acting like it. What is he expecting from me here? My mother was poisoned just feet from where he lives. She died in the annex he owns, and he was amongst those who watched it happen. But for some reason he still thinks that I'd want to speak to him. 'I *can't* talk about it,' I insist. 'Not yet.' *Not with you.* 'Please, just let me deal with this on my own for now.' I walk past him, half expecting him to make a grab for me.

'Sarah, I know your father and I were never related, but he was more a brother to me than the half-siblings I have, those related by blood.' I keep walking, back to him. I don't want to hear it, especially don't want to hear him talk about my dad, the hypocrisy of him saying that when he's here to see my mother. His voice becomes more insistent. 'What I'm trying to say, Sarah, is that no matter what our genes say, you're my niece, we're fam—'

I spin around to face him. 'I know that,' I snap. First Fiona, now him. *We're family.* Like I don't already know it. But family can only take you so far when something like this happens. I take a slow breath. In for three, out for three. 'I know,' I say, just a little more gently. 'But I still need some time.'

And with that I turn my back on him and leave him standing there alone.

Chapter Fourteen

Murphy wishes she'd worn a different shirt. This thick, pale blue one is too hot in the crowded office and she's on edge enough as it is, at her first murder briefing, without feeling like she's in a bloody sauna. She shifts, knocks shoulders with one of the Intels, on loan from Bath, and grimaces her apology. There aren't actually that many people in here, but in an office this small it doesn't take much to make a crowd.

'All right, then,' says DI James from behind his desk. He's leaning back in his faded red swivel chair, a big hole in the fabric obvious just by his left ear. 'You all know why we're here. The Gregory murder is all over the local news so we need to get on it fast. What do we know and where do we go now? Ashby?'

Ashby, hovering to the right of James's desk, clears his throat importantly, looks down at his notepad. 'On 2 October, 999 operators picked up a call from Fiona Gregory at St Lawrence House. The ambulance response time was twenty-three minutes, but Nicola Gregory was pronounced dead at the scene. At the time, it was assumed to be natural causes, heart failure, so we didn't immediately get involved.' A few nervous glances towards James at that, Ashby included. James just waves his hand for Ashby to carry on.

'The autopsy however, revealed that cause of death was poison. Our pathologist hasn't yet been able to give us an exact poison, but found traces of—' he double checks his notes, '—scopolamine and atropine in Nicola's system.' There are blank looks around the office and Murphy has to admit, had she not been present at the medical examination, she'd have no idea what to make of this either. She'd thought she might be squeamish, seeing a body opened up like that for the first time, but found she was able to look at it clinically, listen to what the pathologist was saying rather than focus on the fact it was a human being lying there in front of her. Thank God. She'd have hated it if she'd had to hurl up her guts in front of Ashby.

'Translation?' James prompts.

'Well, scopolamine and atropine are alkaloids, and actually are used in trace amounts in some pharmaceutical drugs. Ironically, atropine can actually be used to treat poisoning in some cases. Here, though—' Ashby carries on quickly, no doubt picking up on James's look of impatience, '—we think it indicates that the poison used was in the plant family Solanaceae.'

'That's good then,' says one of the two other DCs in the room, a tall, lean guy in his twenties and the only DC here who is permanently based out here in the sticks. 'That we already know what the poison is.'

Ashby rubs the back of his neck with the hand not clutching his notepad. 'Yeah, well, sort of. There are 2,700 species of Solanaceae.' A low whistle from one of the Intels. 'Not all of these are poisonous. I doubt she died from eating too many tomatoes, for instance.' He smiles, but everyone just looks a little confused, not getting the reference that tomatoes belong to that plant family. Murphy only gets it because she was with him when the pathologist explained. 'Anyway. A lot of them contain alkaloids and are poisonous, so . . .'

'We need to narrow it down,' James states, as if they didn't already know that.

'We're on it,' Ashby assures him.

'Do we know how it got into her system?' This again from the lean DC. Thomas, she thinks his name is. Murphy bristles, glances at Ashby, then James. She knows the answer to this already, but wonders if she's supposed to be asking things out loud here, just to prove she's thinking.

'As it's a plant, contact with skin or ingesting it are most likely. And as we found traces of it in her gut, we're assuming the latter.'

'Well, that's a start,' mutters James. 'And no chance it was accidental?' Murphy imagines he'd like that. It would mean they wouldn't have to explain to the town why they let it slip through the net to begin with.

'Very doubtful. Victoria – our pathologist – found effects on the body that suggest Nicola was being poisoned system-atically over a number of weeks, though we can't be certain of the exact timeframe. The fact that it was a gradual effort rather than one big hit seems backed up by two different sources – both Sarah Gregory, Nicola's daughter, and Fiona Gregory, her sister-in-law, mentioned that Nicola wasn't feeling well in the run-up to her death, which was likely the poison taking effect. So it seems unlikely that she just took one dose by accident. Added to that, our forensic teams have found no trace of poison at her annex, so . . .' He glances around the room, waiting.

'Why didn't anyone notice then, if someone was feeding her poison all this time?' Murphy really wishes this other DC would stop with the questions.

'From what we've got so far, it sounds like she was going through the menopause, and her symptoms were put down to that.'

Murphy jumps in. 'So the killer might have known she was going through it? Known that some of the symptoms might be masked?'

Instead of looking pleased or impressed by her observation, Ashby frowns. 'Could be, yes.' Murphy tries not to feel put out, tries not to second-guess what he's thinking. And fails, of course.

'So am I right in thinking,' James says in his measured tone of voice, 'that we don't have a time for when the last dose of poison that actually killed her was administered? If it was a gradual affair?'

'Unfortunately, yes, that's right,' Ashby says. 'There was likely a larger dose of poison given to her on the day she died, but with the build-up in her system, it makes it very hard to tell when. Victoria is working on it, and once we can narrow down the poison that should help us gauge how much was needed to kill her, and how fast-acting it was.'

It would help, Murphy muses, if they could actually talk to the victim herself, find out exactly what symptoms she was experiencing. That would make it a hell of a lot easier to narrow down.

Ashby looks down at his notes again, ploughs on before anyone else can interrupt. 'On the day she died, Nicola stayed home from work, presumably because she wasn't feeling well. The poison may have been upped the night before or the morning of to make her feel markedly more ill. We're still working to make sure we know her exact movements that day, but we do know that Fiona, her husband – Nicola's brother-in-law, Benjamin Gregory – and Nicola's boyfriend, Phillip Daley, were all with Nicola when she died. Sarah visited the house earlier that day, but didn't go into the annex. A colleague of Nicola's, a—' he skims the page, '— Mary Webster, also visited Nicola that day.'

James picks up a stray pen on his desk and twirls it in his fingers. 'We've ruled out suicide, correct?'

'We believe so, yes. Nicola visited the doctor, seemed to be asking for help with her symptoms. And as I've said, this was a drawn-out process, giving her a lot of pain over a prolonged period of time. Seems a highly unlikely method of suicide.'

'Someone needs to get on to this doctor, find out more about the visit,' James says.

'I'll do it,' Murphy says immediately, and is relieved when James gives her a curt nod.

'So what's been done so far?' James looks expectantly at Ashby.

Murphy is a little pleased to see him shifting uncomfortably. He should know how it feels – he makes her feel that way often enough.

'Forensics found nothing at the house. Nicola's annex, that is. Fiona wouldn't let us in to search her house, and we didn't push – we didn't feel we had enough to get a warrant at this stage. And even if we could get one, we don't want to make them on edge this soon – they've had plenty of time to hide the evidence, after all.' James gives an approving nod and Ashby stands a bit straighter. 'We've spoken to the daughter – a message on her phone prompted her to come into the station.' And isn't it embarrassing, Murphy thinks, that she was the first to notice something was up? 'And on the back of Murphy speaking to Fiona, we found some flowers in Nicola's rubbish.' Murphy feels a tiny bit smug at the mention of her contribution.

'Flowers?' prompts James.

'With a card. And a note. "Soon".'

'Soon?' asks Thomas again. Murphy resists the urge to scowl at him. She'd be doing the same, if she were him. But it's *her* case, she doesn't want to lose that.

'That's what the card says. Just "soon".' A general muttering goes round the room in a wave.

'Do we know who sent the flowers?' James asks.

'Sadly not. The card has no branding, and though the flowers are in plastic there are no stickers or anything, so we can't be sure where they were bought. We're looking into it.'

'Good,' James says mildly.

Ashby clears his throat. 'Murphy, why don't you run through where we're at with suspects?'

Murphy reaches for her hair, stops herself. Is he trying to show her up, teach her a lesson, by calling on her out of the blue like this? He jerks his head for her to get on with it. She suddenly feels very unsure about what to do with her hands. 'Well, we've got Sarah Gregory,' she says, a little too quickly. 'The daughter.' There's a snort of disbelief from that bloody Thomas. 'Just because she came to us doesn't mean we can rule her out,' she says, echoing Ashby, who nods. 'Fiona and Ben, obviously, as they both lived on the same site as Nicola, could easily have accessed her food or drink, and both were present when she died. Then there's her boyfriend. Phil. He was also there that day, and Fiona mentioned that she thought he seemed controlling at times. It was a relatively new relationship, so that could make sense, timing wise.' She's not sure why she's trying to justify herself – she's not supposed to know who did it yet. The echo of that DC's snort still sounds in her brain. He's got even less experience than her, she's sure of it, otherwise why call her in – he shouldn't be trying to make her feel stupid.

'I think that's it?' She hates how she makes it into a question.

'They're the main ones,' Ashby agrees, and Murphy lets out a silent breath. 'We can't rule out the work colleague either at this stage, but it feels to me more personal than that.' He glances at James. 'Just a hunch, though.'

James sets down his pen – he's been twirling it this entire time. 'Nothing wrong with a good hunch. But cover the bases – check whether she ate at work, whether she could have been poisoned there.'

Ashby nods. 'Of course.'

'Four's a good start, though,' James muses. 'And all would have the opportunity to get into Nicola's home, sneak in the poison. So, who are we starting with?'

'We need to look into this boyfriend,' says Ashby, and Murphy finds herself nodding along with him. 'We can't ignore what Fiona said, and love, or sex, is always a pretty big motivator.'

'Isn't that a bit obvious? Assuming it's the boyfriend?' OK, she definitely wouldn't do *that* in his situation. Who does this guy think he is?

James simply shrugs. 'Just because something is obvious, doesn't mean it's not right.'

Chapter Fifteen

I'm sitting on a high stool at the little round table in my kitchen, a glass of cheap white wine in my hand as I watch Nika cook and try not to wince as the sauce spills out of the saucepan, splattering red both on the hob and the white tiles behind it. Obviously she's just trying to be nice, and she's the one person I actually want to be around right now, so I let her do it. But I'd still rather I was the one cooking, if only because I wouldn't make such a bloody mess.

I take another sip of wine, enjoying the cool feel of it as it slides down my throat. I'm on my second glass and it tastes better now, less acidic. My head is already feeling a little woolly, my tongue just a bit thicker than normal. I'm grateful for it, for the way it dulls the edges of my frayed nerves.

The buzzer for the flat goes and Nika looks over at me, raising one plucked eyebrow. She's always been able to do that perfectly, both eyebrows acting independently of one another. It's something I've often envied – it gives her such a wider range of expressions than me. I start to push off my stool but she waves a hand and unties her apron. I still think it's both adorable and ridiculous that she wears an apron to cook – it doesn't suit her at all, the pinstriped blue and white apron over clothes that, if not expensive, are still always on trend, and always ones that look brilliant on her slim frame and golden skin.

'You stay there,' she says, walking through the kitchen to the corridor. I hear her buzz whoever it is inside. The pasta sauce she's going to the effort of making from scratch is bubbling over and I clamber off my stool, the kitchen tiles cool on my bare feet, to turn down the hob. My fingers twitch at my sides, desperate to start cleaning around her cooking, and I've nearly given in to the urge when I hear the front door opening.

'Come in,' says Nika, and she slams the door shut – we have to, otherwise it sticks.

'Thanks, chick.'

I can't immediately place the other voice and am frowning in concentration when Nika comes into the kitchen, followed by a fat woman with a rather sagging face, wearing the most hideous mustard yellow dress that really doesn't suit her, only accentuating her bulk rather than hiding it. For a moment I think she must be one of the neighbours and wish Nika had made up some excuse to send her away.

'Hello, Sarah chick, how are you?' It hits me then, just in time, and I manage to arrange my face into some kind of recognition rather than an angry scowl.

'Hi, Mary. I'm all right, thanks.' I don't bother asking how she is back – I've learned over the last few days not to, that it seems to make people all flustered – they don't want to say they're fine when clearly I'm not, whatever I say. I wonder how long it will take before everyone stops treading so carefully around me, before I can have a normal conversation. Probably not long. People tend to forget someone else's misery relatively quickly, too tied up in their own lives.

'Well, I just came round to see how you are and, well, I brought some biscuits.' She holds up a clear Tupperware with a blue lid. 'Ginger and chocolate. Nicola always liked them when we had them in the shop, I don't know if . . .'

'That's so nice of you, thank you.' It's easier to make my voice sound grateful with the wine swirling around my head. 'I love ginger,' I lie. I take the box from her, setting it down on the kitchen table. 'We're just about to have dinner, but would you like to come through to the sitting room for a minute?' I shoot Nika a quick look, silently asking her not to invite Mary to stay for food. I'm not sure if she gets my meaning, but she doesn't say anything, just quietly puts the kettle on to boil for the pasta.

Ingrained politeness makes me add, 'Do you want a drink or anything?'

Mary pushes her short hair away from her face. 'Oh no, you're all right, chick, I won't stay long.' I wonder if she would've actually rather just dropped the biscuits and run, whether it's the same forced politeness driving me that's making her stay.

Because it feels wrong to be drinking alcohol when she's not, I leave my wine where it is and lead Mary into our small but perfectly comfortable living room. The flat was unfurnished when I put the rental deposit down but the landlord agreed to buy basic furniture and I got to pick, so the place feels like mine even though it's not. Mary's weight makes the laminate floorboards creak as she follows me and then settles herself heavily onto the smaller of the two black fake leather sofas. Nika hates them, thinks they're too sticky, that they look tacky, but I think they're perfect, complementing the minimalist look I've gone for.

There's silence for a moment and I swear I can see Mary's face contort as she tries to think of something to say. If I were being nice, I'd ask her something first, start up the inevitable small talk. But I'm too tired for that and, all things considered, it's really she who should be making the effort. After what feels like several awkward minutes where the only sound is the clattering of pans in the kitchen, Mary eventually speaks, her chins wobbling as she does. 'Well, Sarah chick, I just came round to see how you were, see if there's anything I can do.'

I hate that, the non-question, the fact that it forces me to repeat what I've been saying over and over again already. So I don't bother to hide the stiffness in my voice as I say, 'I'm fine, Mary. And there's really nothing you can do. There's nothing anyone can do, except the police.'

'The police?' Honestly, her eyes actually widen.

'Yes,' I say slowly. 'It's a murder investigation, Mary.'

She makes a sort of spluttering, gulping noise, and I'm glad I didn't give her anything to drink – she probably would have spilled it. 'Now murder, I know what everyone's saying but you don't really think so, do you, chick? It's awful, not saying it's not, of course not, but sure it must just have been a terrible accident or the like, no?'

I narrow my eyes. 'Oh, really? And how would you know?' She visibly flinches, but I don't have a spark of sympathy. Who is she, this woman I barely know who had some meaningless place in my mother's life, to come in and say all this? To try and convince me I know less about my mother's death than she does? She seems to pick up on what I'm thinking because she flushes, the veins in her cheeks turning redder.

'I didn't mean . . . I just, who would want to do something like that?' I can see her biting down on some emotion that wants to flood her face. Maybe she wants to cry, but doesn't want to do so in front of me. As she bloody well shouldn't – I'm dealing with my own crap right now, I shouldn't have to comfort her, too.

'That's what the police are trying to figure out,' I say.

She sits there, staring at me, her lips parted. I meet that stare head on, daring her to contradict me again. I'm being overly rude, I know it, even if I do think it's entitled. But I'm about to give in and ask her how everything is at work, just to make her feel better, when my phone buzzes in the back pocket of my black jeans. My heart jumps a little as I fumble to get it out, thinking it might be the police, that maybe they've found something. But it's not, and my mouth tightens into a thin line when I look at the caller ID. He just won't give up, will he?

'Do you need to get that, chick?' Her voice is overly hesitant, like she's worried about setting me off again.

I shake my head and press the reject button. No doubt he'll leave a message, where it will sit along with those from the many other so-called well-wishers. Mary is watching me and I pause before speaking, weighing up the value of explaining versus us just sitting in awkward silence. 'It was Ben,' I say on a sigh. 'You know, my uncle. Or step-uncle, I suppose,' I mutter as an afterthought.

'Oh yes, I know Ben,' Mary says, smiling now, something like warmth coming into her voice. No doubt Ben has turned his charm on her at some point – she's the type to fall for it instantly. 'How's he doing?' She leans forward on the sofa, the fake leather creaking with her effort.

'He's fine,' I say shortly. I pull a hand through my hair, make myself carry on. 'We're all just . . . You know. We're all coping.' I fight to keep my face even, but I feel twitchy now, talking about this, like there's a surge of caffeine in my veins even though I've been careful to stay off it recently. I wish I'd brought my wine in with me.

'I can only imagine,' says Mary. 'Murder, gosh . . .' She catches my eye then looks away quickly. 'But, sorry, I shouldn't talk about it, not when it must be so hard for you all. And Ben, he and Nicola were close, weren't they? Even after your dad . . .' She trails off, biting her lip, the realisation of what she's saying clearly washing over her.

A fierce stinging starts up in the back of my eyes and I blink viciously against it. 'Yeah, they were close,' I say, and know that my voice is just a touch too sharp, the emotion inside me needing to come out somehow. 'But I don't want to talk to him right now.' Which he just doesn't seem to get, no matter how many times I hammer it home. Well, no one can say he's not persistent.

'Oh, well, that's fair enough, I'd say, chick. I'm sure he'll understand, we all deal with grief in our own ways.' She says it like she thinks she's being overly wise, like she's saying something I haven't heard over and over already. She has no idea what I'm going through, none at all, but she's still got such a horrible all-knowing expression on her face and I can't fucking stand it. And that's partly why I let my next words slip out.

'Maybe. But he doesn't seem to get that – doesn't seem to get that I just want to be left alone.' I put a hint of emphasis on it, and the sofa creaks again as she shifts uncomfortably.

'I'm sure he's just trying to help, chick. And sure maybe it *would* help, it's not healthy to try and deal with it all alone.'

I want to point out that I'm not alone, I have Nika. But I don't think she'd get that. 'I don't want his help,' I say flatly instead.

'Maybe he wants yours, then.'

I reach my fingertips up to massage my temples, where an all-too-real headache is pressing against my skull. 'I don't think so. I think it's more that he wants to apologise to me,' I say musingly, 'because he can't apologise to her anymore.'

'What? What do you mean, chick?'

'I don't know,' I mumble, closing my eyes so I don't have to look at her. 'There was something weird going on between him and my mum, I think. I walked in on them the other day, and she was all upset, like they'd been arguing or something.' I open my eyes, fix them on her. 'It's bad enough that she was ill, she didn't need him making things worse.'

'Are you saying you blame him?'

She'd love that, wouldn't she? Love to go around telling everyone that I blame my uncle for my mother's death. 'No, I don't blame him. I just don't want to talk to him yet.'

She purses her lips and I can almost see the cogs in her brain turning. 'But you . . . You saw them arguing?'

Why won't she just go away? 'Yes. But they were close, like you said, they were allowed to have an argument every now and then.' She looks a bit taken aback by the abrupt change in my voice, the fact that I'm now leaping to his defence. I grit my teeth. I'm probably not handling this the right way, but it's just so bloody hard to think through this headache. I wonder briefly if this is how my mother felt, in the days leading up to her death, with the poison swirling around her system.

Thankfully Nika chooses that moment to appear in the doorway, apron tied around her once again. 'Umm, sorry to interrupt, but dinner's nearly ready.' I nod and stand up, my legs heavy. Mary gets to her feet, too, though it takes her a fair amount of effort.

'I'll leave then, chick, let you have your tea.'

I force my face into a small smile, muscles aching with the effort. I lead her to the doorway and pull the front door open, letting in a wave of cool, slightly smelly air from the corridor. 'Thanks for stopping by.'

'Of course,' Mary says, her tone full of false brightness. 'And you need anything, you call me, OK? Do you have my number in case?'

'I think so,' I lie, knowing full well that I don't have it, that I wouldn't be calling her even if I did. 'Mum gave it to me.'

'OK, then. And you'll let me know when the funeral is?'

I jolt slightly. Of course I knew vaguely, the way everyone does, that there would need to be a funeral, that I would need to organise it. But I haven't really thought about it in much more detail than that yet. I push the thought aside. I'll deal with it after, when the police have done their job. Her body won't be released until then anyway, no point in thinking about it now. 'I will, absolutely.'

'OK, then,' she says again. She leans in to give me an awkward one-armed hug and kiss on the cheek, then waddles off down the fluorescent-lit corridor towards the lift.

I shut the door behind her and head to the kitchen, where Nika is dishing up slightly over-cooked-looking pasta into two bowls. I pick up the glass of wine I'd left on the table and gulp down the contents gratefully. Nika opens the fridge and fills my glass wordlessly. God, I'm so genuinely thankful for Nika right now. How bloody lucky that she came to look round the flat two years ago, and I didn't get lumbered with one of the other two idiots I'd been deciding between. I can count the genuine friends I've had over the course of my entire life on one hand, and can't quite believe that I now get to live with one of them. In primary school, it used to bother me that I didn't have loads of friends. It was my dad who got me through that, who sat me down one day when I was crying and made me realise it didn't matter how many friends I had as long as the people I *did* have were those I genuinely liked. And he was right – most people just annoy me, they're all so fake, saying one thing and meaning another. That was another reason I got on so well with Dad. He understood – he preferred his own company, too. He never made me feel like I should be going to all the parties, trying to make new friends – not like Mum did. But I have to admit, I'm grateful that I'm not alone right now, that I have someone to lean on.

'Are you OK?' Nika asks.

'Not really,' I answer honestly.

She comes over, puts her arms around me for a gentle hug. 'Just trying to keep your neck up?'

My lips twitch. 'Keep my *head* up,' I correct, though I know she knows full well she's wrong, is only doing it to try and make me laugh.

'Hmm, well, you'd need to keep your neck up in order to keep your head up, really.' I snort. 'I heard what you said to Mary, about your mum and Ben arguing,' she says, a little hesitantly.

'It wasn't really an argument so much as a . . . conversation.'

Another pause. 'Do you really think it's nothing?'

I draw myself up and look at her, her gorgeous brown eyes meeting mine. 'I'm not sure,' I say slowly. 'But I'm not going to tell the police anything until I am.'

Taken from Case File: Nicola Gregory

MARY CATHERINE WEBSTER
EXTRACT FROM RECORDED INTERVIEW

Date: 07/10/2018
Duration: 37 minutes
Conducted by Officers DC MURPHY and DS ASHBY

DC OK, great, and like I said, thanks for coming in to see us, Mrs
Webster, and agreeing to give us an interview. Can you start
by telling us, for the sake of the voice recorder, how you knew
Nicola?

MW We worked at the shop together. Or she worked for me, I
should say. I own it. The little village shop out by The Anchor
– the pub, like. Baubles. Maybe you know it?

DS I know the one. Lovely selection of cakes.

MW Sure, I like to think so.

DC I'll have to check it out while I'm here.

MW Sure, that'd be lovely. I'll save you a slice of Victoria sponge.

DC I look forward to it. So you worked with Nicola. Were you
close?

MW Well, I suppose that depends on what you mean by close.
We got on, yes. And sure we'd go for the odd drink on occa-
sion. I'm not saying we were the best of friends like, but I
knew her pretty well, I'd say. Hard to work with someone most
days for two years and not know them well.

DC So Nicola started working at the shop two years ago?

MW That's right, chick. They needed the extra money, you see. Her husband, Charlie, was getting ill – terrible thing, cancer – and had to cut back on his hours. He was in sales, did very well I think, but he couldn't keep it up, poor guy. So Nicola came to the shop, asking for work, and of course I said yes – did what I could to help.

DS Mrs Webster, how would you say Nicola seemed over the last few weeks, months, perhaps?

MW How did she seem? Not really sure how to answer that, chick.

DS Was she her usual self? Did she seem happy? Well?

MW Happy, don't know about that. Sure she was a bit better recently, but her husband died coming on for a year ago – you don't go through something like that, losing a loved one slowly like that, and come out of it the same, now do you?

DC Of course not. It's a terrible thing, losing someone that way. Understandable if she was still coming to terms with grief, but apart from that did she seem healthy?

MW Well, she was getting a bit confused, a bit withdrawn at times. She's always been efficient at work, but she was tiring a bit more. Sure it's normal, I'd say, as we get older, isn't it? I told her as I'll tell you – the menopause was awful for me, I was terribly forgetful, couldn't go anywhere without a hot flush taking me over.

DS So you didn't think her behaviour was anything out of the ordinary?

MW Can't say that I did, no, chick.

DS All right, thanks. Now it would really help us if we could get a sense of Nicola's rough schedule at work. How often did she work at the shop?

MW Every Tuesday, Thursday, Friday, from open to close, and every Saturday morning. And she'd always cover the extra shift if I needed her to, like.

DS OK, great. And what did she tend to do for lunch, while she was working?

MW For lunch? Well, it varied. She usually brought in her own stuff – leftovers and that. A stickler for waste, Nicola.

DC And where would she store her lunch?

MW I have a little fridge in the back room just for staff.

DC And is it just you and Nicola who have access to this fridge?

MW And Stella, the other girl who works for me – though her and Nicola were never on the same shift, can't afford to have three of us working together these days.

DS What about coffee, teas? Did she make drinks at work often?

MW Ah well, she drank a lot of tea, I suppose. And sure we'd have a cuppa together every now and then with some cake when it was quiet – and I tell you, it's quieter these days than when I first set up. She didn't really drink coffee – hated the stuff, not that I suppose that helps you. Apart from when Phil brought her coffee, that is – she drank a bit of the ones he brought usually, so as not to offend him. Silliness, if you ask me, pretending to like something for a man. Women our age should be long past that.

DC Phil – that's her boyfriend?

MW That's right. She jumped into that relationship about six months ago now, I'd say. Desperate to be with someone, from the looks of things, not that I'd judge. But some people just don't know how to be alone, now do they?

DC You said Phil would bring her coffee? To work?

MW Sure, chick, isn't that what I just said? She told him she didn't like it and all, at first anyway, but then just went along with it. Like I say, I shouldn't judge even if it's silly, a woman her age, pretending to like something she doesn't. But it must be hard, losing your husband the way she lost her Charlie and then trying to get back out on the market at her age. And sure Phil's a looker, I'll give her that.

DC And how often would you say he brought her coffee?

MW I don't know, can't say that I kept track, but it was every now and then. He liked to pop in, catch up with her while she was at work.

DS And how did Nicola feel about these visits? Was she happy to see him?

MW Well, I think she found it all a bit romantic.

DS Mrs Webster, how would you describe her relationship with Phil?

MW I barely knew him, if I'm honest, chick, made myself scarce when he was in the shop, don't like to eavesdrop, you know. And apart from that I only saw him when he was dropping her off or picking her up. He liked to do that a lot. Keen to look after a woman, from what Nicola said of him, and sure she needed that, after all that's happened to her. But I'm not the best person to speak to if you want to know more about their relationship, Nicola wasn't the type to overshare.

DS All right, thanks. Now, Mrs Webster, you visited Nicola on the day she died, is that right?

MW I popped in to check how she was doing, brought her some soup, yes.

DC You brought her soup?

MW I did, yes, thought it might make her feel a bit better.

DS And what time would you say you left Nicola?

MW Oh, I don't know, maybe 8 a.m., something like that? Early, like. Needed to get to the shop, open up.

DS And how did she seem when you left her?

MW Well, sure she was ill. Definitely ill. She thought she had the flu, but wouldn't phone the doctor, silly thing. But I tell you, I never thought it was anything worse, and of course I keep wondering now if I should have noticed. I can't tell you how awful I feel about it, to see her on the day it happened like and not have done anything about it.

DS You couldn't have known.

MW Sure you're right, I couldn't have. Not that it helps poor Nicola.

DC And why did you go round that day? It was a Tuesday, one of her working days. Had she called in to tell you she wouldn't be there?

MW She texted, yes, and I just wanted to check she was all right.

DS That's the only reason you went round?

MW Yes.

DS Are you sure?

MW Yes.

DS Mrs—

MW Ah, look, OK. Now I don't want you thinking anything more of this, you hear me? I only haven't said anything because I feel terrible about it myself and don't want you two judging me, like.

DS Whatever it is, I'm sure we've heard worse.

MW [Laughter] Sure, you're probably right about that. Now, Nicola was a lovely woman, like. Lovely woman. Very kind. And like I said, she'd been through a lot so you can understand it, really.

DC Understand what, exactly?

MW Well, just over a year ago, right when Charlie was at his worst, before he passed, some money went missing out the cash register. I'm very careful with it in my shop, you know – sure didn't I tell you that business hasn't been great recently?

DS Are you saying that Nicola took some money?

MW She did, yes, and she owned up to it straight away when I asked her, paid it all back and that was that. Sure she hadn't meant anything by it, had meant to return it before I noticed – she'd just needed to get her hair done and they were struggling a bit by this point, Charlie wasn't working at all, of course. Anyway, look, I'd thought some money went missing the other day, right before, well, right before she died, and I went round that day to ask her about it.

DC And had she? Taken the money?

MW Well, no, she said she hadn't. And I'll be honest here – bit embarrassing, like, but I think it was actually me miscounting and jumping to the worst conclusion, you know how it is.

DS Sure, it happens. So you went round, accused her of—

MW Ah, sure, 'accused' is a bit harsh.

DS Sorry, asked her if she'd taken the money, she said no, and that was it?

MW Well, now, here's the thing. She was ill, like I said, all pale and shaky, so I didn't want to push it, but I also didn't want to let her get away with it, and there was a bit of cash sitting in the windowsill with her keys so sure I just . . .

DC You took it?

MW Ah now, don't be looking at me like that, chick. Sure hadn't she stolen from me before? I was just taking what was owed, and I'm sure Nicola would have understood it. But that's it, that's all there is to it, you understand?

DS We understand, Mrs Webster. And you've been really helpful. We'll give you a call if we— Yes?

MW Well, now, I don't want you to be reading into this, you hear? But it would play on my mind if I didn't say anything, and Sarah won't – she's a good girl, wouldn't want to say anything to hurt her uncle. This is actually why I came here to see you today, like, but you wouldn't let me get to it right away.

DC Get to what, Mrs Webster?

MW All it is, is I heard – and that's all it was, I didn't see it myself, you understand?

DC We completely understand, Mrs Webster.

MW Well, like I said, I heard that Nicola and Ben had a bit of an argument or something recently. It might not be anything, sure it's probably not in fact, but I want my conscience clear, thought I should make sure someone said something, and it's easier as I'm not family.

DC Ben? That's Nicola's brother-in-law?

MW That's the one, yes.

DS And do you know anything more about the argument?

MW 'Fraid not, chick.

DS All right. Thank you, Mrs Webster. We'll look into it.

Chapter Sixteen

'Detectives, how can I help you?'

The doctor is younger than Murphy expected, with horn-rimmed glasses and floppy brown hair. He flashes her a smile and she gets the impression he's used that smile to charm his way out of a few situations before. He adopts a more respectful expression when he nods at Ashby, no doubt because he's a man, and Murphy decides then and there that she doesn't like him.

'We've come to ask you about one of your patients,' Ashby says, taking a seat opposite Dr Williams' desk without waiting for it to be offered. Murphy chooses to stay standing, making the most of her height for once.

'Oh?' Dr Williams raises his eyebrows in an expression of polite interest, but Murphy can tell from the way his eyes flicker away from them that he already knows.

'Nicola Gregory,' Murphy says anyway. 'Do you remember her?'

'Well, I . . .' He clears his throat. 'Yes. I saw her a few weeks ago, yes.'

'Are you aware that she's since been murdered? And that cause of death was poison?'

'I . . . Yes, I read about it in the news, yes. And it's a terrible, terrible thing. But you can't . . . I mean, the paramedics didn't notice it was anything out of the ordinary when she died, did they? That's why you took a few days to discover it was murder?' The bloody local newspaper, Murphy thinks. It's far, far worse than the national press, investing way more time in a story like this. It means everyone knows everything about the case almost before they do.

'That's right, yes, but—'

Dr Williams cuts Ashby off. 'So you can't expect me to have noticed anything out of the ordinary, can you? If they didn't when she actually died?' A little on the defensive, isn't he?

'We're just trying to find out a bit more about her symptoms, Dr Williams, that's all,' says Ashby calmly. 'No one is blaming you.' But maybe they should be, thinks Murphy. She hopes it doesn't show on her face, though. Ashby is right to take the soft line, she knows. They want his help, not to get his back up.

'Oh,' he says, visibly relaxing. 'Her symptoms?'

'Yes, what did she come in here for? What was she complaining of?'

'Well, I . . . Well, she was experiencing a few things. Headaches, stomach cramps, hot flushes. All normal symptoms around the time of the menopause,' he adds quickly, clearly trying to reassure them that he shouldn't have noticed any sign that something was quite severely wrong.

This is what Nicola experienced, Murphy realises. This lack of attention, the eagerness to find an easy solution. The willingness to brush everything aside and blame it all on 'women's problems'. She's literally walking in the dead woman's shoes, and for the first time on the case, she feels a shiver run down her spine. Because it's only now that she's actually thinking of Nicola as a real person, not just as a way for her to prove herself. As a woman who tried to get help and was ignored. Whose pain was too easily dismissed. She feels the sadness of that, striking her right in her stomach.

She wonders how the murderer felt, when Nicola came to see the doctor. They've already established that the murderer was close to Nicola, saw her regularly enough to sneak the poison into her food and drink. They wanted to be close by, to see her deterioration, to know the poison was working. So they must have known that she'd been to the doctors, surely. Were they worried about that, worried the doctor might find something? Did they try to stop her going?

'So you told Nicola her symptoms were down to the menopause, is that right?' Ashby's voice pulls her back to the room.

'Well, look, a woman her age – what would you think?' Murphy notices how he directs his question to Ashby alone. 'I also thought she might be experiencing a bit of depression.'

'Is that so? What made you think that?'

'Well, the difficulty sleeping, the fact that in her notes it said she'd suffered with depression before.'

Murphy frowns. This is new to them. 'She'd suffered from depression in the past?'

Dr Williams flushes. 'Well, she said she hadn't, but it was in her notes that it could be a factor.'

Murphy fights to keep her expression even. So once again, Nicola's own feelings were ignored. She's behind Ashby, but she wishes she were next to him so she could see his expression, gauge what he's thinking. 'It's a big biological change,' Dr Williams insists. 'It would be normal for Nicola to have experienced mood swings, changes in behaviour, and that could have been made worse if she had, well, depressive tendencies.'

'Was there anything else that indicated she could have been depressed?' Murphy asks. 'Did she say anything, complain about feeling down, show any other clinical signs?'

Dr Williams glances at his screen again, though it's too fleeting for him to be legitimately checking anything. 'Well, no, not exactly. But she'd also suffered a great loss recently – her husband, I don't know if you . . .?'

'We know about that, yes,' Murphy says shortly, and the doctor's face falls. She imagines he'd have preferred to be the one to tell them, to direct attention away from the array of mistakes he clearly made with Nicola.

'All right,' says Ashby, his voice much calmer than hers. 'So stomach cramps, headaches, hot flushes. You said she was also having trouble sleeping. Was there anything else?'

He does actually click on his computer screen this time, and Murphy finds her disrespect for him increasing. If it were her she'd have memorised Nicola's visit, gone over it in her head to see if there was anything she'd missed, so she didn't make the same mistake again. For God's sake, this woman was being poisoned, and this idiot doctor failed to notice. But unless one of her family call him up on it, he won't face any charges.

'Nausea,' he says. 'She also complained of nausea.'

'And that's also a side effect of the menopause, is it?' Murphy asks. She can't help herself. She notices Ashby shift his weight, wonders if he's annoyed with her.

'It can be,' he says defensively. 'It's less common, but it can be.'

'OK,' says Ashby, in that same even voice. 'What about hallucinations?'

Dr Williams frowns. 'Hallucinations? No, no she didn't say anything about that.'

Murphy feels a jolt of disappointment. The three main poisons they're looking into all tend to cause hallucinations.

'Constipation or diarrhoea? Dizziness? Any vision problems?'

He's shaking his head now. 'No, no none of that. Just what I've told you.'

'All right,' Ashby says, standing. 'Thanks, I think we have all we need. We'll need a print-out of her medical record, if that's OK.'

'Of course.' He hands it over, then, as they're about to leave, says, 'You mustn't think badly of me. You have no idea, the number of patients we have to see in a day, the pressure we're under with the NHS these days.'

Right, Murphy thinks. Like they don't understand pressure in their jobs.

'Thanks for your time, Dr Williams,' is all Ashby says as they shut the door behind them.

'Well?' Murphy asks, the moment they're in the car, away from where anyone can overhear them.

'Doesn't hugely help us narrow down the poison, does it?' He rests his head back against the passenger seat. She was surprised by it at first – that he'd let her do the driving. She'd assumed when she first met him that he'd be the type to want to be in control of that, maybe not to trust her with the car.

'Headaches, nausea, hot flushes . . .' Murphy taps her fingers against the steering wheel, not switching the car on yet. 'All of that fits with our top three, right? Belladonna, jimson weed, mandrake.' All part of the nightshade family, all deadly if taken in the right dose, but survivable in small quantities. People even take jimson weed as a drug in some places, from what her research has dug up.

'No hallucinations,' Ashby says.

'But all three of them cause hallucinations.'

'Common in all,' Ashby agrees, 'but perhaps less common with mandrake.'

'So you're leaning towards that?'

'Maybe.' He sighs, pinches the bridge of his nose between his thumb and forefinger. She knows how he feels.

'She could just not have told the doctor. I wouldn't have, if he was the one I was talking to.'

'You're right,' he says, surprising her. 'Just because she didn't tell anyone, doesn't mean she wasn't experiencing them. I still say we're looking at just two – mandrake or belladonna. Jimson weed is harder to grow here. I think our next point of call is finding out what types of food she ate, drinks, that kind of thing.'

Murphy nods, doesn't ask why. Belladonna is known for being sweet, mandrake more bitter, so knowing her taste preferences might help them know how the poison was masked – masked enough for her to keep consuming it over a number of weeks.

'Do you know, I've been thinking,' Ashby muses. 'There are lots of ways to kill someone and make them suffer – so why poison specifically? Why plant poison?' She's not sure whether he actually wants her opinion, or if he's just thinking out loud. She's less sure on him now than when they first met, is starting to think she read him a little wrong.

She answers anyway. 'Plants are easy to get your hands on, I suppose?' He grunts, which she takes as agreement. 'And poison, well, it's less gruesome, isn't it? And the psychological impact is worse for the victim – not knowing what's wrong with you. Especially when no one would believe her.'

'Our killer can't have known no one would believe her.'

'They took a guess, I suppose, that the menopause would hide it. Fiona and Mary both commented on it, didn't they? On the fact that she was ill or whatever but that no one thought anything of it because it's something everyone goes through.' Fiona in particular had seemed annoyed about it, Murphy remembers.

'Ah yes, good old Mary Webster.'

Murphy wrinkles her nose. It wasn't ideal that Mary came

148

to them before they were ready, but they still got quite a bit out of the interview yesterday. 'Are you thinking she had anything to do with it?'

'No. Are you?' It sounds genuine, the question.

'I don't know,' she says slowly, trying to think objectively, to weigh it all up. 'Nicola could have been poisoned at work, I suppose – Mary adding it to her food or drink there. And brought the soup as the final dose?'

'She could,' Ashby concedes. 'Apart from the soup – we tested that, remember. No trace of poison.'

'Oh yeah, right.' Murphy taps her fingers on the steering wheel. 'There's still this thing with the money.' Ashby just waits for her to reason it out. 'But I don't know, it all feels a bit dramatic just to get her back for nicking some money out of the register. And, I mean, it can't have been much, can it? The second time around, she was taking what she was owed from Nicola's windowsill, and people don't tend to leave giant wads of cash lying around there.'

'I'd say you're right about that.' About it all or just the last part, Murphy isn't sure. 'So what would you do?'

'Do?'

'About Mary – as a suspect?'

'Well, get someone out to the shop, I guess? Check for any traces of those plants, at least rule it out?'

'Great. Do that.'

'Me?'

'Sure. Just make sure you have them report their findings back to me, too, OK?'

'Sure. Yes, OK.'

'Now I'm more interested in what Mary had to say about our other suspects.'

'The argument with Ben.' Another grunt. 'Think there's anything in it?'

'I think we'd be idiots not to ask him. But right now, I'm more concerned about the boyfriend. Controlling behaviour, didn't Fiona Gregory say?' Murphy nods. 'And Mary has backed it up – picking her up, dropping her off. We know she had a car, right?'

'A Ka. It's still sitting on the drive.'

'Right. And he was always going to visit her, and—'

'Bringing her coffee,' Murphy finishes. 'Which could hide the taste of the mandrake, as it's so bitter, or, I suppose, the belladonna if she took it with loads of sugar.'

'Exactly.'

'And the flowers,' Murphy muses. 'The note.'

'We don't know for sure that has anything to do with it,' he says evenly.

'I know, I know.' She waves an impatient hand in the air, then starts up the ignition. They still haven't been able to trace the flowers. She spoke to the local florist, who conceded that the now dried bunch of flowers *could* have been from the shop, but there was no record of Sarah, Phil, Ben or Fiona having bought any flowers from there recently. So either the flowers were bought somewhere else entirely, or whoever bought them paid in cash – careful not to leave a trail. 'But she seemed spooked about them, Fiona said. And—' Murphy ploughs on, raising her voice a little, '—if it was a threat, a way to make her scared, which would fit with the killer's MO you have to admit, then flowers are a very *lover's* thing to do.'

The eyebrow rise. This time she finds it less infuriating. 'A *lover's* thing to do?'

She flicks the indicator on. 'You know what I mean. Plus,' she adds, a fizzing of excited energy firing up under her skin, 'I did my research this time around.' He waits and she smiles. 'There's something else you'll find interesting about Phillip Daley.'

Chapter Seventeen

'I feel sick already.'

I glance at Nika, who is sitting in the chair next to me in the hospital waiting room. I have to admit, her face is a little paler than usual, making her look a sort of yellow-brown. 'You'll be fine. Honestly, it's no big deal and you'll feel great afterwards, knowing you've done something to help someone.'

'After I'm done feeling sick and shaky,' she mumbles.

'Not everyone gets like that. I don't. If it was something horrible, I wouldn't be encouraging you to do it, I promise.' I shoot her an encouraging smile. She doesn't return it, but I think her face regains some colour. I know this is something she'd never usually do. She gets squeamish at so much as a papercut. She's only here to keep me company because I refused to cancel the appointment, even with everything going on. But I couldn't cancel. My dad died of leukaemia, and there's a chance that if more people went to give blood, then he could have been saved, or if not, he would have had just a little longer, and I would have had just a bit more time with him. Nika knows all this, of course. It's why she won't back out, no matter how sick she feels.

Two people come out of the blood donor room, a couple, from what I can gather, and head to the refreshment area, then the nurse comes out to call me in. She beams when she reads my name and glances around the room, her gaze quickly settling on my face. 'Sarah, how are you? So lovely to see you.'

I walk over to her and she grasps my hand in greeting. 'Hi, Helen.' I smile, glad it's her this time. I like her, she has a kind smile that fits her round face, and even though I've often seen dark circles under her eyes, she never sounds tired, is never anything other than incredibly friendly. 'My friend also has an appointment today but it's her first time and she's a bit nervous – can she come in with us?' I gesture towards Nika, who gets uncertainly to her feet.

'Of course, of course, not a problem.' She turns her beam to Nika, whose face flickers into a brief smile. Helen has that effect, able to bring out a smile in even the grumpiest of people. Nika trails behind us into the donor room and I see her balk when she spots the chair.

'Maybe your friend should go first, hmmm?' says Helen, bustling about with something on the white counter. 'That way it's over and done with. Sit on the chair, my love.' Her voice is friendly but firm, and Nika obeys. Helen shoots me a wink and I smile. 'Now, can you just confirm your name, address and date of birth for me?' She holds up a clipboard and runs her finger down it as Nika replies.

'Lovely. Now, I'm just going to put this pressure cuff here on your arm, to make it easier for us, OK?' Nika just nods. 'Good girl,' she says, sounding a little like she's talking to a well-behaved dog. While Helen fixes the cuff on Nika's arm, she looks over at me. 'So how are you, Sarah, you're keeping well, are you?'

'Oh, I'm fine,' I say, shrugging. 'You know, the normal.'

Nika raises one eyebrow at me. I give her a little shake of my head, not that I think she'd actually say anything. I don't want to tell Helen about it all, though. Right now, I just want to pretend that none of it has happened, that my life is not in pieces, that this is just an average day for me. And because we're over in Bath – the nearest permanent donor centre – the news is unlikely to have reached Helen, so my family disaster will not be as big a piece of gossip as it is in our small town.

Helen pumps some gel into her hands and rubs them together, the smell of antiseptic filling the room. 'Now, I'm just going to clean your arm with this wipe, my love, it won't hurt. Nothing to worry about at all, as I'm sure Sarah's told you.' I zone out, having heard all this before, and wander towards the window, staring out at the bleak hospital car park, the rows and rows of cars evidence of how many people are ill right now. Nika sucks in a breath and I glance over to see they've put the needle in. She has her eyes squeezed shut, forehead crinkling in the effort not to look at the blood. Helen pats her hand reassuringly. 'Not long now.'

Unlike Nika, I can watch it, the blood seeping from her vein into the tube. It's calming, the way it flows through into the plastic, turning it from something devoid of colour to a deep red. I watch its steady progress to the clear plastic bag where it settles, seeming to swell to fit the space. Amazing, really, that this is all it takes. That this could be the difference between someone living and dying.

'You sure you're all right, Sarah?' Helen whispers it, like Nika's asleep rather than just refusing to look, but I jolt anyway. The way she's looking at me, I wonder if she has heard after all, if perhaps my mother's death is not just the small-town gossip I'd thought it was. I haven't been paying attention to the national news, too lost in the hour-to-hour hell I'm living right now. Helen could have read it, could have made the connection. Or maybe I'm just quieter than usual, maybe the constant tension I'm feeling is evident in the way I'm holding myself.

'I'm fine,' I say. I know my voice is too stiff to be believable, but I don't want to talk about my mother. Not now, not while it's all still going on. Not until the police have made an arrest and I can start to put it all behind me. 'I just . . . I'm just thinking about my dad.' Not a lie, given the fact that every time I come to give blood, I do it for him. Helen nods, her face the picture of empathy. She already knows about him. She was one of the nurses I told, feeling the need to explain, the first time, why I was here. 'Every time I'm here, I always wonder if there was something more I could have done.'

'There wasn't, you know that,' she says gently. 'You did everything you could. If your blood types were incompatible, it wouldn't make a difference how much you donated.' I know this already, it's something I've been carrying around with me for the last year – the knowledge that, just because I was born with the wrong blood, I couldn't save him. His parents died when I was young, and he had no siblings. No *real* siblings, anyway. Ben tried, but wasn't a match either. And we had no luck finding a non-family donor. Not enough to go around, apparently. 'But you can make a difference to someone else,' Helen says softly. 'You do, every time you step in here.'

Nika has her eyes open now, watching me, and it's that – the concern on her face – that makes my throat sting so much I have to look away. The agitator scale beeps and Helen claps her hands. 'All right, then, that's you all done!'

'How do you feel?' I ask.

She flinches a little as Helen removes the needle and her gaze stays fixed resolutely on me, rather than on the arm that Helen is now applying a plaster dressing to. 'Fine, I think.'

'You did brilliantly,' says Helen, smiling as she puts away the blood bag. 'And there's somebody out there who is going to be ever so grateful. Now, I'm going to do the same with Sarah, but rather than you sitting in here watching, why don't you head out to the refreshments, take a seat out there and have a warm drink and something to eat, hmmm?'

'Oh, OK.' Nika glances at me and I nod encouragingly.

'Are you OK to stand?' Helen asks, putting a hand under Nika's arm to support her. 'You tell me if you feel too faint, OK?'

'Thanks. I'm OK,' Nika says, and she does actually look better now than when she walked in.

'All right, then.' Helen holds the door open for Nika and hovers there, clearly watching to make sure she gets to her seat OK. When she turns back to me and says, 'Your turn', she smiles at me as usual, but I'm sure it's not just my imagination that her smile is less bright than usual. I was stupid, I suppose, to pretend I could escape it all, to think that the weight pressing down on me might lessen, if only for a moment. So fucking stupid.

An hour later, after many cups of tea and a few chocolate bars, Nika and I are sitting in my car, whizzing down the A4 away from Bath. Nika's welcome pack sits on her lap and she turns the key ring she was given over in her fingers. 'I wonder who will end up getting it,' she says, looking out the window rather than at me. 'My blood.'

'Does it matter?'

'I suppose not,' she says musingly. 'But I'd quite like to know, you know?'

Something squirms in my stomach, and I don't reply right away. The problem is, I've thought about that often enough myself: who my blood might be going to. And I've had the uncomfortable thought, more than once, that my blood might be going to save the wrong person, someone who doesn't deserve to be saved. So I don't answer her.

Now that we're on the way back home I feel jittery all over again, my fingertips bouncing off the steering wheel, my stomach churning in a way that is urging me to do something. I shouldn't have had any tea. Even that small amount of caffeine seems to be enough to put me on edge. Needing to do something to distract me, I reach over and take Nika's hand where it's sitting in her lap, give it a brief squeeze. 'Thanks for coming with me today. I'm sorry if I've been a little off.'

'Don't be thick. If I were you I'd be in a far worse state, I think you're doing brilliantly.' She pauses and I feel her gaze sweep over my face. 'Are you . . . OK, though? I mean, duh, stupid question, but is there anything else I can do?'

'I just need time. I'm sure eventually I'll be happy as Larry.'

'You know, I've never met a Larry who's particularly happy.' She pauses, tapping her nails against the window. 'Our assistant at work is always happy though. She's called Claire.'

My lips twitch. 'OK. I'm sure in no time I'll be happy as Claire, then.'

She grins, but it drops off her face almost instantly, and I know it's because she's thinking that there's no way that can be true, that someone doesn't lose their dad to cancer then almost exactly a year later find out that their mother was murdered, and come out of that fine, let alone happy.

'So, I need to do something before I go home. Do you want me to drop you off first?'

'Umm, no . . .' She raises a questioning eyebrow at me but I say nothing, the effort of maintaining a normal conversation becoming a bit much for me. I need to save it up, for when I really have to speak. She doesn't ask me anything more until I turn into the police station. 'Sarah, what are you . . .?'

'I just want to know where they are with it all. They won't tell me anything on the phone, so I thought if I just came in . . .'

Nika looks like she wants to dissuade me of it, but then just nods. 'Do you want me to come in with you?'

I bite the inside of my cheek, trying to decide if having her with me will help in any way. 'It's probably better if you just wait in the . . .' But I stop talking, staring out the windscreen, as someone else gets out their car on the other side of the car park.

'What?' Nika follows the direction of my gaze. 'What is it? Who is that?'

'It's Phil,' I murmur, trailing him as he lumbers from his jeep to the glass entrance of the station. 'You know, my mother's boyfriend. They must have called him in to speak to him.'

'Shit,' Nika mutters, and ducks her head to her knees.

I frown down at her. 'What on earth are you doing?'

'I don't know. Aren't we being, like, stealth-like or something?' The sight of her, bent over, looking up at me imploringly, makes me want to burst out laughing for one glorious moment. But the urge fades when Phil disappears inside the station.

'We don't need to be stealth-like, we're doing nothing wrong. I'm entitled to ask what they're doing to catch my mother's murderer.'

Nika sits up straight again. 'You're right, I'm so sorry, you're totally right. I wasn't—' She stops talking when I turn the engine back on and pull out the parking space. 'Aren't you going inside, then?'

'No.' I edge out the police station, but instead of turning left towards our block of flats, I turn right.

'Oh. Umm, where *are* we going then?'

'To Phil's house.'

'Right. But, ah, we just saw him at the station . . .'

'I know. But I want to know why the police think he's guilty. They won't tell me if I ask, so I'm going to find out myself.'

PHILLIP DALEY
EXTRACT FROM RECORDED INTERVIEW

Date: 08/10/2018
Duration: 27 minutes
Conducted by Officers DC MURPHY and DS ASHBY

DS Thank you, Mr Daley. Now, also present is . . .

SOLICITOR Rachel Moore. Here to act as legal advisor.

DS Thank you. So, Mr Daley, do you mind telling us how long you and Nicola had been seeing each other for?

PD Seeing each other?

DS Yes, I mean—

PD I know what you mean. We were in a relationship for about six months.

DS And how did you meet?

PD What's that got to do with anything?

DS We're just trying to get a bit of background, build up a picture of Nicola's life.

PD Right, fine. At the little corner shop – Baubles, you know it?

DS We do.

PD Well, I just popped in to get a few things and she served me. We got talking, and I asked her out.

DC You were married previously, is that right?

PD Yeah, that's right. No law about having another woman after that, though, is there?

DC No, no, of course not. Do you mind telling us why you and your ex-wife got divorced?

PD Yeah, I do mind, actually. None of your damned business.

SOLICITOR You don't have to answer anything you don't want to.

DS Of course, Rachel is right. We're really grateful for you coming down to meet us, we know you didn't have to do that. But all of this really does just help us paint a picture, so that we can get to the bottom of what happened to Nicola. I'm sure you want that, too.

PD Well, asking me about my divorce is hardly helping Nicola, is it? All right, all right no need to look at me that way, I get it, you want to build a picture. We just drifted apart. That happens.

DS Yes, it does, sadly. We did notice, though, that your ex-wife – Shirley, I believe? – filed for a restraining order a few years ago.

PD That was all bullshit – I was just trying to keep things friendly, you know, thought I could get to know her new husband, and she went ape shit about me coming round the house.

DS So that was it? You just went round her house a few times?

PD That's right. Damn woman completely overreacted.

DS Did you have a key? For Shirley's house?

PD It was my house, too, before she got it in the divorce, which I had to remind her of.

DS So you kept the key?

PD So what if I did?

DS And what did you do, when you went round her – that is to say your old – house?

PD I don't have to answer that. Isn't that right?

SOLICITOR That's completely right, yes.

PD Well, that's that, then. I don't want to talk any more about Shirley. It's got nothing to do with Nicola's death and won't help you in the slightest, so I don't have to sit here explaining it to you.

DC Fair enough. In that case, let's talk a bit more about your relationship with Nicola. A couple of people we've talked to have commented that you seemed rather protective of Nicola. Would you say that's fair?

PD Nothing wrong with being protective. Are you saying you wouldn't want your man to take care of you? Do you even have a man, working woman like you? Bet it's all about the career, isn't it?

DC I don't think that's any—

PD Nicola liked it, and it was about time someone took care of her.

DC And how exactly did you take care of her?

PD You need me to spell it out for you?

DC I—

PD I drove her to work, picked her up. Made sure she didn't spread herself too thin – she was always trying to make everyone else happy, not herself.

DC Right. And how often did you drive her to and from work, would you say?

PD Don't know. Most days she was working, I suppose. Unless I was tied up at a site.

DS Nicola had her own car, is that right?

PD Yeah, so?

DS And the shop was close to her house, close enough to walk?

PD I don't see what you're getting at here.

DS I'm just wondering why you made a habit of driving her to and from work if she could get there herself.

PD Just because she could, doesn't mean she wanted to. I've told you, she needed taking care of after all the crap she'd been through – and there was certainly no one else going to do it.

DC No one else? What about her daughter, Sarah?

PD Yeah, right. She'd be better off without that girl in her life, I told her that. Nothing but trouble.

DC Trouble? How do you mean?

PD Well, she didn't treat anyone with respect, in my opinion. Too caught up in her own life, only saw her mum when it suited her. No, she certainly wasn't going to take care of her, it was down to me.

DS Mr Daley, did you ever send Nicola flowers, as another way of taking care of her, perhaps?

PD What? Flowers? Yeah, I guess I brought her flowers every now and then – women like that, don't they?

DS And did you send her any flowers in the week or so before she died? We found some in her rubbish, you see, and are just trying to figure out who sent them.

PD Well, look, I wouldn't have sent her them – I'd have brought them round with me. But no, I don't remember giving her flowers in the last few weeks.

DS So you didn't write her a card with the word 'soon' written on it?

PD What? No. No idea what that's about.

DC All right, thanks, Mr Daley. We've also spoken to Nicola's boss, Mary, and she mentioned that you tended to bring her coffee to the shop. Was this another way of taking care of her?

PD Yeah, it was. What are you getting at?

DS How often did you take her coffee, do you think?

PD What kind of ridiculous question is that? I didn't keep track. I wasn't tallying up the nice things I did for her. Do you have a woman?

DS We're not here to talk about me.

PD I bet you don't. Is that because that's the type of thing you do? Tally up all the favours you do for a woman, so she can pay you back? Free tip – women don't like that.

DC So, back to the coffee.

PD For Christ's sake, what more do you want to know about the bleeding coffee?

DC Well, Mary seemed to think Nicola didn't like coffee.

PD She never mentioned that to me. Was always grateful when I brought her one.

DC What kind of coffee did she like?

PD Oh, for Christ's . . . I always got her a cappuccino, which she certainly never complained about.

DC Did she take sugar?

PD No. She was watching her figure, so I never added any sugar.

DC She was watching her figure? She told you that?

PD Didn't have to tell me.

DS All right, thanks, Mr Daley. Now, the night Nicola died, you were there, is that right? Along with Ben and Fiona?

PD That's right.

DS Mr Daley, did Nicola say anything that evening, anything that you think might help us at all?

PD Well, she wasn't very coherent, if I'm being honest. Nothing she was saying made a lot of sense.

DS Can you remember any of it? It might not have seemed relevant at the time, but it would still be really helpful to know.

PD I can't remember much of it. She was saying a lot of people's names – she said Charlie's name a few times, though none of us knew why. And she made some weird comment, about eyes.

DS Eyes?

PD Yeah, something like 'it's all in the eyes'. Something along those lines, anyway. Like I said, none of it made any sense.

DC All right. Do you mind telling us why you were there that night? Had you made plans to see her?

PD No, no plans. I hadn't heard from her all day, and I knew she hadn't been to work because I'd called in to check on her, so I went by to see if she was OK.

DC And when was the last time you saw Nicola, before that night?

PD I stayed round the night before, was there when she woke up.

DC How did she seem that morning?

PD She was no worse than the night before. Obviously, if she'd seemed really ill I would've taken her to the hospital or something. Do you not think I'd have done that? I really wish she had seemed worse, because maybe I could've prevented it somehow and I'd be with her right now rather than talking to you clowns.

DS I know this is difficult, Mr Daley, but—

PD You know shit. Instead of you being out there doing something useful to find out who killed her, you're in here with me asking all these bullshit questions that won't help anyone.

DC I can assure you, we are doing everything in our power to—

PD Yeah, yeah. Have to rule me out as a suspect, don't you? I know how these things work, I've seen *Luther*. Already made your mind up, have you, decided it's me? Nicola, though. She was fine that morning.

DC And yet she wasn't well enough to go to work?

PD She didn't actually tell me that herself. I only found out later when I called to check on her.

DS What time did you leave her, roughly?

PD I don't know, I . . . Look, I'll be honest here and tell you we had a bit of an argument that morning. So I left a bit earlier than usual, maybe around seven, seven-thirty.

DC An argument?

PD Yeah, and you really think I'd be telling you if it were some big deal? She wanted me to leave, rather abruptly at that, and I was a bit cross about it, that's all. That's why I went round later, to apologise, to make up with her. I'd actually gone to buy her something nice that day, down at the jewellery shop in town, been planning it as a surprise for a few days to cheer her up – you know she hadn't been feeling great.

DS We do, yes. So you went to buy her a present that day – which shop, exactly?

PD Images. Look, I need to use the loo, are we done, can I go?

DS We'd like to ask you a few more questions, if possible, but of course you're free to use the facilities. For the sake of the recording, this interview is being paused.

DC Interview is being resumed. The time is 3.43 in the afternoon by my watch and present in the room are myself, DC Murphy, DS Ashby, Rachel Moore and Phillip Daley.

DS Thanks, Detective Murphy. Mr Daley, how would you say you got on with Fiona and Benjamin Gregory?

PD Barely know them.

DC Did you like them?

PD Like I said, barely know them.

DS A general impression, then.

PD Fiona's all right. Can't say I like Ben too much, if I'm honest.

DC Why's that?

PD Does there need to be a reason?

DC Well, no, I suppose not.

PD Look, it was clear he had a thing for Nicola. If you speak to anyone else I'm sure they'll tell you the same.

DC You mean he was having an affair with her?

PD No, I don't think so. Well, I don't know. Yeah, I don't know, and that's the honest truth. I'd like to think Nicola wouldn't have done that to me, and would have at least told me if there was something going on. She said they were just good friends, but he was always sniffing around her, like a dog in heat, even though she was with me. Couldn't take a hint, that guy. Bit intense, if you ask me. I tried to put Nicola off him, to show her what kind of guy he was, but I don't think I ever really got through to her.

DS You tried to put her off him? How exactly did you do that?

PD I just told her what kind of guy he was. Might have said I saw him looking through her stuff, that kind of thing. She needed to know what she was dealing with there.

DS And did you?

PD What?
DS Did you see him going through her stuff?
PD Look, just because I didn't see it, doesn't mean it wasn't true.

Chapter Eighteen

'But, Sarah, we don't even know if the police *do* think he's guilty.' Nika has her 'trying to be reasonable' voice on, but I can hear the mild panic underneath as I whizz along the little lanes towards Phil's house. I've only been there once before, when I went to pick my mother up, but I still remember where it is, like somehow I knew one day I'd need to come here again.

'He could be at the station for any number of reasons,' she continues, her voice becoming ever so slightly higher. 'I mean, the police talked to you, didn't they?'

'Yeah, well, I'm not so sure they didn't think *I* was guilty, too,' I mumble, to which Nika shakes her head disbelievingly.

She changes tact. 'How are you even going to get in? And please don't tell me you're going to break the door down, because even if that were in any way not a terrible idea, I'm not actually sure it's feasible.'

'Don't be ridiculous. I have a key.'

'You have a . . .' She pulls both hands through her hair.

'My mother had one.'

'Yes, but how do *you* have it?'

I glance at her out of the corner of my eye but don't reply. Somehow I don't think she'll like the fact that I took my mother's set of keys after I'd got to her annex the night she died, far too late, of course.

I pull up on the kerb by Phil's house. I don't even worry about what the neighbours will think, if they're in at this time of day. I have a key, and I don't exactly look like the breaking and entering sort. I get out, make sure I grab my handbag out of the back, then peer at Nika, who is still sitting in the passenger seat, looking mildly shell-shocked. 'You coming in?'

'I, shit, I . . .'

'Maybe better if you stay here, actually,' I say. 'You can keep a lookout, text me if he comes back.'

'Oh, for fuck's sake, Sarah.'

'Chill, I won't be long. I need to do *something*, Nika. I can't just sit around when my mother has been murdered.' I expect that to shut her up, to tap into some sympathy, but clearly she considers this way beyond that.

'You need to let the police handle it,' she snaps. I slam the car door shut, but she opens it again. 'And what am I supposed to do if he *does* come back?' she hisses. I wave my hand over my shoulder and march straight up to Phil's door. The key is out of my handbag and in my hand by the time I get there. I'm greeted by a musty smell, the one you get in a bedroom when it hasn't been aired out in too long. It's disgusting and I wrinkle my nose against it.

Nerves jump in my stomach as I head straight for the kitchen. I'm aware, despite ignoring Nika, that this is a little reckless, that I'm pushing the boundaries of rational behaviour. I've got no idea how long Phil will be at the station, or if anyone else has a key who could rock up at any second. I take a breath. All that means is I've got to be quick. In and out. I don't think the police have looked here yet – I'm sure I would have heard on the grapevine somehow, it would be big news around here. But I have my own reasons for being here.

I glance at the garden through the glass back door when I get to the kitchen. It's so sparse, no plants, just a small concrete patio leading onto a square of grass, which looks like it hasn't been cut in months. I know it's a tiny garden but he still could have done something with it – small gardens can look great if you know what to do with them, as I've learned from Fiona.

There are dirty plates stacked on top of what is presumably a full dishwasher, and a congealed mess sits in a pan on the hob – last night's dinner, I assume. Really, could he be any more of a cliché? But then, the house wasn't in this state last time I was here – my mother's influence, perhaps, or maybe he's grieving for my mother in his own way. I try and fail to conjure up a spark of sympathy at that.

A faint off smell emanates from the fridge when I open it. Hardly any food in here, just a couple of cartons of milk, some tomatoes that look like they're going mouldy in the bottom shelf and a half-empty tub of Utterly Butterly. I stare at the contents for a moment, wondering if the detectives will have the same thought I'm having right now.

When I'm done in the kitchen I re-adjust my handbag and check my phone, but ignore the barrage of WhatsApp messages from Nika telling me to get on with it. I get it, I have to be quick. But I'm here now, and if the police *are* thinking Phil might have killed my mother, then I want to check if there's anything in his house that might substantiate that thinking, if and when they decide to search it. Because *I* might think that poison makes no sense for a guy like Phil – too subtle, too drawn out – but that doesn't mean the police will think the same. Then there's the jealousy. I saw it, the night he and I walked in on Ben and my mother looking shifty. The fact that he's a complete knobhead doesn't help – if the detectives are talking to him, they'll see that. And who knows, the idiot might have said something, done something to make them think he's guilty – something I don't know about yet.

My heart is beating faster as I run up the stairs. I can feel blood pulsing in my fingertips, can hear a faint ringing in my ears but shake my head against it. I've got to think logically, like the police would do. I check the bathroom, the tiny second bedroom. Nothing jumps out at me as suspicious, no notepads with 'I hate Nicola' written on.

There's the sound of something slamming outside and I freeze. But no, no, it was too far away, it can't be Phil's car, not yet. I run through into the master bedroom and check through the window, just in case. No one is there. The street is still empty.

The musty smell of the whole house is stronger in here and there are clothes piled on the floor in a corner, two half-full glasses of water on the bedside table, alongside an empty beer bottle. I stare at the bed. My mother must have slept in it. Something curdles in my stomach at that. Yes, I made a show of being all supportive over the last few months but, really, what was she thinking, a guy like *him*? He's nothing like my dad, who was kind and gentle, and never jealous or possessive.

I hear the sound of an engine and jump. At the same time, my phone lights up in my hand, showing more incoming messages from Nika.

Phil is here
I'm serious he's here he's driving in now get out of there

Shit. *Shit!*

I run out the bedroom, but I already know I'm too late. I can hear the car pulling up onto the small driveway in front of the house. Any moment now and he'll walk in and see me. Yell at me, demand to know what the hell I'm doing. Shit, maybe he'll even report me to the police – *that* would look just great, wouldn't it?

I dial Nika as I sprint down the stairs. She answers immediately.

'Distract him,' I hiss.

'What?'

'Nika. Phil is about to walk in and see me. I need you to go up to him and distract him, so I can get out of here.' I'm surprised at how calm my voice is, how fucking cool I am in a crisis. I hang up, not giving her the time to answer, hoping like hell she'll just do it.

I reach the hallway at the same time as a key is jammed into the lock. A male grunt of frustration follows it.

To the kitchen. My breathing is now coming so fast, it feels like I'm hyperventilating. I look out at the garden through the clear-paned back door. Fucking hell, if only my mother had a back door key too. I glance frantically around the kitchen – surely there's a back door key somewhere?

There! On top of the microwave, a metal set of keys seems to glint at me, advertising their presence.

I lunge for them, but I can hear the front door opening. The sound of bottles clinking. I'm going to be too late, just seconds too late.

And then, God fucking love her, I hear Nika's voice. 'Umm, hello? Excuse me?' She is breathless, too high-pitched, and I can just imagine her expression. 'Sorry, excuse me?' she repeats, louder now. On high alert like I am, I swear I can hear her breathing, almost as frantic as mine. I hold my breath as if to compensate, every muscle in my body strained. I've got the keys in my hand but I don't dare use them yet in case I make too much noise. 'I'm really sorry to bother you,' she says, and I can tell she's right at the door now. 'I can't seem to get my car to start, and there's no one else around. Is there any chance you could take a look?'

'Look, lady, today's been a really long—'

'Please?' she says, and I can just imagine her batting her eyelashes. Thank fuck she's attractive. 'I know it's a lot to ask, but I could really do with some help. I've called my sister, but, well, she knows about as much about cars as I do.' She laughs, a little manically if I'm honest, but I know she's nailed it even before Phil answers.

'All right,' he says gruffly. 'Show me what the problem is.'

'Oh, thank you *so* much,' she says. I hear the front door shut and jump into action, fumbling with the keys and trying them one by one in the back door. The third one works, and I actually let out a squeak of excitement. I quickly dump them on top of the microwave, shove open the back door and shut it behind me. Hopefully he'll just think he forgot to lock it.

I sprint down the length of the garden, let myself out the back gate, and keep running until I'm just round the corner from the road which leads onto Phil's, far enough away that he'd have to walk right up to the end of his road to see me. My head feels light and I get an irrational urge to laugh. Fumbling with my phone, I send Nika a quick text, telling her I'll meet her on the main road and she'll have to drive my car to come and get me. Then I start walking, keeping my head down, just in case.

It doesn't take long until I hear a car and turn to see my green Clio. Scowling at me, Nika gets out the driver's seat, and without a word walks round to the passenger side. I get in, fasten my seatbelt. Only then do I notice that my hands are shaking.

'Thanks,' I breathe as I pull out.

She says nothing.

'So the car started immediately, I'm guessing?'

Again nothing, though I can't help but grin, the adrenaline buzzing inside me setting me off, making me want to laugh. I can't remember the last time I felt something close to this, and the urge to give myself over to it is almost unbearable.

Nika seems to struggle for a moment, her arms crossed tight over her chest, her eyebrows almost comical the way they're darting all over the place independently of one another, refusing to settle in one expression. Then she lets loose. 'I can't *believe* you. You are completely insane. You could have been caught, do you *get* that? Breaking and entering is *illegal*, and . . .' On and on she goes, and though it has the effect of killing my buzz, I manage to drown her out.

Because now that I'm out safely, my mind is back on what I was thinking about, staring into Phil's fridge. I wonder if it will occur to the detectives, too, if I should tell them my theory, or if that's a bit too pushy, even for me. It might have taken a while for me to realise it, but it's obvious to me now. That whoever was spending time with my mother, eating the same food or drinking the same drinks as her, could well have ingested poison that was meant for her without knowing it. So all the police have to do is check who does and doesn't have poison in their system. Right?

Chapter Nineteen

'Well, that was interesting.'

Murphy glances at Ashby, who comes up to where she's staring at the wall of the office they've turned into a board for the case. Phil's photo is looking out at her. She knows she was on edge during the interview, feels like she didn't do her best work. She tried not to let it get to her, how he looked at her compared to how he looked at Ashby. Tried to stay calm. But she knows she didn't quite pull it off, and she's waiting for Ashby to say something about it.

'I know,' she says. 'What's with the eyes comment?'

'No idea. Not sure we should read too much into it. Maybe it means she was having hallucinations after all – if she wasn't coherent, mentioning her dead husband's name, talking about eyes . . .'

'Yeah, you might be right.' A good thing, she supposes, given it fits with their poisons. Ashby goes quiet and she feels the need to keep talking. 'He wouldn't give us his phone,' she says. Unnecessary to point out, given Ashby was there when he refused, but she'd rather detract attention away from herself right now.

'Yeah, because "God knows what we might be looking for".'

'It's that damned *Daily Mail* article, I'm telling you,' she mutters.

'To be fair, him not wanting us to look at his phone doesn't necessarily make him guilty – plenty of people would be the same, I think. I *know,*' he corrects himself. 'I've seen it before.'

'I know that,' she says impatiently. 'But it doesn't look good either, does it?' She wants it to be him. She knows that's wrong, knows she should be more objective. But she really wants it to be him. 'And there's still the fact he was bringing her coffee.'

'Hmmm. He didn't really get his back up about it, though.'

'I suppose so,' Murphy mutters. 'Well, no more than the rest of it, anyway.'

'Exactly. He wasn't being overly helpful, but I didn't sense he was especially worried about us asking about that in particular.'

'So maybe he really didn't know she didn't like it.'

'In fairness, we only have Mary Webster's word to go on for that. Besides, regardless of whether she did or didn't like it – if she was drinking it then he still could have hidden the poison there.'

'Yeah, that's true.' She makes a sound of disgust. 'Watching her figure. I bet she never said anything of the sort, bet he just didn't want her having sugar for his own reasons.' Ashby raises his eyebrows, says nothing, and she flushes, clears her throat to cover it. 'The jewellery store checks out, by the way. He did go in that day, buy her some earrings. They've got the footage.' Ashby nods, considering, and Murphy sighs. 'Does it make sense, for him to buy her something the same day as kill her?'

'We don't know he was definitely buying something for Nicola,' Ashby points out. 'Just because he says that's what he was doing.'

'Right,' says Murphy enthusiastically, willing to get on board with that theory. 'Plus he was with her in the morning, could have upped the dose of poison then, especially as they'd had an argument.'

'And he was obviously the controlling type.'

'Yeah, exactly. Plus the restraining order doesn't look good for him, does it? The fact that he wouldn't let go of his ex-wife.'

'True. Shows a history of obsessive behaviour, perhaps.'

'So what if Nicola was going to break up with him? And he got angry?'

'The poisoning had been going on for several weeks at least, likely planned long before then. If she was going to break up with him, we'd be questioning her ex, not her current boyfriend.' She frowns. He's right about that.

'Do you definitely think he's the type?' Ashby asks. 'Remember our killer is someone who has been thinking about this for a long time, who planned it and waited it out deliberately so Nicola would suffer. That doesn't speak of someone who acted in the heat of the moment – it's someone clinical, able to stay detached from it all as Nicola suffered over weeks. There's got to be a strong reason for someone to do that.'

'It could be a jealousy thing? The whole "if I can't have her no one can" scenario? Or maybe, "if I can't have her *exclusively* then no one can"? He was clearly unhappy about Ben, didn't trust Nicola – otherwise why would he try and put her off him like that?'

Ashby's gaze travels to the photo of Ben. 'Yeah, I've been wondering about that.'

'And then there's all of this "I had to take care of her" crap, it just sounds like he was possessive over her, doesn't it? Like he didn't want to share her with anyone – did you see how he reacted to Sarah? It just sounded like he wanted Nicola to himself.' Murphy moves her gaze to where

Sarah's pale green eyes stare out at her, unnervingly direct even in a photograph. 'Wonder what she thought of him,' she thinks aloud.

Thomas, the DC she doesn't like, chooses that moment to rock up, clutching a brown folder in hand. She swears he's just put whatever it is in a folder for effect – what's wrong with carrying round a piece of paper? 'Thought you'd like to see this, sir,' he says to Ashby, pressing the folder into his hands. Really, what's with the 'sir'? Ashby only outranks them by one position – James is the only one they need to call sir around here. Blatantly just sucking up.

Ashby takes a look, smiles. 'Well,' he says, turning from the other DC and looking at her. 'Looks like we've now got an excuse to go and ask her about it.'

Chapter Twenty

I'm sitting on my bed with my duvet around me, hugging my legs to my chest as I try to figure out the best way to go forward. I need to keep doing things, things that feel constructive, otherwise there's a chance I'll go legitimately mad waiting for the police to figure everything out. I can hear Nika clattering around in the kitchen and grit my teeth against the noise. It's not her fault, but sound really carries in the flat, and right now I want quiet. The adrenaline from the near miss at Phil's house has gone and all I'm left with is a chill.

I press my forehead to my knees. I just want this to be over. Why can't it be over?

There's the sound of the buzzer to the flat ringing and I squeeze my eyes shut. Nika can deal with it. Hopefully it's just someone delivering an Amazon package – she orders a disproportionate number of things from there. I hear her open the front door, then there are murmured voices that I could probably make out if I tried hard enough. The sound of the door slamming, followed by footsteps creaking on the wooden floorboards.

There's a tentative knock at my door. 'Sarah?'

'Tell them to go away.' My voice is muffled against my knees.

'I, umm, can't,' she mumbles.

I groan, and push up off my bed. 'What do you mean you can't?' I ask as I open the door. 'I don't want to talk to anyone.'

Nika twists her hands in front of her, slim fingers entwining together. 'Sarah, it's the police,' she whispers.

My heart thuds painfully against my chest, firing my system back into full alert. She looks at me with round eyes, and I meet her gaze, knowing she's thinking the same thing, wondering if the police somehow know I was at Phil's house earlier, wondering if they've come to question me about it. Shit. Maybe I shouldn't have done it, maybe it was too risky.

I take a breath. Tell myself to get a grip. 'OK.'

We walk along the landing and to the sitting room. Just before we head in, Nika takes my hand, gives it a gentle squeeze. I squeeze hers back without looking at her, the warmth of her touch lingering, making me a little calmer.

The detectives are sat next to each other on the bigger of the two black sofas. Murphy looks at ease with one leg, encased within black trousers, crossed over the other, while Ashby sits right at the edge of the sofa, leaning forward. I wonder if that's because he thinks his stumpy legs won't reach the floor if he sits too far back.

They both stand when Nika and I enter. I take a breath. In for three, out for three. 'Hello, detectives. How can I help?'

'Sarah.' Murphy smiles at me, flashing a set of perfect teeth. 'How are you doing?'

'Well. I could be better,' I say stiffly.

Nika clears her throat from where she's hovering in the doorway. 'I'll leave you to it, then.' She hesitates. 'Do you . . . want a drink or anything?'

'Oh no,' says Murphy graciously. 'Don't worry, we won't be long, I hope.'

Nika scurries out the room. I look the detectives straight in the eye, and gesture for them to sit back down, waiting until they do so before I take a seat on the smaller sofa.

I make sure my movements are calm, unhurried, so as not to let on at the nerves bubbling under my skin at their arrival.

'So. Have you found out who murdered my mother yet?' I spit it out, the question bitter on my tongue, before they can say anything. My stomach squirms as I wait a beat for them to answer – for one tiny moment, I'm not actually sure if I want to hear the reply.

'We're still working on it,' says Murphy calmly. Great. So they are no closer, have done nothing. 'Have you had any other thoughts about who could be responsible?'

I have a feeling she's asking me out of courtesy, to keep me satisfied that I'm in the loop, rather than actually wanting to hear my theories. But I hesitate anyway. I think of what I told Mary, about walking in on Ben and my mother. And of Phil, of the fact that I was just at his house, the theory I had while there. 'No,' I say eventually. 'If I knew who did it, I would tell you.'

'Well, in that case . . .' She clasps her hands on her lap and glances at Ashby. He gives her a little nod. 'We're actually here to talk to you about your mother's will, Sarah.'

I frown. 'Her will? What about it?'

Ashby picks up the thread. 'Well, you're named as the only beneficiary there.'

I nod slowly. I haven't given much thought to her will, in all honesty, haven't bothered to push the solicitor on it. It's so far down my list of priorities right now. 'Well, I'm her only family. Unless you count Ben and Fiona, I guess. But I'm the only one left related by blood.'

'Did she speak to you about it beforehand?' asks Ashby.

'No. We never spoke about it. Why would we have? She wasn't expecting to die.'

'Do you know if she spoke with anyone else about it?' Murphy's voice is calm. A little *too* calm, actually – like she either already knows the answer, or doesn't care about it.

'No,' I say bluntly. 'Why would I know that?'

'You're right, of course, you wouldn't necessarily know,' says Ashby. 'I suppose we're just wondering if you can think of anyone who might have expected to be in the will? Who might have been put out they weren't named?'

I cock my head. 'Detectives, have you actually read the contents of my mother's will?' I don't give them the chance to answer. 'Now, I haven't, but I can guarantee there's not a whole lot in there, certainly nothing of any huge value. Why do you think she was living in an annex across from her brother-in-law? For fun? She lost everything when my father died. Everything.' My voice cracks on that, an image of our old family home, of all the memories it held, flaring up in my mind.

They don't say anything immediately to that, and I feel a spark of impatience, though I manage to stop myself tapping my foot on the floor. 'Look, are you trying to ask me if I think someone was angry they weren't in the will, so killed my mother because of it? Because not only does that not make sense given how little she had, but surely it would only make sense for someone to kill her if they *were* mentioned in the will?'

They exchange a look that I can't read, and my stomach swoops. Because maybe that's it. I'm the only one mentioned there, so maybe they think that gives me motive, ridiculous as it might seem to me that someone would kill her for a few household items. I ignore the tingle of nerves that kick in at that. All it proves is that they are bloody incompetent, if they think that.

I deliberately straighten my back, stick my chin in the air. 'Do you actually have something of significance to ask me? Because, really, I'm going through enough right now that I don't need you showing up at my house, getting my hopes up that you might have found something, only to drop something like this on me.'

'You're right, Sarah,' Murphy says, her voice deadly smooth. 'The truth is, while we did want to talk to you about her will, we also wondered if we could get your opinion on something.' I raise my eyebrows, waiting. 'We wondered how you felt about your mother's boyfriend, Phil.'

My heart sends an uncomfortable thrum of electricity around my body, but I try not to let it show. They are calm, so I will be, too. There's no reason to suspect they know what I was doing only hours ago. 'What about him?'

'Did you like him?'

I shrug. 'No. Not really. Not at all, actually. But my mum seemed to, so I put up with him.'

'And your mother was happy with him, was she? She didn't say anything to you about him over the last few weeks before she died?'

I sigh. 'Look, I know what you're getting at. And no, I don't think he killed her. I don't like him – and I'm pretty sure the feeling's mutual – but he genuinely seemed to care for my mother, and she certainly never said anything bad about him to me. Besides, they'd only been going out, what, like six months? I don't know, I just . . . I don't see what could have happened to make him . . . make him do that to her.'

Murphy nods slowly, and I get the impression my answer isn't one she wanted to hear. So I was right. They think it was Phil. First suspect's usually the right one, or something like that, isn't it? But they've already questioned him and haven't made an arrest, so surely they can't be certain, otherwise they wouldn't be here, asking me about it. I press my tongue to the roof of my mouth to avoid snapping out words I'll regret later. But for fuck's sake, they are dragging their heels here. It's their job to figure out who did this to her, but it's like I want it solved more than they do, like I'm having to do the work for them. Actually, that's stupid. *Of course* I want it solved more than they do. I just have to be patient. But really, isn't it as obvious to them as it is to me that a guy like Phil isn't behind a murder like this?

'And Sarah,' Ashby picks up the thread, 'we heard that your mother may have had an . . . argument, perhaps, with your uncle Ben, a few nights before she died. Do you know anything about that?'

Another jolt from my heart. It's going to cut years off me, the way it's working so hard at the moment. They know about that, then. I wonder who told them – Phil or Mary. Bet it was Mary. You can't say anything in this town unless you want it shared. 'Sounds like you already know everything I do,' I say evenly. I choose my next words carefully – whatever I'm feeling, I don't want to be the one to land Ben in it. 'Phil and I walked in on them the other day, but it wasn't all that dramatic – and we didn't really see anything, so I can't even tell you if it was an actual argument, or if they were just talking.'

'And Phil,' Murphy picks up. 'How did Phil seem, seeing them . . . talking?'

'I don't know,' I say with a sigh. 'He didn't say anything out loud – and it's not like he'd open up to *me* if he was annoyed by it, but he didn't yell at Ben or my mum or anything – and he was still around after it, so . . .'

Murphy glances at Ashby, and they seem to come to an unsaid agreement, standing up in unison. 'All right,' says Ashby. 'Thanks, Sarah. You've been really helpful. We'll show ourselves out, shall we?'

'Oh,' I say, feeling that the end to this conversation has come rather abruptly. But then, maybe that's a good thing. It means they can't know what I was doing only hours ago – means I got away with it. 'No, it's OK, I'll let you out.' Ashby glances around the living room as he follows me, and I can't help wondering if he's looking for something in particular, or just being curious.

'That's a nice selection of plants you have out there,' Murphy says conversationally.

I turn to see her gesturing to our small balcony, where I've arranged various potted plants. I can sense she's trying to be casual, but there's something in her tone that sets me on edge. 'Oh, thanks. I wish I had a garden, really, but, well.'

'What type of plants are they? I know nothing about gardens.'

'I don't know a huge amount either, in all honesty. I only got into it recently – Fiona's been teaching me. She and Ben are both big gardeners.' I see her exchange a look with Ashby, though I think she's trying to be subtle. I really wish I knew what they were thinking right now. 'Those ones, though, that's a geranium, and that one's a tomato plant, not that I've had any joy there yet. I'm lucky, or so Ben's told me – we get quite a lot of sun on that balcony.'

We reach the front door and I hold it open for them. 'I'm sorry I couldn't be more help,' I say, feeling awkward. I wish I hadn't lost my temper early on now, maybe I stopped them from telling me something.

Murphy smiles, though it doesn't seem real. It seems like the type of smile I've been trying to put on recently. 'You've been very helpful, Sarah, not to worry.'

Ashby follows her out the door, giving me a curt nod, his expression mild. He turns to go, but Murphy stops after only a couple of steps, angling her head in a way that makes her cheekbones look fantastically prominent, despite the roundness of her face.

'Sorry, Sarah, can I just ask one more thing?' She ignores what seems like a questioning look from Ashby. 'This might seem like a silly question, but I wonder if you could tell us how your mother liked to take her tea?'

I frown, glancing from Murphy to Ashby and back again. Neither of their expressions give anything away, but I know this isn't just a throwaway question. Know that this must be them looking into the poisons – and not telling me. I curl my hands into fists at my sides, nails biting flesh. But my voice is calm as I answer. 'Milky, I guess. And sweet. She liked it sweet.'

Chapter Twenty-One

Murphy jangles the Corsa keys as the two of them step out of the block of flats. She turns to look at Ashby, as if to say *Well?* 'I don't think the will has anything to do with it,' Ashby says eventually.

Murphy blows out a breath. It surprises her that it's already cold enough to mist up the air. 'It was a long shot. Would have been nice, though. Easy.'

Ashby offers her a rare grin. 'Where's the glory in that?' They walk across the car park together. 'You asked about the tea,' he states. But as Murphy opens her mouth to speak, he cuts her off. 'Don't give me that look, I'm not cross, not about to tell you to back off.'

'I wasn't—'

'No, I imagine you weren't.' Murphy frowns, and Ashby's lips twitch before falling back into that straight-faced expression he does so well. 'I imagine you weren't going to say anything,' he elaborates. 'That's the problem – you don't say it, you just think it. I'm not annoyed that you asked about the tea,' he reiterates, as she squirms a little. 'It was a good call. It doesn't change the fact that someone could still have been giving her the poison in something she didn't like, but . . .'

'But it makes more sense for the killer to disguise it in something she *did* like, right?' She doesn't point out that this would make it less likely to be Phil. She doesn't really want to say that out loud yet.

'Yeah, it would. More guarantee she'd actually get it in her system.'

'So in that case . . . Could we be looking at belladonna? Be easy to hide that in sweet tea for sure.'

'Seems a likely possibility, yes. And it's a better-known poison, easier to cultivate, perhaps.' Murphy feels an electric jolt of excitement as she unlocks the car, the thought that they might have their poison.

Ashby makes no move to get in, so she leans against the driver's door. 'So if it's belladonna, I'm pretty sure we're looking at least an hour between ingesting the poison and death – it's not instantaneous from what I've read.'

'All right, good to know.' He pauses. 'You pointed out the plants in her flat.'

Murphy nods. 'Sarah didn't seem worried by it, though. I was waiting for a reaction.'

'And none of them are poisonous.'

'And none of them are poisonous,' she agrees. 'And . . .' She cuts herself off, not sure if what she's thinking is actually worth anything.

'Go on.'

'Well, I remember something from reading about belladonna. It grows more easily in the shade – hence its other name, deadly nightshade. So it wouldn't be ideal to grow on that balcony anyway.' Ashby grunts and she leaves it at that. 'She seemed pretty certain it's not Phil,' she says instead.

'Yeah, which is interesting given how much she clearly doesn't like him. But I have to say . . .'

'You agree with her?'

'Well, I'm not saying we should rule Phil out altogether. But I think there's enough pointing us in a different direction that we would be idiots to cling on to him just for the sake of it. It doesn't fit his personality, and there's no sign of him being interested in gardening, whereas—'

'Ben?'

'Yeah, that's what I'm thinking. I don't think we can ignore that his name keeps cropping up, that he was living just metres away from our victim. He's got the opportunity, and if there was something going on with Nicola, that might give us motive.'

Murphy nods in agreement. She'd initially thought they should get Fiona and Ben in right away, but Ashby thought – and the DI agreed – that they shouldn't put them on alert, should make them wait a bit, wondering what was going on. When she gets into the driver's seat, she closes her eyes for a second. She's so damn tired. She's not sure she's ever been this tired before. How has it only been four days since the investigation started?

'You OK?' Ashby slides in next to her.

'Yeah.' She drops her hand, not wanting to seem weak in front of him. 'Just thinking about Ben.'

'Yeah. That interview is bound to be interesting.' Murphy grimaces, thinking about the interview with Phil. Like he's somehow reading her thoughts, Ashby adds, 'Hopefully he won't be quite as big a dick.' She glances at him, a little surprised, and he just raises his eyebrows. 'You didn't think I'd notice what kind of person he is?'

'No, I just . . . I don't know what I thought,' she admits. 'I guess I didn't think you'd admit it to me, is all.'

Ashby runs a hand across his jawline. 'Look, I know you don't like me much.'

'I never—'

He cuts her off, and she uses the excuse of reversing out the spot to avoid looking at him. 'I know you think I've been unfair, calling seniority on you or not trusting you or

whatever. And I just want to be clear – I'm not a dick.'
Murphy squashes down a snort. That's not quite what she
expected him to say. 'I'm not trying to stop you getting
involved – if I was, I would have said right at the outset
that I didn't want a DC on a murder case that was all over
the town, especially not one that doesn't know the area,
or that I didn't feel comfortable with you in the interview
room, given your lack of experience.'

Murphy grimaces. She knows of course that he could
have done that, she just doesn't like hearing it out loud.
'What I'm saying,' he carries on in that frustratingly even
tone, 'is that I *am* giving you a chance, OK?'

She nods, swallows down a bit of pride. Apparently she
hasn't exactly been the Queen of Subtlety. 'I'm sorry. I'm
grateful to be involved, honestly. I just thought . . . I don't
know, it just seemed like you were judging me, or not
trusting me or something.'

'Well, I was,' he says, shrugging. She frowns across at
him. 'Of course I was. I don't know you that well, and
this is a big case for me, too – one that James is letting
me take the lead on. You come in, a DC who's never been
on a murder case, who doesn't know the town – of course
I was judging you. And I'll keep doing that, and so will
the DI. But that doesn't mean you shouldn't keep trying
to prove that you can add something valuable.' Murphy
opens her mouth but can think of nothing to say, so she
shuts it again. 'So are we OK? Or are you going to keep
being silently resentful?'

He says it so damn evenly, but she can't help wanting
to snap back. She supposes that's the problem. 'We're OK.
I'm sorry. I'll stop.'

'Well, just try to stop. You're still allowed to be pissed
off every now and then – a privilege of the job.'

She smiles. 'Noted.'

'All right, then. Let's stop at Burger King, can we? I want a coffee.'

'And I need sugar. Did we even have lunch?'

'You had a Coke and an egg sandwich from Sainsbury's.'

'Right. The food of Gods.' Partly to clear the now slightly awkward air, she says, 'This is why I'm still single, you know. I haven't stopped thinking about the case long enough to remember if I ate – when am I supposed to find time for the damn apps my sister keeps telling me about?'

Ashby, perhaps wisely, says nothing. Murphy sighs as she pulls into the drive-through. 'I keep thinking that this should be easier, simpler, you know?'

'It would be easier if there was an easier murder weapon,' he mutters.

'Yeah. Which I suppose might be another reason they chose poison.' She edges a couple of inches forward as the car in front moves. 'There's still the voicemail. The one Nicola left Sarah. I keep trying to figure out what it could be. Like maybe it could be Nicola wanting to tell her something bad about Phil, that she couldn't get out the relationship, and then Phil overheard, upped the poison or something.'

'You're trying to make it fit with what you want, not the facts.' But he says it kindly, not a reprimand. Besides, he's right.

'Yeah. Well. Maybe our little chat with Ben Gregory will open up a new lead, then?' He nods. Her whole body feels twitchy, eager to get on with it. 'I'm actually a little excited by it.' She glances at him, and his lips twitch.

'And I think *that's* the reason you're still single.' She's so surprised, all she can do is let out a bark of laughter.

Taken from Case File: Nicola Gregory

BENJAMIN THOMAS GREGORY
EXTRACT FROM RECORDED INTERVIEW

Date: 08/10/2018
Duration: 53 minutes
Conducted by Officers DC MURPHY and DS ASHBY

DS So, Ben, you were Nicola's husband's brother, is that right?

BG Well, I mean, I'm still his brother now, even if he's not here anymore. But yeah. Step-brother, technically.

DS Step-brother?

BG Yeah, you know, as in not related by blood.

DC So you're related by marriage?

BG Yeah. My dad married his mum, when I was about five. Charlie was older, twelve.

DC And you got on well together?

BG Really well, yeah. Charlie was a fantastic big brother. He used to drive me to school and everything when I was a kid and we hung out a lot later on. We helped each other out when we lost our parents and everything. And that's why I stayed around town – I wanted to be near him.

DC All right, thanks, Ben. You were with Nicola on the night she died, is that right?

BG Yeah, that's right. Along with Phil and Fiona. We were the ones to call the ambulance.

DC Your wife, I believe, was the one to talk to the paramedics on the phone?

BG That's right.

DC And did you all walk in on Nicola together, to see her in need of medical attention?

BG In need of medical attention? She was dying.

DS Sorry, Ben, we know this must be difficult.

BG Yeah, it is. Sorry. It's just, talking about it, makes me think about it all over again, you know?

DS We understand. Losing a loved one is never easy. I just hope we can help you find closure by finding out who did this to her. Would you like a brief pause, have a drink of water?

BG Thanks.

DS No problem. Just let us know when you're ready to continue.

BG It's fine. You can go on.

DC We were just asking if you were all with Nicola together, before the ambulance arrived.

BG We all waited with her together, yeah. I went over first because Sarah had asked me and Fiona to keep an eye on her – we all knew she wasn't doing great, not that we thought it was anything that serious. But I . . . I saw her and she didn't look well at all, so I went and got Fiona. Then Phil came round maybe five or ten minutes later because he hadn't heard from her all day. We all waited until the ambulance came but it was . . . it was too late.

DC So you were with Nicola alone, before the others came in? How long would you say you were alone for?

BG God, not long at all. I tried to get her to drink something, and then went and got Fiona – she works at the hospital so I thought she might be able to help.

DC Ben, why did you wait until your wife arrived to call an ambulance? Why didn't you call one right away?

BG I don't know. I wish I had. I keep wondering if it could

have made a difference, those extra few minutes, you know? But I guess I panicked. I didn't realise it was as bad as it was.

DS Ben, how would you describe your relationship with Nicola?

BG She was my sister-in-law.

DS And were you friends?

BG Yeah. Yeah, of course we were friends. She was married to my brother for over twenty years.

DS So you only knew her through your brother, is that right?

BG Well, yeah, I guess. But it was so long ago that they got married that she feels – felt – like my friend as much as his wife, if that makes sense.

DS And after your brother passed away – you remained friends with Nicola?

BG Of course. She lived in my annex, looked after my kids.

DC Apparently you and Nicola had an argument a few days before she passed.

BG What? No, we didn't.

DC Something that Sarah and Phil walked in on?

BG Sarah told you that?

DS We didn't say that.

BG I bet it was Phil. Bastard. He was always jealous of Nicola and me.

DC Jealous of Nicola and you? Why was that?

BG Well, it's like I just said, we were friends for a long time. Phil didn't like competing with that.

DS And was he competing with that?

BG What do you mean?

DS Were you and Nicola something other than friends? Something more than that?

BG I'm married.

DS That's not what we're asking.

BG We were good friends, OK?

DS So if we asked your wife, asked your niece, would they say the same thing, that you and Nicola were just good friends? If we looked at your messages to Nicola on your phone right now, would they support your claim that you were just good friends?

DC I'm sorry, Ben, do you mind answering the question?

BG Look, we were together a while ago, OK? But not recently.

DC You mean you had been having an affair with Nicola?

BG It's not— Yes. Technically, yes. But it was over.

DC When did it end?

BG Years ago.

DS How many years? Roughly?

BG God, look . . . I don't know. Before Sarah was born and she's, what, twenty-three? So there you go. Over twenty-three years ago.

DS But Nicola was married to Charlie at the time?

BG Yeah, she was, and I know what you're thinking, that that makes us terrible people, but it was . . . Their relationship wasn't perfect and we . . .

DC We're not thinking anything like that, Ben, we only care about finding out what happened to Nicola. So were you also married at this point?

BG No. No, I met Fiona much later, around ten years ago.

DC So between Sarah being born and you meeting Fiona, you never resumed the affair?

BG We didn't . . . It wasn't . . . Look, we might have got together a few times. You have to understand, Charlie and Nicola were so young when they got married and I don't think either of them thought they were in the best marriage – they stayed together because of Sarah, I'm sure of it.

DC Nicola told you that?

BG She didn't have to tell me, I was there. But look, it ended when I married Fiona. Then Fiona and I had the girls, Charlie got ill and . . . We didn't start it up again, not through all that.

DC All right. Ben, we found some flowers in Nicola's rubbish bin
– do you know who might have wanted to send her flowers?

BG What? I don't know. Phil, maybe?

DC So you didn't buy her flowers in the run-up to her death?

BG What? No. No, I don't know anything about any flowers.

DC Did Sarah know about the affair, Ben?

BG Sarah? I don't know. She never said anything to me if she did.
Nicola was worried that she'd walked in on us . . . close . . . when
she was younger, but I don't think she saw anything. Why?

DC Nicola left a message on Sarah's phone right before she
died, saying she wanted to tell Sarah something.

BG What, and you think she wanted to tell her about me? I doubt
it.

DC Can you think of anything else Nicola might have wanted to
tell Sarah?

BG Jesus, I don't know. But it wouldn't make sense for Nicola
to want to tell her about me now. She didn't want to start up
again so . . .

DS But you did? You wanted to resume the affair?

BG I . . . I don't know. But that's all irrelevant now, isn't it?

DS Does your wife know about you and Nicola?

BG We've never talked about it. But I've told you, it was over
before I met Fiona.

DC Yet you wanted to resume the affair recently? Since Charlie
passed away, perhaps?

BG That's not what I . . . Look, I've told you, nothing actually
happened, we didn't start up again.

DS Is that so?

BG Look, I know what you're thinking.

DS Do you now?

BG I would never have done anything to hurt Nicola. Never. I
loved her.

Chapter Twenty-Two

I can't get out the car. I stay sitting where I'm parked on the gravel driveway, headlights switched off, behind Ben and Fiona's car. My mother's car is still here, too, her tiny beat-up Ka looking a little sad on the driveway, like it knows that no one will take it now that my mother is dead. I need to sort that, I suppose. Another thing to add to the list. But for now I just stare at the house, faintly illuminated by the porch light.

I didn't think it would be so hard, coming here for the first time since she died, and now that I am here I find I don't want to see the annex after all, don't want to speak to Ben or Fiona, don't want to have to try to pretend in front of them.

There's a knock on the passenger window, loud enough to make me jump. It's Fiona, her face paler than usual as she squints at me, wearing a big blue puffa jacket. She's come from behind me, rather than out of the house as I would have expected. I unstick my hands from the steering wheel and roll down the window. I've been sitting here without the engine running for at least five minutes, so it's not exactly hot in here, but the cool air I let in makes me shiver. The nights are definitely getting colder. Either that or I am.

'Sarah?' She makes my name into a question, even though it's obviously me.

'Hi. I just came round to, well, see you, I guess.' It's as close to the truth as I can get. The main reason I came round is to clear the air, to bridge the gulf I can feel widening between us the longer this goes on. But that sounds too awkward, calls attention to the fact that my mother was murdered right here, and the police think it was one of us.

'Oh, I'm so glad you came. We've been so worried about you, my darling.' She shoves her hands in her coat pockets. 'I was just out walking, you know, wanted to get some fresh air.' Another pause, and I can't think of a single fucking thing to say. 'Do you want to come in? The girls would love to see you.'

Well, I drove all the way here so I'm hardly going to say no, especially not when I do genuinely want to see Lily and Emily. Besides, this is the chance I wanted to get inside the house – because the police must surely be looking round it at some point?

I get out the car and Fiona envelops me in a tight hug. I stand rigid for just the briefest of seconds, then allow my arms to creep around her, too, resting my head on her squishy coat. She feels so strong, so solid. So unlike my mother was towards the end of her life. 'I'm so sorry, my darling,' Fiona whispers, her breath hot on my exposed neck. 'So very sorry. It isn't fair, it's not fair at all.'

'No,' I breathe. 'It's not fair.' None of this is fair. And that's partly why I don't ask whether Fiona is really sad now my mother is gone, or whether she thinks life will be just that bit easier without her. Because I know, even in the state I'm in right now, that I don't want to destroy things with Fiona, after everything else I've lost. I know I'll regret it in the long run if I do give voice to the darker thoughts swirling around inside me.

My throat is tight when she pulls away. Turns out it's Fiona, with her motherly concern, who can bring me the closest to breaking point. 'Come on, my darling, let's go inside and I'll make you a cup of tea.' I grimace, thinking of the way my mother died, but do my best to straighten it out as I nod.

Fiona unlocks the front door and ushers me inside. 'Lily? Emily? Sarah's here!'

There's the sound of little feet running down the stairs and I look up to see Emily grinning as she leads the way. She launches herself at me and I pick her up and spin her around, making her giggle. 'Hello, Trouble. How are you?'

She grins. 'Trouble!' She takes hold of my hand. 'Daddy bought us a castle, do you want to see?'

'A castle? No way.'

She nods in earnest, her eyes wide. 'It's in our room.'

I glance at Lily, who is standing by the bannister, staring at me. I smile at her as I approach, dragging Emily with me. I prod her gently in the side, and she relents, giggling. I know I looked more like Lily, but I wonder briefly who I was more like – the loud, confident child or the one hovering in the background, waiting to decide who to trust. Now there's no one left to ask. Except Ben, I suppose. But I don't want to ask him.

'Come up with us?' Emily pleads.

'In a minute. I just want to get a drink first.'

'Then you'll come up?'

'Yes,' I assure her. Emily seems satisfied because she races back up the stairs, past Lily, who stumbles after her big sister.

'Come on, let's get you a cup of tea,' Fiona says, and though her voice is warm, I can sense the effort to make it so. She takes me through to the kitchen, but I insist on making her a drink, telling her, truthfully, that I need to stay busy.

'Do they know?' I ask, keeping my voice low.

'I've told them she died, yes,' she whispers. She doesn't need to add the rest – that she hasn't told them how, exactly. Hasn't told them that their aunt was murdered.

'They seem . . . OK.'

The advantage of being the one busy in the kitchen means I don't have to look at her as she answers. Still, I hear it, the strain this is all taking on her. 'I'm not sure they completely understand. Emily, I think, gets it. And they were sad when I told them. Sometimes they bring her up, like they're still trying to figure it out. But if not, I don't want to . . .'

'It's OK. I get it. I wouldn't want them to have to know it all either.' I cross the kitchen to the kettle when it starts to bubble. 'Where's Ben?' I ask, partly to change the subject and partly because it's making me on edge, not knowing.

'He's upstairs, lying down. He, well . . . I'll go and get him in a minute, he'll want to say hello.'

'If he's sleeping then . . .'

'He'll want to see you.' She says it firmly, no room for argument, though it sounds more like she's telling him that, even though he's not here.

I hand her a mug, but the moment I'm done being busy I find that I can't do this, I can't stay still, talking about it. My main problem right now is my inability to be still, to be patient, it seems. 'Fiona, I'm sorry, but do you mind if I go round to the annex? I haven't been there since . . . And I just wanted to, well, see it, I suppose.' Not true, but it gives me time to clear my head, get some air.

'Of course. I'll get Ben but take your time, and give me a shout if you need anything.'

I turn back to her when I'm nearly at the back door, unable to keep the question in. 'Fiona, did the police . . . Have they looked round the house at all?'

She bites her lip. 'They looked around the annex, yes. But not . . . not here.' She doesn't add anything else, but looks down, away from me and I wonder if the police just haven't asked to look round the house, or if she – or she and Ben – have refused to let them in. It makes me worried, either way, that they haven't looked round yet, and a familiar pulsing under my skin starts up again, urging me to do something.

'And have they . . .' I swallow, hating how difficult this is to talk about. 'Have they spoken to you? At the station, I mean?'

Fiona blanches, making the dark circles under her eyes more obvious, but her voice is steady. 'They've spoken to Ben at the station, yes. They asked me a few questions when they were here, but I've not been in to see them. Not yet, anyway.' She makes it sound so pleasant, not like we are all being interviewed about the murder of my mother. I nod slowly. I'm glad they've spoken to Ben and not her – I don't want them to be considering her as a suspect. Fiona's next words come out in a gush. 'Sarah, if I knew anything, I mean, if *we* knew anything, we'd tell you right away, you have to know that. This is as much a shock to us as to you, and I don't want you thinking—'

I raise a hand to cut her off. I'm nowhere near ready to have this conversation. 'I know,' I say simply. 'It's OK.' Even though things are not OK, not by a long shot.

Unfortunately, I'm not quite quick enough getting out the back door after that.

'Sarah?' Ben's voice is rusty, like he's forgotten how to speak.

I force myself to straighten out my face as I look over to where he's hovering in the doorway. I keep the door open behind me, even as the cool air bites through my clothes.

'Hi,' I say, as calmly as I can. 'I'm just going round to the annex, but I'll be back in a bit to say goodbye before I leave.' I know my voice is clipped, almost rude, but I can't help it.

'Are you . . . all right? I tried to call you, after I saw you at the church.'

'I know. I'm sorry.' There I go again, apologising to people when I shouldn't have to.

He looks terrible. His stubble has grown out and is going grey in places, all muscle definition that he had just a week ago is seemingly lost. I wonder if it's just grief, making him look like that, or if it's something else. If it's guilt.

Fiona is probably expecting me to say something, to try and comfort him the way everyone keeps trying to comfort me. Hell, maybe Ben's expecting it too. But I can't. Instead I ask the one thing I do want to know. 'Ben, my mum rang me on the night that she . . .' I swallow. 'On the night that she died.' He frowns, waiting. 'I didn't see it until too late, but she left me a message, saying that she needed to tell me something.' He just stays still. Too still, actually, and I can feel Fiona watching us both in the wings. 'Do you . . . I mean, you were with her when she . . .' I wrinkle my nose, annoyed at myself for my sudden inarticulacy. 'Did she say anything to you that night, about what she might want to tell me? Do you know what it might have been?'

'No,' he says, but he says it too quickly. 'I'm sorry, Sarah.' His voice sounds wrong, like it's only just broken. 'I really don't. I wasn't with her when she tried to call you. And she . . .' He rubs a hand over his face and it makes a scratching noise on his stubble. 'She wasn't very coherent that night. I'm sorry,' he says again.

I watch him for a moment more, waiting to see if he'll break. But he just looks at me with round, sad eyes that make me want to punch something.

'Sarah, I think maybe the three of us should—' But I block out Fiona, rude as that might make me, and shut the door behind me without a word.

My breath comes out as mist as I cross the garden towards the annex, choosing to walk on the grass, through the plants as an act of defiance. They seem to shrink back from me as I march on, whether because they're allowing me space to pass through or protecting themselves from me I don't know. Well. This just confirms what I already suspected, doesn't it? Ben is a fucking liar – he *must* know something about the phone call, surely. He's just another person who's lying to me, just like the police won't tell me what they know, won't tell me if they've figured out what poison it was yet. All I want is for people to be honest with me, is that so much to ask?

It's because I'm raging about this that I don't notice someone walking towards me, don't hear the sound of footsteps until they are almost on top of me.

I spin around just in time to see Phil's burly figure not two metres from me. 'I knew it,' he snarls. 'It's your car, isn't it? In the drive? The same car that that European chick made me look at. Isn't it?' Absurdly the only thing I want to do right now is point out that 'European' is a somewhat vague term, but looking at his purpling face makes me decide better of it.

'I don't know what you're talking about,' I say instead, keeping my voice as even as possible to hide my shock that he's turned up like this when I was so sure I'd got away with it. 'It's my car on the drive, yes, but I don't know what you mean by that last part.'

He sneers. 'Oh yeah? Well, you know what I think, I think you're a lying bitch.' I bristle at that, the venom there. 'And I think you were round my house. What were you doing there?'

'I don't know what you mean,' I repeat. 'Surely I should be asking you what you're doing here, not the other way around.'

He takes a step towards me, but I refuse to back up, despite the warning prickles running up my forearms. 'No business of yours, why I'm here.'

'I'd say it is, given you're no longer welcome here. Just let yourself in, did you, through the gate? You're not allowed to do that anymore.' I try for firm, but it comes out scathing, almost taunting, and his eyes flash in response. Damn it. *Control your fucking temper, Sarah.*

'I saw your car there.' Ironically, his voice is a hell of a lot calmer than mine. 'I deserve an answer as to why you were at my house.'

'I wasn't,' I say simply.

'I'll go to the police, tell them you were there.'

I laugh, but stop when it sounds a little manic. 'Oh really? And what proof do you have? Did you take a photo of the number plate? Do you have CCTV footage?' He glares at me, but I know I've got him. Of course, it could all fall apart if he ever finds out that Nika is my flatmate, but that's future Sarah's problem. 'You still haven't told me why you're here. I'd wager that's a lot more suspicious than a car that looks similar to mine outside your dump of a house.'

'I'm allowed to drive past, aren't I? Allowed to fucking grieve. *You* might not miss her, ungrateful bitch, but I sure as hell do.' He spits the 'b' of bitch so that his spittle flies past my face, narrowly missing my cheek.

This time, I'm the one to step towards him so that we're almost nose-to-nose, close enough that I can see his overlarge pores. 'How *dare* you?' I growl. 'How *dare* you talk to me like that?'

'Came here to see what you got in her will, did you? Seeing what everything's worth?' He laughs bitterly. 'I told her not to give everything to you, but she ignored me.'

That makes me hesitate. 'You knew? You knew she was going to leave everything to me?' Admittedly, 'everything' sounds a hell of a lot better than it is, but this certainly doesn't look good for Phil. I wonder if the police know yet.

'Of course I fucking knew,' he says, his chest swelling, and clearly *he* doesn't think this looks bad for him. 'And she wouldn't listen when I told her you didn't deserve it, the way you treated her. Disgusting, it was, leaving her to fend for herself after her husband died.'

A ringing starts up in my ears. 'After my *dad* died, you mean.' I shake my head and my shoulders seem to collapse in on me. 'You know what, I don't deserve this. And I sure as hell have better things to do than standing out here talking to you.' I drag my hands through my hair. 'You really think I want anything in there?' I gesture to the annex door. 'I've lost my *mother*, for Christ's sake, and the last thing I'm thinking about is what stuff I might get as a result. You care so much about it?' I demand, fishing the key out of my pocket. 'Here.' I toss it to him, though he doesn't react in time and it lands with a clink at his feet on the paved stone he's standing on. He doesn't bend to pick it up. 'Take it. Help yourself to everything, you insensitive fucking bastard.'

I walk past him, intending to leave him standing there, but, even knowing that I shouldn't, that it won't accomplish anything, I can't help a few last words. 'You couldn't stand it, could you?' He swivels to look at me, his face hidden in my shadow. 'Sharing her. Is that why the police think you did it?'

He clenches his hands into fists. 'You know shit.'

'Do I now?' I cock my head. 'So they didn't call you into the station, then?'

'How do you know that?'

I shrug, though I'm not sure I pull off the casual look, not with every muscle in my body wired to breaking point. 'I have my sources.'

'Well, you little bitch, given I'm still out here and not locked up in some cell, I think it's safe to say you're wrong about your theory, don't you?'

'Don't call me a bitch.'

He laughs, the sound ugly and menacing, and the first pinpricks of genuine fear trace their way down my neck. 'Don't accuse me of murder, then.'

I go to step away but he grabs my shoulders. I try to pull free, but he holds firm. Icy heat flushes through my veins and I hitch in a breath. Fuck, maybe I had this all wrong, maybe he really is dangerous, really would do something to me. 'Let me go.' I hate the way my voice quivers.

'Take it back,' he growls.

'Let me go.'

'I don't want you spreading nasty rumours about me, do you hear?' This time, when he spits, it lands just to the left of my mouth. I grimace, unable to wipe it way with my arms bound by his.

'What on earth is going on here?' Warm relief chases away the ice in my veins at the sound of Fiona's voice. Took her long enough. Phil lets go of me, looking over my shoulder, and I turn to look at Fiona, too, wiping my face with my jacket sleeve. Right behind her, barefoot, is Ben.

'Nothing,' snarls Phil, and barges past me.

'It didn't look like nothing,' Fiona says warily, glancing at me. I reach up a hand to brush away angry tears that I've only just realised are there. I will *not* give Phil the satisfaction of knowing how much he's got to me.

Phil slows down when he gets to Fiona, like he might say something, but Ben steps out in front of her. 'You really should leave now. And don't even think about coming back. You're not welcome here anymore.' Ben's voice might be gruff, but it's firm, no hint of weakness there and he draws himself up to full height – he might not be as well-muscled as Phil, but he's taller.

Phil laughs again, the bitterness emanating from him almost palpable. 'As opposed to before, when you were so welcoming?' He casts a glance around at all of us. 'She deserved better than you three.' He stomps his way to the gate, and none of us say anything as we watch him. But he's not done. 'I know, by the way,' he says with a glance over his shoulder. 'I'm not as thick as you seem to think I am.' He's looking directly at Ben. 'I know you were trying to fuck her. And I know you were angry that she didn't want you, that she chose me instead.' With that, he swings the gate open and leaves, his footsteps heavy on the gravel driveway.

In the darkness, I still manage to catch Fiona's eye. Still manage to exchange a look that tells me, yes, Fiona knew about Ben and my mother. What isn't so easy to tell is whether she's wondering, in that moment, if Ben could have anything to do with her murder. Whether the seed of is doubt there. I lose my chance to figure it out when she jerks her head at me to follow, then puts a hand on Ben's arm as they walk back to the house together. I crick my neck one way then to the other to try and release some of the tension.

Well. If she's not going to, then I'm certainly not going to be the first to say it.

Chapter Twenty-Three

'The affair changes things, right?' Murphy says as soon as she arrives at Ashby's desk. She holds out a Diet Coke to Ashby, keeps the regular one for herself. She feels two sets of eyes – the two uniformed police officers – watching her, and knows they're eavesdropping.

Ashby takes the Diet Coke, leans back in his chair. 'Well, I think it means we've got two strong suspects, both with a serious motive now.'

'So we're saying a definite no to Phil? Despite the fact he could have found out Ben and Nicola were thinking of starting up again and got jealous?' She knows, even as she says it, that there's something wrong with that theory, as much as she wishes it were true. So she holds up a hand when Ashby goes to speak. 'It doesn't really make sense, I know. Besides the fact that both Ben and Fiona are serious gardeners and Phil isn't – they were only going out for six months, which isn't that much time for something to go seriously wrong, for him to plot and carry out a prolonged murder. I know,' she repeats, then sighs. 'So we're back to Ben being angry that she wouldn't start up the affair – gets jealous, kills her, or Fiona finding out about it, getting jealous and killing her?'

'We don't *have* to prove motive, you know,' Ashby says evenly. 'We just need to prove who did it.'

'I know that. But isn't it easier if we have it?'

He shrugs. 'Sometimes.' For a second she feels like shaking him, just to rile him up, to get him out of his calm demeanour. He takes a sip of his Coke. 'All right, let's look at Ben. This affair has been happening on and off again for nearly twenty-five years. Then Nicola's husband dies, perhaps she's caught up in guilt about cheating on him, so she refuses to start up with Ben again even though he wants to.'

'Right,' says Murphy, tapping her fingernails, painted dark red today, on the Coke can. 'So he can't deal with the rejection, especially when she starts going out with Phil. Six months ago – maybe when she started seeing Phil, that's when he started to plan it out?'

'Could make sense,' Ashby concedes.

'*And*,' Murphy adds, 'maybe he didn't actually up the poison, actually kill her, until he knew for sure she was going to reject him? Maybe he wanted to watch, see what she'd do?'

Ashby raises his eyebrows, says nothing, and she knows she's reaching. She blows out a breath. 'I don't like that he didn't call the ambulance right away.'

'Could be that he just panicked, like he said, or that it really didn't seem as bad as we're now thinking it did. Easier in hindsight and all that.'

She knows he's just playing devil's advocate, that they need to consider it from all angles, but it feels like he's just contradicting her. He gives her a look that says he knows exactly what she's thinking, and her lips twitch involuntarily. 'There's the voicemail, too,' she says. 'Nicola could have been trying to tell Sarah about the affair? And Ben didn't want her to, so he upped the dose of poison?'

'We don't know when Nicola called Sarah, though – to me, it reads like Nicola only called her once she felt the effects of the poison kick in, which wouldn't give someone a motive to kill her for whatever she was going to say.' Ashby swivels on his chair as they think in silence. 'For what it's worth,' he says, 'my money's on the wife.'

'Fiona?' Something twists her gut at that. She liked Fiona, she doesn't want it to be her. But . . . 'Well, I can see how the jealousy would eat away at her, having Nicola right next door like that, knowing about the affair. Would make sense, if she'd been harbouring resentment towards Nicola for a while, but the opportunity to poison her only came once she moved right down the end of the garden.'

The garden, Murphy muses. The beautiful, elaborate garden, with plants she couldn't begin to recognise. After the interview with Ben, the revelation of the affair, they applied for a warrant to search the house, the garden, but until it's granted their hands are tied, given Fiona wouldn't let them in. Of course, they might have already got rid of the poison by now.

'And poison,' she continues, pushing that uncomfortable thought aside, 'it's not as messy, you don't need to have physical strength or anything to use it.' She hates how much sense it makes.

'The woman's weapon of choice,' Ashby muses.

'Well, I mean not really,' Murphy says, staring across the office at the board, at Sarah and Fiona's faces this time. 'It's only something like the sixth most common murder weapon used by women.' Ashby raises his eyebrows and she flushes. 'I looked it up.'

'But women are still statistically more likely than men to choose poison as a murder weapon,' Ashby says.

'Yeah, but if we're going by statistics then the killer's far more likely to be a man – so actually *all* murder weapons are used more commonly by men, including poison.' Ashby concedes that with a grunt, not that it helps them either way – whatever the statistics say, they don't help with making the arrest on an individual case. Murphy stares at the board again, at the two female faces looking out at her, a set of warm, brown eyes and cool, misty green ones that seem to change colour depending on where in the office she is. 'Are we ruling out Sarah, as well as Phil?'

'We're not ruling out anyone for certain, not until we make an arrest. But as it stands, we've got no motive for her, do we? And she lost her dad a year ago, so what, she just turns around and kills her mum just for good measure? And . . .' Ashby sighs. 'And even though I said otherwise at the beginning, she did come to us. If she killed her and it looked like the coroner was just going to rule the death as heart failure, then why the hell would Sarah then demand it be looked into as a murder? Why not sit back, hope everyone accepted that it was natural causes?'

Murphy downs the rest of her Coke. 'So we're getting Fiona in then?'

'Yeah. Be interesting to hear her side of it, if *she* thought the affair had ended, like Ben's telling us.' He swivels back and forth in his chair. 'What about the phones? Ben let us have his, right?'

'Yeah, they're running checks on it now. Sarah's came up clean.'

'Good to know.' He rubs his hands across his face. 'The DI wants an update on where we are.'

'What will you tell him?'

'That we're working on it. See what he thinks, he might have a few ideas himself.'

Ashby's phone rings and he raises his eyebrows at Murphy when whoever's at the other end of the line answers. The caller's voice is too quiet to hear so she only gets his side of the conversation, which is infuriatingly clipped. 'Ashby here . . . Is that so? . . . When? . . . And they're sure? . . . All right, thanks.'

He hangs up, smiles grimly at Murphy. 'Well. You'll never guess who just got admitted into hospital for, wait for it . . . belladonna poisoning.'

Taken from Case File: Nicola Gregory

FIONA GREGORY
EXTRACT FROM RECORDED INTERVIEW

Date: 09/10/2018
Duration: 41 minutes
Conducted by Officers DC MURPHY and DS ASHBY

DC So, Fiona, how well would you say you knew Nicola?

FG Well enough. I met Ben over ten years ago, so I've known
Nicola since about then. And of course when Charlie passed
away she moved into the annex, so . . .

DC That's right. Very kind of you, to let her live there.

FG Well, it was Ben's idea, really.

DC Ben was the one to suggest she move in?

FG Yes. He offered. Nicola couldn't afford the mortgage on her
house after Charlie died – they didn't have any savings, I
don't think.

DS How did you feel, about Ben offering?

FG Well, I mean, I wasn't thrilled about sharing the space, but I
was hardly going to leave her on the street after her husband
died, was I? And Nicola was really helpful – she was brilliant
with the girls.

DC Did you get on with Nicola, Fiona?

FG Well, I definitely wouldn't call us the best of friends, but we
ticked along OK. Like I said, she was great with my daughters

and she used to babysit a lot for Ben and I once she moved into the annex.

DC Why do you say you weren't the best of friends?

FG We just . . . We didn't click, you know? We spent a fair amount of time together – our husbands were brothers, after all. But we would never hang out just the two of us or anything like that.

DC Why do you think you didn't click?

FG Well, you don't get on with everyone you meet, do you?

DS Fiona, were you aware that your husband was having an affair with Nicola?

FG I— Yes. He was having an affair with her – as in, he hadn't been recently. That all stopped after he and I got together.

DC So he told you, about his relationship with Nicola?

FG No, but he was hardly going to admit to sleeping with his brother's wife to a new girlfriend, was he? He didn't have to tell me, it was obvious if you paid enough attention, watched the two of them on nights out. I'm still surprised Charlie never knew, though maybe he did and chose to ignore it.

DC And could this be a reason why you and Nicola didn't 'click'?

FG Well, yes, knowing that Ben had been sleeping with her didn't exactly help things, I'll admit. I tried to get past it but it was difficult, always having her around.

DC And I suppose that would have become more difficult, once she moved into the annex?

FG Yes, look, I'll be honest – it was hard having her there, having the constant reminder of her and Ben's history. But the affair was over for a while now, I believe that. I have to believe that Ben has been faithful to me since we've been married. He would have told me, or at least I would have noticed, if they'd started up again.

DS All right, thanks, Fiona. Can I ask, do you know much about gardening?

FG What? Well, I . . . I know a bit, yes. Both Ben and I like to spend time in the garden.

DS An enviable skill. I don't know much about the garden, myself. What about you, Detective Murphy?

DC Oh, no, nothing. Always thought I'd like to get more into it, if I had the time. And I'd need a garden, I suppose. What kind of plants do you have in your garden, Fiona?

FG I'm afraid I really couldn't list them all off the top of my head.

DC Daisies, perhaps? I think I saw some lilies, by the pond when we were there?

FG Yes, yes, I have both. I'm not really sure what this has to do with anything, though?

DS I spotted some purple flowers there, too, when we were there, didn't you, Detective Murphy?

DC Yeah, I think I did. What are the purple ones called?

FG You mean the teasels?

DC No, I'm not sure they're the ones I'm thinking of.

DS Me neither. I was thinking of deadly nightshade. Belladonna. Do you have any of that in the garden, Fiona?

FG I . . . I don't know. We've got so many plants, Ben and I are always buying new ones, I really can't remember them all.

DS I see. Fiona, Phil said that Nicola said something about eyes, just before she lost consciousness?

FG What? Eyes? Yes, yes, I suppose she did – but she really wasn't making any sense at all by that point. I barely remember what she said, if I'm honest – we were all a bit panicked by that point, as I'm sure you understand.

DC So you have no idea what Nicola could have been referring to?

FG No. No, I'm sorry, none at all.

Chapter Twenty-Four

Fiona is waiting for me under the overhang of the entrance to the police station, her head hunched, both hands stuck in her blue puffa pockets. She's staring at the concrete ground in front of her so hard that she doesn't notice me pulling into the car park until I stop right in front of the glass door entrance. She walks around the front of the car to get to the passenger door in a rather zombie-like manner.

She stares straight ahead without saying anything as we leave the ugly brick building behind. I glance at her when we get stopped at the first red traffic light. Up close I can see how tired she is – her face looks gaunt, there are dark rings under her puffy eyes and her chocolate curls have lost their shine. Safe to say she's looked better.

'Do you want to talk about it?' I ask, keeping my voice as neutral as possible. I'm not really sure how to handle it, the almost electric tension that's buzzing in the car between us, louder than whatever Radio 1 is playing right now.

'I really don't.' She's staring out the window rather than at me. 'I'm sorry, my darling. Is that OK?'

The traffic light turns green and I nod as I shift the car into first and drive on. 'I understand.' Partly true, I suppose. I do understand, theoretically, why she doesn't want to talk about it, with me at least. But that doesn't mean I like it. It's making me twitchy again, not knowing what they asked her, not knowing if they gave anything away about the case.

And I want to know what she said to them, too. I fucking hate this. I hate not being able to talk openly with her, hate the wedge this is driving between us.

'I'm sorry I had to call you to pick me up,' she adds after a moment. 'Ben has the car – he's gone to pick up Lily and Emily, and I can't call him because the police, well, the police still have his phone.' She glances at me but quickly looks away, like she's admitting his guilt by telling me that.

'I don't mind picking you up,' I say, still with the same carefully neutral tone. They should take my mother's Ka, really – it's not like anyone else would want it, and it would make their lives a hell of a lot easier, rather than having to juggle a car between them.

'Oh,' she says suddenly. 'I have something to tell you. I meant to call you to tell you but I got, well, distracted.' She clasps her hands together in her lap and looks at me properly for the first time since she got in the car. 'Phil went into the hospital. He's . . .' She wrings her hands. 'Well, it seems he's been poisoned.'

I stare at her. 'What?'

'Watch the road, Sarah!'

I snap my attention back to the road, notice I'm dangerously close to the middle, and take a breath as I steady the car. 'What do you mean, he's been poisoned? Were you there, at the hospital? Did you see him come in?'

Our roles shift, and she becomes the calm one. 'I was in briefly this morning just to drop something off before I had to, well— I didn't see it myself, but one of the nurses told me about it. My friend Becky – you've met her, remember?'

I don't actually remember, but I don't care about that right now. 'Is it serious? Is it the same poison?'

'I don't know,' she says softly. 'It . . . it was plant poison, I think, but I don't know any more than that. I suppose the police will be looking into it, though they mentioned nothing to me.'

'Maybe they don't know,' I murmur. I'll have to make sure they find out, if that's the case. Plant poison. A jolt runs through me. And the police were asking me about the plants at my flat. So it's a good guess that they already know that much, at least. So why haven't they done something about it – what are they waiting for? My nerves feel jittery, the need to do something active rather than just sit around waiting is building once again. I keep talking, trying to distract myself. 'So, is he OK?'

'He's fine. He went into hospital last night after he . . .'

'After he came round,' I finish, and she nods.

'Apparently he was complaining of a stomach ache, but he was also ranting about poison, about his girlfriend, and, well, I suppose the doctors took him seriously. They've probably seen about . . . it all . . . in the news, so I imagine that helped. He's completely fine, though,' she reiterates. 'Apparently it was only mild traces of poison, something that probably would have gone undetected if he hadn't been so insistent about it.' She flicks me a glance and I get the impression that 'insistent' wasn't the word that this nurse used to describe him. 'I think they're letting him out today.'

I go quiet, thinking. I'm surprised he went into hospital so quickly, because of something so mild. And it had to be mild, the dose he must have ingested. But then, he'd been watching my mother getting worse and worse and no one noticed anything until it was too late – maybe that would make anyone paranoid. So now, if he's in hospital because of poison, then surely that drives him lower down the suspect list. Because he wouldn't poison himself, and surely the detectives must realise that whoever was poisoning my mother was likely to be careful not to ingest the same stuff that was killing her, given how planned out this was.

'I'm sorry,' Fiona says quietly. 'I know it's difficult to hear.' I frown, wondering why she'd think that – neither of us are exactly fond of Phil. But then it clicks, far too late, showing how bloody distracted I am. He's fine. He noticed something was wrong and went to hospital right away. Surely that adds credence to the idea that if my mother had done that, she would have been fine, too. I swallow and nod, for her sake.

I search around for another topic, desperate to change the subject. It doesn't take me long. If we can't talk about what the police are doing, then maybe we can clear the air around something else. 'Fiona,' I say hesitantly. 'I know that my mum and Ben were having an affair.' She must know that I've guessed, but even so, the words seem to stick heavily in the air and I clear my throat to try and move them along. 'I just wanted to say that I'm sorry, I guess,' I mutter.

Her neck seems to elongate as she stretches her head towards me with a jerk. 'What? Why on earth are you sorry?'

'I just meant—'

But she talks over me. 'Sarah, you have nothing to apologise for. Do you hear me? *Nothing.* You are not responsible for your mother's actions, you do not deserve any part of the blame, OK?' I purse my lips at this, wondering if that means she thinks my mother was the one who should have taken the blame, if, perhaps, she deserved what she got because of it. Fiona seems to pick up on my thoughts from my expression, and carries on quickly. 'Not that I . . . I didn't mean . . .' She pushes her curls back from her face. 'It's takes two, OK? Maybe even more than two. It happened, and I don't like it, of course, but your mother wasn't a cruel person, she didn't—'

I lift my hand from its resting position on the gearstick and squeeze hers where it sits in her lap, cutting off this rant before it can go any further. I don't want either of us to think too much further down this line. Fiona smiles at me gratefully.

We go the rest of the journey in, if not comfortable then at least tolerable, silence and I only speak again when I pull onto the driveway. 'I bought some books for Lily and Emily – do you mind if I drop them off while I'm here?'

'Of course. Ben doesn't seem to be home with them yet, but you can come in, they should be back soon.'

'Great, thanks.' I grab both my handbag and the tote bag full of books off the back seat, try for a smile as we walk to the front door. 'Bribery, you know.'

Fiona smiles back, though for some reason it looks a little sad. 'You don't have to bribe them, they love you already.'

Once inside, I pause for a second. 'You know I'm here, right? If you ever need my help looking after them, I mean. I know my mum . . . That she helped.' The sight of Fiona's eyes, shining with unshed tears, makes an uncomfortable guilty feeling flare up in my stomach. I swallow to try to push it away. 'And I know I wasn't around a huge amount after my dad died,' I continue, 'that I cut myself off a bit, but I don't want it to be the same this time.'

'Thank you, my darling.'

Angry with myself for the lump that's growing in my throat, I look down to the tote bag. 'Shall I put the books away?'

Fiona seems to pick up on my need to escape this conversation. 'You can leave them in their room if you like.'

I glance at the stairs, but shake my head. 'I'll put them on the bookshelf.' I head to the living room and Fiona snorts quietly, but not derisively, behind me. I know what she's thinking, that I'm being overdramatic in my need to have everything in its rightful place.

'Sarah?' I look back at her. She's not smiling anymore. 'We understood, you know. That you needed time alone after your dad died. Your mum understood that, too.'

I nod, blinking back the burning in my eyes, grief but also that too-familiar anger where my parents' deaths are concerned. I turn away before she can say anything else. I cross the living room to the bookshelf, which is next to the TV. It's only half full of books – the top shelf is made up of framed photos, positioned around a pot plant in the middle. I stare at one of the photos – Fiona, Ben, Lily and Emily all grinning at the beach. I feel a stab of pain looking at it – because it reminds me of my childhood, but also because of the thought that there's a strong chance that Lily and Emily's perfect childhoods might soon be ruined. I press my lips together. I'll make sure I'm around, that I'm here for them, to help them through it.

I take the books out the bag and search for the right place to put them, my fingers itching to rearrange everything in height order. I bend down to look at the children's books on the bottom shelf – mainly picture books still, even though Emily is at school now. They won't know which books I've brought them, I realise, and reluctantly leave the two new picture books – *Giraffes Can't Dance* and *Room on the Broom* – on the floor in front of the bookshelf. Fiona can point them out, and hopefully they'll think of me when they read them. I straighten up and run my index finger along the other books, lingering on the gardening ones. I take a few out to look at them when I can't see the title. One of them I bought Fiona for Christmas two years ago. I frown as I trace the spine, thinking. It's there again, the buzzing in my veins, driving me to do something.

'Sarah?' Fiona's voice again, calling to me from the kitchen, makes me jump and I shove their books, along with the ones I brought, back in line. 'Do you want a cup of tea?'

'No, thanks! I've got to get going, actually.'

I pick up my now-empty tote bag and stick my head around the kitchen door, where Fiona is bustling about, slippers having replaced her practical shoes. 'I left the books on the floor by the bookshelf, so you can show the girls when they get home.' My words tumble out my mouth a little too quickly, my mind still on the other books there. 'I'll come round to see them another time.'

'They'll love that.' She smiles at me, but I see the effort it takes, and know that I'm doing the right thing, leaving her alone. I don't think either of us could stand any more forced conversation, trying to pretend that things are fine. Until the police make the arrest, I know it won't get any better.

'I'll see you later.' I lift my hand in an awkward half wave and back away even though I sense she wants to give me a hug. 'Got to dash!' I say, overly jovially. I grimace at how I sound, how completely unlike me.

I let myself out the front door, hesitate in the driveway. But the hesitation is unnecessary. I've already decided what I'm going to do. The buzzing in my veins intensifies, urging me on. I tiptoe across the gravel and open the side gate as quietly as I can. Fiona wouldn't have a problem with me going into the garden, but I don't want her to see.

And there it is. On the far side of the garden, through the gate, fenced off so that the girls can't get in here, play in here. In the part of the garden that lives mostly in shade, left to its own devices almost all year round because of it. Green leaves, reddish-brown flowers, just beginning to wilt, and berries with a waxy sheen. Belladonna. One of the plants in the book on Fiona and Ben's bookshelf.

I look behind me, half expecting Fiona to burst out of the back door, to ask just what the hell I think I'm doing. When I look back at the plant, I realise my hands are shaking. I should have done this long before now – come to the garden – but I presumed that the police would do a thorough search, would have noticed something when they did. It seems not, however. Apparently, I'm the only fucking person actually committed to the investigation. And so, if they won't get off their asses to come and look, then once again I'm going to have to do the work for them. Because I can't leave it down to chance, not now.

I reach into my handbag and bring out the scissors I always carry round with me for trimming the ends of flowers at my dad's grave. Being careful not to touch the plant, I clip off a few cuttings. I bend down and, wrapping my hand in my jacket sleeve, dump the flowers unceremoniously into my bag.

I leave quickly, rushing across the lawn to the gate, keeping my head down like an ostrich – if I can't see Fiona, then she can't see me. My heart is beating fast, my mouth dry as I start the car. I wonder what she'll think – only just hearing the engine now. Whether she'll even realise.

I don't think she'll notice what I've done to the plant. I think it's subtle enough – and surely she wouldn't go looking? I reverse out the driveway, my handbag seeming to throb with heat from the cuttings inside it. Shit, I really do hope she doesn't find out what I've done, what I'm about to do.

And with that thought dancing around my mind, I set off, not towards home, but towards the police station.

Taken from Case File: Nicola Gregory

SARAH ELIZABETH GREGORY
EXTRACT FROM RECORDED INTERVIEW

Date: 09/10/2018
Duration: 21 minutes
Conducted by Officers DC MURPHY and DS ASHBY

SG I can't believe you're still sitting here. I brought you evidence that Ben has been growing a poisonous plant – a plant that may very well have been used to kill my mother – and you're still waiting around, talking to me!

DS Ben?

SG Yes, Ben, it's his garden.

DS But isn't it also Fiona's garden?

SG Fiona would never have done anything to my mother.

DS They didn't get on too well.

SG Yes but it's Fiona. She would never hurt anyone. And Ben was mad at my mother, I know it. She didn't want to carry on the affair – and yes, I know about that, too.

DC You know about the affair?

SG Yes. I guessed a while ago. Then Phil came round to Ben and Fiona's house the other day, accused Ben of it right in front of me and Fiona. So it's all out in the open now.

DS All right. Sarah, why do you suspect that belladonna was the plant used to kill your mother?

SG A few things. You asked about plants at my house, the other day, so I thought maybe that might be to do with the poison. And then I found out today, about an hour ago, that Phil went into hospital because of plant poisoning.

DC How did you find out about that?

SG Fiona works there, she told me.

DS All right, but that doesn't explain why you suspect belladonna, out of all the possible poisonous plants out there?

SG Yeah, well, I was at the house – at Ben and Fiona's house – just now, and I saw a book on plants on their bookshelf and it . . . it made me think. It made me realise I'd seen one of the plants – one of the poisonous plants, I mean – in their garden before. Fiona was teaching me a bit about gardening so I'd spent some time out there and I . . . I remembered. And when I went to look, it was right there. All of it seemed like too much of a coincidence. I know you've talked to Ben, I know you think it was someone close to my mum, who killed her. So I just . . . I figured it out, and I came straight here. Am I right? I'm right, aren't I?

DC Belladonna is one of the plants we're looking at, yes.

SG [Inaudible]

DC Sarah? Are you OK?

SG No. No, I'm not OK. My mother is dead and you're not doing anything about it. I'm telling you all this and you are still here, doing nothing. It's like you don't even want to catch her killer, it's like I'm the only one who cares. And I have a headache.

DC I can assure you, you are not the only one who cares.

SG Fine. Then prove it.

DC Would you like some water? I think I have a paracetamol somewhere.

SG No. I took some about an hour ago.

DS Are headaches a common occurrence for you, Sarah?

SG At the moment, yes. The doctor thinks it's grief. That once I give in to it, I'll feel better.

DS Do you mind if we take a sample of your blood? Just a pinprick?

SG Why?

DS It's just to help with the investigation. I can't tell you exactly why, not at this stage, but I hope it will help us to draw some conclusions, and soon.

SG All right. Yeah, that's fine.

DS Great, Detective Murphy will do that for you.

DC If you're squeamish about blood—

SG I'm not. I give blood all the time.

DC Oh. That's a good thing to do.

SG It is, yes. It can save lives. Do you know my dad died of leukaemia?

DC We do, sadly, yes.

SG Well, then, you know why it's important to me – my blood couldn't save him, but it might save someone else. Do you? Give blood? You really should. [Inaudible]

DC Sarah?

SG Sorry. It's the headache.

Chapter Twenty-Five

'Well, it's a good thing the warrant came through,' says Murphy as she grabs her phone and purse off her desk, nerves thrumming with excitement. Still, she wonders what the DI will say when he finds out the plant was in the garden the whole time. If he'll blame the bronze team for not finding the belladonna when they first went round. If someone will blame Ashby somehow. Or her.

'You got Sarah's blood sample off to the lab, right?' asks Ashby.

'Yeah, I told them it was urgent, to test it alongside Fiona's. I called Ben, he's on his way in for us to take a sample. He'll be here imminently, apparently. I assured him it wouldn't take long – he's got his daughters with him.' They exchange a look at that. This is a father they're talking about. Or a mother. Still, that doesn't exclude you from being a murderer.

'Great. You ready to go?'

'Now? What about the forensic team?'

'It's going to take them a while, but I think we should get out there first – they can meet us there.'

'OK. Don't you want to wait for Ben?'

'Thomas can handle it.' Great, the DC she doesn't like. Still, she'd far rather be at the house with Ashby than sitting around waiting for a tox result to come back.

'OK, then, yes.' She hesitates when Ashby makes to walk out of the office. 'Is it suspicious, do you think, that she showed up with the plant, just as we're about to search the house?'

'She couldn't have known we were about to search the house,' he points out. 'And her explanation makes sense to me – if she found out that Phil was in hospital for poisoning but that he survived, I can see how that would set her on edge a little. I've seen this happen before – people hate the waiting and something snaps. Plus her dad only died a year ago, too. Losing both parents that quickly has got to do something to you.'

She murmurs a vague agreement. Perhaps she should be feeling more sympathetic towards Sarah. She just doesn't like that she seems to have been doing her own investigation right alongside them. Though she supposes that might say something more about her than Sarah, wanting to solve it all herself.

She crosses the office to join Ashby by the exit, glances over at the board one last time, to the photo of Nicola in the centre. 'Do you think she knew?' she murmurs. 'That someone had done it to her? Do you think she knew at the end *who* did it to her?'

'I don't know. Wish we could ask her.'

Soon. The message on the flowers. If she was spooked by that, if it was a threat, then why not tell someone? Why not report it? *What were you afraid of?* But, of course, the dead can't answer.

'At least we can get her some justice.' When she looks doubtful, he claps a friendly hand on her shoulder. 'We've got this, you'll see. You're about to help close your first murder case. Don't stress about the things you didn't see – enjoy the high of it, for now at least. There'll be plenty of times in the future where you don't get to the bottom of it.'

'Excellent. Thanks for that.' They walk out the station together. 'We still don't know which one it is, though. Ben or Fiona.'

'Yeah.' His voice is still over easy, but she can tell from his expression that it's bothering him, too. 'Sarah seems pretty confident it's Ben.'

It's true. She had indeed seemed *very* confident, and it makes her think again there's something they're missing here – like Sarah knows something they don't, something she doesn't want to tell them for some reason, that's making her so sure Ben is guilty. 'She has a good relationship with Fiona, though, doesn't she?' She glances at Ashby who, of course, is raising his eyebrows. 'Well, I saw her picking Fiona up from the station – don't you think that says something?'

'It says Fiona needed a lift. You're reaching if you think it's anything more. We'll be able to get both of them in for questioning properly, after we search the house, find the poison.'

'But Fiona *lied*. If Sarah is right, then Fiona lied about there not being belladonna in the garden.'

'True,' Ashby says with a sigh. 'But we don't know why – could be she's covering for her husband, or maybe she honestly couldn't remember.'

'Maybe it's both of them. In it together.' She senses he doesn't really like that theory. She's not sure she does either to be honest. Why? Why would they work together on it? Murphy glances around, but there's no sign of Sarah in the waiting room. 'You think she's gone home, is waiting for us to call her and let her know we made an arrest?'

'No, I think she's probably parked round the corner, waiting to see if we follow through.'

Murphy starts to answer him, but stops when someone calls out behind them. She turns to see DC Thomas striding towards them, clutching a green file and looking like he's having to hold himself back from running.

'What's wrong?' Ashby asks. 'Is it urgent?'

'It is,' he says breathlessly. 'The techs have the full reports from Ben and Fiona's phones, I said I'd run it over as I was around.'

'And?' Ashby sounds neither excited nor impressed by this.

Thomas hands over the folder and Ashby opens it. He takes a look, and his eyebrows shoot up practically into his hairline. He shoves it into Murphy's hands. 'Well. Why don't you see what you make of this?'

Chapter Twenty-Six

The police are taking a fucking age. What are they playing at, dragging their heels like this when I've literally just dumped everything in their laps?

I told Fiona that I thought I'd left my phone at her house, which obviously she accepted without question, and then agreed to stay for a glass of wine so I have the excuse to be here. I'm now sitting in their living room, though neither of them are here – Fiona is in the kitchen, getting the wine, and Ben, having got back only moments ago, immediately took Lily and Emily upstairs, seemingly unable to be in the same room as me. It's like he knows, somehow, despite the fact I've said nothing. But then, maybe he has his own reasons for not wanting to be in the same room as me.

Fuck, this room feels too claustrophobic. The heat is cranked up high and it's almost unbearable, unnatural compared to the chill outside. My stomach curdles. Maybe I shouldn't have gone to the police – what if that threw them off? I fight the need to get up, move in some way or another. I probably shouldn't even be here now, should probably just be waiting out of the way somewhere. I'd find out the outcome, sooner or later. But I can't. I need to be here, need to see first hand how this plays out.

Then I hear it. A car pulling in. The doorbell. I jump to my feet.

'Hold on!' calls Fiona. I peer around the doorway and see the detectives walk into the hallway when Fiona opens the front door. Ashby doesn't seem to notice me, Murphy flicks me a glance. Nothing registers on her face so I can't tell what she thinks, finding me here. Well, too fucking bad if they don't like it.

'Umm, hello,' Fiona says cautiously.

'Hello, Fiona,' Ashby says in a would-be pleasant voice. 'We were wondering if we could have a quick word.'

'I don't—'

'We have a warrant,' Murphy says, equally pleasantly. Without waiting for Fiona to answer, she manoeuvres around her so that Fiona has to step aside. 'We need to search the house, I'm afraid,' Murphy says, squaring her shoulders in a way that makes her seem even more imposing, more confident than when I first met her.

'What? Why?' I wonder what Fiona's thinking right now, why she looks panicked. Is there a chance that she, too, thinks Ben is guilty, and has just been covering for him all this time? I'm not sure I actually want to know the answer to that.

'Detective Murphy is going to search the garden,' Ashby says in answer. 'It would be easier if you all stayed in one place.' He glances at me as he speaks. Fiona stares at me, too, noticing me watching for the first time. I keep my expression blank. I don't want her to know I'm the reason they're here, don't want her to blame me.

Fiona gets the girls and Ben from upstairs. Ben seems to accept it all without question and I have to admit I'm a little concerned that he's not putting up more of an argument – it doesn't do anything to help calm the thrumming under my skin. So close. I'm so close now to getting the closure I need.

We wait in the kitchen in total silence. Even Lily and Emily seem to pick up on it, huddling by Fiona, not saying a word. I don't look at any of them. Right now, this has to be all about me.

I stare out the kitchen window and watch Murphy as she walks the length of the garden, straight over to the bit that's sectioned off by a gate. She doesn't bother asking for the key, just vaults over.

She walks straight to it. Right up to the belladonna.

Chapter Twenty-Seven

Murphy sucks in her breath. There it is, right in front of her, almost identical to how it looks on the Internet. So this little plant is the murder weapon. It's kind of pretty, though the flowers are wilted now, the plant coming to the end of its summer life. Almost like it knows it's done its job.

She didn't ask Ashby how to play this in the car, and she's not actually sure if she should go straight back into the house or not. So she calls him. He answers on the first ring. 'Well?'

'I'm standing in front of it. It's definitely deadly nightshade. Or belladonna. Whatever.'

'All right. And I've found a book on poisonous plants on their bookshelf. Not exactly bulletproof evidence, but will be interesting to see how they react.'

'What now, do we get them into the station?'

'Let's ask them a few questions here first. I spoke to James just now, he said it was fine. But I think we've got enough for the arrest – the phone, the book, the plant.'

'All right.'

'Keep looking, just in case. Check the bins, the compost, anything else out there.'

'Got it.' She's about to hang up when she feels her phone vibrate in her hand. 'Hang on,' she tells Ashby. She looks down at the screen. 'It's the lab guys! Could be about the blood results?'

'Answer it. I'll stay on the line, I want to hear this.'

She glances behind her to the kitchen window. It's too far away for her to make out expressions, but she can feel them all in there, watching her. She switches lines on her phone. 'Murphy speaking.'

'You said to call you as soon as the blood results were in.' It's a cool, female voice, and she doesn't even introduce herself. But right now, Murphy doesn't care.

'And?'

'And you guys were right. There's only one person without the poison in their system.'

Chapter Twenty-Eight

It doesn't take long before both Murphy and Ashby join us in the kitchen. Ben and Fiona have had a muttered conversation in the meantime, but I haven't bothered to listen, too intent on Murphy in the garden. They exchange a look when the detectives come in. They seem united in that moment and it worries me.

'Sarah,' Fiona says, her too-calm voice making me jolt, 'would you mind taking the girls into the living room, popping the TV on for them?'

'I— Of course,' I say, trying to make my voice easy, to hide the fact that blood is pulsing in my fingertips, faster and faster. It's not exactly like I can refuse her, is it? Not without making a scene, without seeming unreasonable. She doesn't know what I know, wouldn't understand how much I want to be in the room right now.

'Come on, Trouble,' I say to Emily, who smiles uncertainly at me. Lily looks between me, her mum and her dad. To save time, I haul her up in my arms and prop her on my hip. She doesn't protest, so I grab Emily's hand and take them both into the living room. I'm surprised to find I feel a little numb. I can feel my heart reacting, its pulse unnervingly quick, but it's like I'm detached from it. Like my brain has decided I can't react, not yet, not until I know how it all plays out.

I plop Lily down on the sofa and Emily scrambles up next to her. I hear Fiona asking if she can make some tea and the skin along my forearms tingles in anticipation. I log into Amazon on the TV and press play on the first thing I see there – *Moana*.

'I don't like this one,' Lily complains instantly. 'It's scary.'

'No, it's not,' I say, putting the control on top of the TV. 'It's great, one of my favourites.'

'Will you watch it with us?' asks Emily.

'I'll be back in a minute, OK?' I walk quickly to the kitchen. I can't miss this.

I arrive in time to hear Murphy speaking. 'Mr and Mrs Gregory, are you aware that there's a belladonna plant in your garden?' Back to Mr and Mrs now, the formality of it only increases my anticipation.

Ben frowns. 'Yeah, of course. We have a few plants of it, so what?' Murphy and Ashby exchange a look, and I fight the urge to hold my breath. This is it. This is fucking it.

'Well, you see, Mr Gregory,' says Ashby conversationally, 'that was the plant that was used to poison Nicola.'

There's a sharp intake of breath from the counter and I snap my gaze to Fiona. All colour is draining from her face and she doesn't seem to know where to look.

'What?' Ben's voice is hoarse. 'But . . . but it can't be from *our* plant.'

No one speaks. The kettle hits boil and switches itself off, but Fiona doesn't move to do anything with it. I feel like I can't breathe, like if I make the slightest of movements it could fuck things up somehow.

Murphy breaks the silence. 'Fiona—' Fiona's whole body jerks at the sound of her name, '—you said previously that you didn't think you had any belladonna in your garden.'

'I . . . I forgot,' she mumbles. Impossible to tell right then if she's being truthful. Why would she lie? I'm back to it then, the uncomfortable thought that she could have thought Ben did it, have been covering for him.

'Do you mind telling us when you planted the belladonna?' asks Ashby.

Ben looks at Fiona, but she doesn't return it this time, only stands there, gripping the counter behind her. She looks like she's about to pass out. 'About a year ago,' Ben says reluctantly. 'Didn't you say you liked the way it looked, Fiona?' Fiona jerks at this, but doesn't answer. It's smart, I suppose, if he means to do it – putting her in the firing line. The bastard. My nails bite into the flesh of my palms, the sharp pinpricks of pain helping to keep me grounded.

'Were you both aware it was poisonous?' asks Murphy.

'Well, yes.' Fiona's voice trembles. 'We've been drilling it into the girls, not to touch it, you know. It's why it's in the locked part of the garden – so the girls can't get to it.' She trails off, hugs herself with both arms. She looks like she's about to start rocking any second.

'You can't think – you can't think we used it to kill Nicola?' Ben looks back and forth between the two detectives, then gives me the most fleeting of glances. I'm surprised neither he nor Fiona have told me to leave yet. Maybe they know I wouldn't go.

'Well, perhaps we'd be willing to entertain the possibility that you didn't, had we not also found this.' Ashby picks up a book that had been face down on the kitchen table, unnoticed by all of us. My lips twist into an expression I know must look ugly as I read the title. *Handbook of Poisonous and Injurious Plants*.

Ben stares at it, and the dark circles under his eyes seem to deepen so that his face looks even more ashen. 'We have lots of gardening books,' he says hoarsely.

'Yes, that's right,' murmurs Ashby, setting the book face up on the kitchen table for all of us to look at. Which we all do, like we're mesmerised. 'You're a keen gardener, aren't you?'

'We both are,' says Fiona, her voice a little harsher now, some confidence there. What the fuck is she doing? Is she trying to defend him? 'I couldn't tell you the list of gardening books on our shelf right now – people buy them for us as gifts all the time. A book doesn't mean anything.'

'No, no of course not,' says Ashby, holding his hands up, palms out. 'But, well, it's not just the book, is it? Not just the plant in the garden either, actually, come to think of it.' He sucks in a contemplative breath. 'As you know, we asked for a sample of each of your blood.' He includes me in his sweep around the room, the first time he's acknowledged that I'm lurking here. My heart quickens at the mention of blood.

'And?' Fiona demands.

'And Ben,' picks up Murphy, 'was the only one without the poison in his system.'

Chapter Twenty-Nine

For a few seconds no one speaks, even the kitchen itself seems to be holding its breath, waiting. Then Ben breaks the perfectly still silence like he's smashing a glass window. 'What? What do you mean?'

'Well, what we *think* it means is that there's a very good chance you were the one administering the poison.' There. Murphy's said it. The first time it's actually been voiced out loud. Where I was detached before, everything now zooms into focus so that I'm hyper-aware of every little movement, the jerk of Ben's head, the little spasms of Fiona's hands. I'm tense, almost in pain from how rigid my body is. I can't relax. Because it's not over, not yet, not until they say the final words.

'No,' says Ben. 'That's ridiculous. I told you, I'd never do anything to Nicola.' He starts pacing. For a man who thinks it's 'ridiculous', he's doing a good job of seeming worried. I trace his movements with my eyes, sure he'll break any second now. 'I *loved* her,' Ben stresses, either ignoring or not noticing the way Fiona flinches at that. 'This doesn't mean anything, it means nothing at all.'

Fiona's swallow is audible. 'Does this . . . Are you saying that the rest of us, that me and Sarah, that we've . . . been poisoned?'

Murphy's voice is kind when she speaks. 'It means there are traces in your systems, yes. But there's not enough to hurt you. It will pass out your body naturally in a few days, provided you're careful not to ingest any more.' She turns her attention on Ben, who actually takes half a step back under the force of her gaze. I feel a thrill of satisfaction at that, at the way he's acting panicked. Guilty. 'It *means* that you were very careful when poisoning Nicola, weren't you? You were careful not to eat any of it yourself, but less so about leaving traces in the annex, where other people might accidentally ingest it, isn't that right? The likes of Phil, Sarah, even your wife?'

'No.' Ben shakes his head frantically. 'You've got this all wrong. If this is true then I don't know how it happened, I don't!'

'The girls!' exclaims Fiona desperately.

'We'll go to the hospital, get them tested,' I say quickly. I wait for her to meet my gaze head on. 'They'll be OK,' I whisper. And here's the first trickle of relief, the slight relaxing of my muscles. Because we acknowledge something in our shared gaze – we're in this together now, Fiona and I.

'Look,' says Ben, and though he's clearly trying for a reasonable tone, he doesn't pull it off. 'I don't know what all of this means, but I didn't kill Nicola, OK? I didn't, I couldn't have.' His firm voice gives way to desperation at the end. Good. He should know what it's like to feel that. 'I never really ate round the annex, so maybe it just got into the others' systems, and I got lucky.'

Fiona opens her mouth, about to say something, but Ashby cuts her off. 'Maybe that's true,' he says, and for a second all tension returns to my body. 'But then there's this.' He slides a brown folder across the kitchen table, though none of us make to pick it up.

'It's a print-out of your phone records,' says Murphy, like she knows we won't actually look at it. 'It took a bit of time, but our experts were able to pull even the deleted data from your phone, deleted Internet searches, for instance. Like the one searching belladonna, searching specific doses of the poison, how much poison is needed to kill and how much would just cause someone to feel ill.'

'What? I never looked anything like that up. Or even if I did, it must just have been to do with the garden!'

But neither detective seems at all moved by what he's saying. Ashby walks around the kitchen table to Ben. He clasps Ben's shoulder with one hand, produces a set of handcuffs with the other. I watch it, as if in slow motion. It's happening. It's really happening – I'm finally getting justice.

Ben is still shaking his head, mouthing the word 'no', over and over, as he looks down at the handcuffs, seemingly paralysed.

'Benjamin Gregory, you are under arrest for the murder of Nicola Gregory.'

Chapter Thirty

It is barely a second before Ashby is speaking again, yet it feels like eternity. Just like that, the crucial moment is over. This point I've been building up to is gone, with barely enough time for me to even register it's happening. 'You do not have to say anything, but it may harm your defence if . . .'

I don't hear the rest of the caution statement. The ringing in my ears is eclipsing all else, the utter disbelief that this has happened, that it's over. Fiona is saying something, her voice on the verge of hysterical, but my mind somehow drowns her out. The kitchen seems to blur in front of me, and my legs feel shaky. Fuck, I think I might collapse.

'Mummy?' It's Emily's voice that snaps me out of my daze. I'd almost forgotten the girls were there, just in the next room. I want to say something comforting, but I can't think of what it would be. In my peripheral vision I see Murphy walking round to join Ashby by Ben's side. See the two of them leading him away.

'Go back to the living room, Em,' I say, but she stays there, hovering, and seconds later Lily appears, too. Guilt weighs heavily on me in that moment. They're innocent in all this – they don't deserve it, shouldn't be watching their dad being taken away like this. Even if I do think they'll be better off without Ben in their lives. I look over to where Fiona is now following Ben, like she's attached to strings, pulled along with him, through the hallway towards the front door. She seems to be in a daze, no noise coming from her, like she can't believe this is happening. 'Fiona? Come on, you don't want to watch this.'

But she ignores me, her silence breaks. 'No.' The word is a whisper and I'm sure I'm the only one who hears her. 'No,' she says again, loud enough now for Ben to look back at her. His face is an ugly pale yellow, like he's about to be sick. 'This can't be happening,' she says desperately. I watch her carefully, waiting for her to stand up for him, to protest his innocence. But she doesn't. 'How *could* you? How could you *do* this to us?' Her cheeks are a bright, blotchy red, her eyes so wide her pupils look almost dilated. She seems to be completely unaware the children are right there.

'I didn't!' Ben shouts, craning his neck to try and look back at us from where they are leading him down the driveway. At her. 'Fiona, shit, I didn't, this is all a misunderstanding.' He's trying to stay calm, but his voice shakes and a grim satisfaction creeps through me at the sound of it.

'You bastard,' Fiona whispers. 'Why wasn't I enough for you? Why did you have to do this?' I see now that she's started crying, the porch light softly illuminating her tears. I wonder yet again if she's suspected him, all this time. Why else would she be so willing to accept that her husband is a murderer?

'Fiona—' But Ben doesn't get to finish because Ashby is shoving him in the back of their car, not seeming to care that he's quite literally tearing a family apart right now. Fiona lets out a heaving sob and Murphy turns towards her at the sound.

'You should go back inside,' Murphy says gently. 'Take a bit of time to get your head around this.'

'Mummy?' Lily's cartoon voice seems unnaturally loud, high and clear in the chaos surrounding us.

Fiona gasps, runs back to her and Emily. 'My girls,' she whispers, pulling them towards her. 'I'm so sorry, my darlings. Don't worry, it'll be OK, it'll all be OK.'

Emily frowns, definitely not buying that. 'Where are they taking Daddy?'

'It's OK,' she whispers again. Her hand shakes as she strokes Emily's head. She looks up at me from where she's bent down with the girls. 'Sarah, I . . . I don't know how to . . .' Her voice breaks and the guilt inside me intensifies. I've got what I wanted, but that doesn't stop me from wishing there wasn't this collateral damage.

'Don't,' I whisper back. I can't think of anything else to say. After so long of wanting to get this point, I am utterly at a loss as to what to do now

'I'm so, so sorry, Sarah. I can't . . . I just can't believe this is happening. It's not . . . Maybe they got it wrong and this is all just a horrible, horrible mistake. Maybe they'll let him go.'

'Maybe,' I say. But my tone of voice makes it clear what I think and I know – from how Fiona was with Ben, from the way she doesn't seem to believe what she's saying – that she agrees with me. She can believe that Ben did it. There must have been so many more cracks in their marriage than the ones they let show.

'What's a mistake, Mummy?' Emily asks and the sound of her little voice sends me close to crying, just like Fiona is now.

'Ssshhh, my darling,' Fiona says, stroking Emily's hair. I can see her trying to pull herself together for the girls. It gives me hope that she'll get through this, because she has them to pull her through. 'We'll be OK.' It's all she can seem to say to the girls, and I wonder how she'll do it, how she'll explain to them where their father has been taken and why. I glance towards the driveway, through the still-open front door. Their dark car has gone now. Neither Fiona nor I noticed it leaving. Just like that, he's gone. It feels so anticlimactic. Though I suppose it's all still to come. The trial, the conviction. They've got enough, though, I'm almost certain of it. The evidence is stacked up against Ben, surely there's no way he'll get off.

'You *will* be OK,' I say to Fiona, trying to convince myself of it at the same time.

She nods. 'I know.' She gives her daughters another big squeeze, reluctant to let go of them, it seems. 'We'll be absolutely fine, just us girls, won't we?' She manages a smile as she says it and for the briefest of seconds it looks real, looks like she's almost *glad* about the prospect. Or maybe that's me just imagining it, hoping for it. Because if she's glad then I have less to feel guilty for.

'I'm hungry,' Emily says after a beat, hesitantly, almost like she's trying to diffuse the tension.

Fiona stands up. 'Why don't you go back to the living room for a minute, I'll bring in some popcorn and we can have movie night, how about that?' Lily and Emily exchange a glance that seems too old for them and I feel a pang watching it. I remind myself that, given what type of person Ben is, they will be better off without him, in the long run. 'Go on,' encourages Fiona. 'I'll be there in a minute. Please.' When they still don't move her voice changes, becomes more commanding. 'Emily, be a big girl, take your sister in to the sitting room.'

That does it, and Emily grabs Lily's hand, gives it an almost defiant yank and the two of them leave Fiona and I alone in the hallway, the cool outside air wrapping around us from the still-open front door. I hear the girls start arguing about what to watch almost immediately. Fiona walks to the front door, shuts it silently. The click is too loud, seems to echo through the house, like it's signifying something. An end to something, a big change about to happen. She takes a breath, like she's pulling herself together, and when she turns back to me, when she takes both my hands in hers, her eyes are dry. She's in shock, I'm sure, her pale face, her too-calm voice evidence of it. I wonder what will happen, when the adrenaline leaves her.

'We mustn't let this destroy our family, Sarah.'

I shake my head. 'We won't.'

'We need each other. The girls need you in their lives.' Her gaze is very direct, enough to make me a little uncomfortable.

'I know,' I say, as calmly as I can. Surely this isn't the time – her husband has just been led away for my mother's murder, we *both* need to deal with that before we talk about moving forward together. Lily is crying now, her sobs carrying through to us, a despairing noise indistinguishable from when she cries about Emily taking her toys, only this time it seems justified.

Fiona doesn't seem to notice, her eyes too intent on my face, her gaze resolute. 'Sarah, you're family.'

'I know,' I stress, and pull my hands away from hers. I take a breath. I love Fiona but, really, this is all a bit much, this talk of families. Right now I just want to sit in a dark room and not speak to anyone.

She shakes her head. 'No.' The word is firm, and I know then, that something is about to change. The skin on the back of my hands buzzes, the ringing in my ears starts up again. 'You don't get it. You really are their family.' She glances towards the living room, drops her voice. 'I – your mum wanted to tell you, I think, before she . . .' She takes a breath, and the moment before she speaks feels eternal.

But I make myself keep looking at her straight in the eye as she says the words that have the power to change everything.

'Ben is your father.'

PART THREE

—

Fiona

Benjamin Gregory, 47, of St Lawrence House, Frome, has been convicted of the murder of Nicola Gregory, 53, following a five-day trial at Bristol Crown Court. Mr Benjamin Gregory and Mrs Nicola Gregory were related only through marriage, Mrs Gregory having been married to Mr Gregory's late step-brother.

The court heard that Mr Gregory and Mrs Gregory had previously had an affair, when Mrs Gregory's late husband was still alive. The jury were also told that Benjamin and Nicola Gregory had a child together, Sarah Gregory, 24. Ms Gregory was previously unaware of her true biological father, thus the prosecution argued that Mr Gregory killed Mrs Gregory both because she would not resume the affair, and because she was going to tell Ms Gregory the truth about her conception, something Mr Gregory wanted to be kept secret.

The cause of death was poison, specifically the use of the belladonna plant, or deadly nightshade, which was found in abundance in Mr Gregory's garden.

Mr Gregory pleaded innocent to the charge of murder, but guilty to the charge of manslaughter, maintaining that he did not mean to kill Mrs Gregory and must have poisoned her accidentally. However, there was evidence that

Mrs Gregory was ingesting poison over the course of many weeks, suggesting this was pre-meditated.

The jury found Mr Gregory guilty of murder. He has been given a life sentence, to be served at HMP Bristol.

Det. Sgt. Ashby with the Avon & Somerset Police said, 'We are satisfied with how the trial went, and are confident that the public will be safer with this man behind bars.'

Mr Gregory's wife, Fiona Gregory, declined to comment, however his niece and biological daughter, Sarah Gregory, said, 'I am still in shock that this could happen, that Ben could be guilty of such a thing. But I can find some closure in the fact that he's been put away, and can't do any more damage to me or what's left of my family. Now maybe we can move on from this nightmare and start to put it behind us. We just ask that the community leave us be and let us try to come to terms with what's happened in our own time.'

Chapter Thirty-One

It felt wrong, somehow, that the sun was shining, that she was wearing a flowing lilac skirt and a white vest top, her shoulders bare for the first time this year, warm. Fiona thought perhaps that it should be raining, or at least grey – that the weather should reflect the reason she was here. Of course, objectively, she realised that was nonsense, an example of people desperate to feel that the world around them somehow cared, was somehow attuned to their wants and needs.

Still. She blew out a sharp breath as she walked up the path to the church, trying to keep her steps light, respectful. The plastic encasing the flowers crinkled beneath her fingers as she tensed her hands. She wouldn't give in to the desire to turn back, as uncomfortable as it made her to be here. She turned right, onto the grass and into the graveyard, the ground hard beneath her pumps. Though she tried to control it, her heart beat a little faster as she approached the two headstones, one dark, one ashy grey, sitting side by side.

It was pure nonsense that she should feel like this. They were gone now, Charlie and Nicola, there was nothing they could do to her now.

Still. Yes, that word again, still. Knowing that they were gone, objectively knowing the truth of it, didn't stop the gnawing of guilt that started right in the middle of her stomach and seemed to travel outwards so that it made her insides pulse. She stopped in front of Nicola's grave and a shudder ran down her spine. She was standing right on top of Nicola's body, her flesh perhaps gone by now, eaten away by worms, but her bones still there, separated from Fiona's shoes only by a layer of dirt. She tightened her grip on the flower stems in her right hand. It was the first time she'd been here, the first time she'd been able to make herself come – because, really, the hypocrisy of it, that she was here when her husband was locked up for killing the woman.

And there it was again, that pulsing guilt. It clawed at her these days, reared up just when she thought she'd beaten it down. Because there were so many things she'd done wrong, so many things she should have done differently. Perhaps if she'd just paid more attention to what was going on right under her nose, she wouldn't be here, laying flowers on the grave of a woman she'd never really liked.

No. Fiona closed her eyes briefly, the warmth of the sun stroking her eyelids. That wasn't fair. Certainly, she hadn't liked Nicola when she was alive, because she was someone Ben had had an affair with in the past, because of the way Ben had still looked at her, had clearly still felt about her. But she understood that she'd been more mad at Ben than Nicola. Furious, really, that he would still act that way around Nicola, that he clearly still wanted her. And yes, there was a bitter, ugly part of her that was all the more hurt that he'd feel that way about someone older than her. She didn't know why, but it was strangely more insulting that way.

In her more reasonable moments, she'd understood that it wasn't Nicola's fault, the way Ben felt about her. But she'd been unable to take it out solely on him in case she risked ruining their marriage completely – and that was something she'd never have done to her daughters. So it had been easier to blame Nicola, to see her as the demon in all this. Even now, now that Nicola, not Fiona, was certainly the victim, she found it tricky to separate her feelings, to know whether she had disliked her fundamentally as a person, as opposed to what she had come to represent.

Fiona bent down, stared at Nicola's name engraved on the gravestone, the lighter flecks sparkling a little in the sun, almost mocking, reflecting some happiness Nicola hadn't enjoyed, certainly not at the end. There were flowers there already, in that metal vase. Dead, wilting flowers. It seemed worse, somehow, that there were old flowers there, rather than none at all.

Fiona glanced around the graveyard. Only a handful of gravestones had fresh flowers, some of which were potted, so as to stay there longer. Charlie's was one of those graves – someone had come here recently, topped up the flowers. Topped up his but not Nicola's – a colleague, perhaps, or old school friend. Surely here was a sign that he'd had more friends than her in life. She frowned at herself. She was still finding ways to put Nicola down in her own mind. She shouldn't do it, she had no need to, not now. And anyway, it might not be that at all. It might just be that there was no scandal in the way Charlie had died, whereas *murder*, well, that made people uncomfortable to say the least.

Silly, she supposed, to think that the dead would care whether flowers lay atop their bones. Silly, but still, a little sad. And so, despite everything, despite that clawing, pulsing sensation in her gut, Fiona felt a sob try to force its way out her throat and had to press her lips together firmly to stop it from escaping. Hypocritical, to be crying for Nicola. She blinked to clear the blurriness of her eyes as she reached for the metal vase on Nicola's grave, unscrewed the top and carefully took out the dead flowers. Lilies, by the looks of things. White lilies. Clearly someone who hadn't known her very well – Nicola always said she hated white flowers. Maybe Phil – she'd seen him bring her white roses a few times, seen the fake smile Nicola had plastered to her face when he did.

God, Phil. She hadn't thought about him in so long now. Unlike her, he'd escaped the horror of the trial, dismissed by the police and everyone else as just Nicola's lover, someone who would grieve and move on with his own life. Unlike her, he hadn't had the intimate details of his family life put on show for the whole county to read about in the papers, hadn't lost friends because of it, friends who had, preposterously, said that 'they'd never liked Ben', or that 'there was always something weird about their marriage'. Things that were said behind her back, but which without fail got back to her anyway, in a town like this. An ugly sensation swirled at the thought of it, a dark fog infecting every part of her, try as she might to keep it at bay. Nonsense, all of it. Because no one *had* disliked Ben, no one *had* thought she and Ben had anything other than an idyllic family life – a big house, a car, two beautiful daughters. Yes, a few close friends had known of Fiona's doubts about Ben and Nicola because she'd needed to talk about it, but even then . . .

She pulled the metal vase, warm from the sun, out of its holder and straightened. She walked to the corner of the church, leaving the bunch of flowers – shamefully bought at the local Sainsbury's petrol station on her way back from Bristol – between Nicola's and Charlie's graves.

God, being here was bringing it all back. The way she'd felt during the trial, the horror of having to sit there, listening to her husband try to defend himself. Having to answer the lawyer's questions until she felt like someone had scooped away her insides, felt like she didn't even understand her own answers. At times, she still felt numb from it, even now. Felt utter disbelief that it had all really happened, that it had come to this. In the shock of the arrest she'd initially accepted it – the weight of the murder investigation, still having to deal with the fallout of Ben and Nicola's relationship, it had been pressing down on her, so that it had all somehow seemed to make sense. And there was all that evidence . . . But now, with the space she'd had to breathe, she found it unbelievable, really, that the father of her children had been convicted not just of manslaughter but of murder.

Murder. The word rolled around the inside of her mouth and she wanted to spit it out like sour milk and be rid of it.

She filled the metal vase up with water from the old, rusted tap, then started back to the grave, a bead of sweat at the base of her neck sliding a few inches down her back. She set the vase down, then folded herself neatly onto the ground, too, not caring if her skirt got dirty because of it. She sat there, the silence a little eerie despite the bright day, and took the plastic wrapping off the flowers. She hadn't bought scissors. How stupid of her to forget that, given she spent half her free time in the garden, knew perfectly well you needed to trim the stems.

Though she was not – according to that superior prosecution lawyer, to those detectives before her – as good a gardener as Ben, who had apparently harvested the deadly nightshade over many months, gave it to Nicola in small doses, just enough to give her pain, to make her delirious, even, but not enough to kill her. According to the prosecution, Ben had wanted to make Nicola suffer before he killed her. Make her suffer because he was in love with her and she didn't love him back, wouldn't take him back after Charlie died. Killed her because she was going to tell Sarah the truth – that he was her father.

The jury hadn't bought the manslaughter plea, the one that the defence lawyer they'd hired had been so keen for Ben to make. Mark Barrett, a young, up-and-coming lawyer. He'd insisted that it would be better for Ben to make the plea, even though he hadn't initially wanted to. Had said the evidence didn't look good, that it would be better if they tried to get off on manslaughter, that they had more of a chance of that than saying he'd done absolutely nothing wrong. And Ben had agreed. Fiona hadn't understood when Ben had tried to explain it to her. He'd tried to use the same arguments as the lawyer, that he thought it was the best shot, yet at the same time he was still insisting, again and again, that he hadn't killed Nicola. But to Fiona, refusing to plead innocent had been like admitting to her that he did it, and it was that, really, that made her truly give up on him.

Clearly the jury had been thinking along the same lines, because now he was in prison. For life. *Life*. And even if he did get out early, he wouldn't see his girls grow up, they wouldn't know their dad, would only have fleeting childhood memories of him. She blinked furiously against the stinging in her eyes – not for her this time but for her beautiful daughters, who still didn't really understand what had happened, why they couldn't see their dad, why he wasn't there to read them a bedtime story anymore. There was no way she'd take them to see him in prison. No. She didn't want them thinking of him in there, didn't want them telling other children that their dad was locked up, wouldn't have them victimised because of it. She wouldn't have them known as the children of a murderer. Better they didn't know, better they just thought Daddy had gone away for a bit, as painful as that was. She'd explain it to them when they were older.

Her fingers shook a little as she arranged the flowers in the vase. It was times like this – the quiet, alone times – that were the hardest. When she was with the girls, she managed to get through it, to be their mother, to put on a smile for them. But as soon as she didn't have someone to pretend to, that's when she had to face up to what she was feeling, had to try and deal with the misery, the anger. It was getting worse, now. Funny, perhaps, that it was worse now than the long months leading up to the trial, the trial itself. During those days, a strange hollowness had settled into her and stayed there, so that she had seemed to be looking at everything through smeared glasses. Since the moment she'd watched those detectives handcuff him, marking him out as a killer. But now that hollowness was lifting, making her realise just how shredded her life was. Making her realise that he'd done this to her, to her daughters – he'd ripped apart her life, and all he could say in response was how much he loved the woman he'd killed.

She did her best to take a slow, steady breath, to fight the need to scream or sob, as she put the metal vase back into its holder. She glanced at Charlie's grave. Poor Charlie. She hoped that wherever he was, he wasn't watching this, hoped he didn't know what had happened to his family after he died. She'd liked Charlie. Perhaps even more so because she felt they were both in some ways victims of the connection Nicola and Ben shared. She hoped he hadn't known the true extent of it. Hoped he had truly believed Sarah was his daughter. He'd been quiet in general, around most people, but with Sarah he always lit up – they brought each other to life, those two.

God, Sarah. She closed her eyes briefly, fighting the stinging that was starting up again. She didn't want to cry, didn't think she deserved that release. She'd wondered, again and again, if she'd done the right thing, telling her that way. She should have waited, should have found a better moment. It was the stress of the investigation, of hiding her knowledge from the police, that had made her do it, made her blurt it out, like someone had taken a lid off the secret and set it free, the moment she saw Ben in handcuffs.

Because he was the reason she'd kept quiet. She'd known, even if no one else did, what Nicola had wanted to tell Sarah that day. She'd known what Nicola had meant when she'd talked about eyes. Because Sarah's eyes were nothing like Charlie's cobalt blue – no, they might be stormier, more expressive, but they were almost the exact colour of Ben's, of Lily's. And the timing of the affair – they were together in that year before Sarah was born. But she hadn't said anything about her suspicions – historically because she hadn't wanted another block in her and Ben's relationship, and it was easier to pretend it wasn't true. And while Charlie was alive . . . She wouldn't have done that to Charlie, to Sarah. It wasn't her place. And then, once the police started asking questions, once it was clear they thought one of them had killed Nicola, well. She was ashamed to admit that she'd kept it secret to protect Ben. Because she'd been worried that it would look bad for him, because she didn't want to give the police undue reason to suspect him, not when she wasn't sure he'd even known about it himself. She hadn't wanted to complicate things. And now she felt like an idiot for doing that, for handling the whole thing so badly. She'd wanted to protect her husband, yet he'd proven since then, over and over, that he hadn't cared one bit about her. She shouldn't have done it. Shouldn't have misled the police for a man who turned out to be guilty, shouldn't have told Sarah the way she did, shouldn't have stayed with Ben despite her suspicions about Nicola.

Shouldn't, shouldn't, shouldn't. She crossed her arms and dug her nails into flesh, fighting the hot ball of anger inside her. She swallowed slowly, knowing the feeling would fade, that she'd be able to get through it. She'd survived this long, she could keep doing it, keep just putting one foot in front of the other. Besides, if Sarah could do it, so could she.

Thank God for Sarah, really. If it hadn't been for her, she didn't know how she'd have got through these past months. She'd been an absolute star helping out with girls, but then, they'd always loved her. She'd thought that the trial, and all that led up to it, would have driven her and Sarah apart, but Sarah had surprised Fiona with her ability to keep it together, with how determined she was not to let it ruin her, ruin their relationship. It had helped enormously, having someone else going through a similar thing – they'd both been lied to, both had family who had betrayed them, and both had to stand up in front of a jury and talk about their personal lives. Another reason she'd hadn't been to see Ben, she supposed. It felt like disloyalty to Sarah, who had left no doubt in her hatred for Ben, despite her ability to forgive Fiona. Sarah, who was looking after the girls right now so Fiona could go on to her leaving drinks. The gnawing guilt was back now, knowing what she was about to do. She checked her watch. She needed to leave. It was only 4 p.m. but she had one stop to make before she headed to those drinks.

She stood up, shook the dust out of her skirt. 'I'm sorry,' she whispered to Nicola's name. Despite herself, a single tear escaped, traced a line of salt down her bare cheek. 'If it makes any difference, I'm sorry.' And with that she turned, head down, and walked back towards the car, brushing aside the evidence of that tear.

Chapter Thirty-Two

Ben was waiting for her at one of those awful grey tables in the visitors' area of the prison. He looked terrible. Worse even than he had at the end of the trial. It was like he'd had the life pumped out of him, the very essence of what made him *him* scooped away. Nothing like the man she'd met in the pub, who had charmed her from the instant they started talking, had made her dance when usually she hated it. She'd fallen for him so hard in those first months, had been beyond ecstatic when he'd asked her to marry him after only eight months of dating. That was part of the problem, she supposed – it had been so unequal, their relationship, right from the beginning. She should have known that she was just a stopgap, a way to fill the hole left by Nicola. But she hadn't wanted to see it.

She tried to keep calm as she sat opposite him, but was too aware of the guards everywhere, watching them. She wondered if they knew who she was. Wondered if they judged her – either for being here now, or not coming sooner. In that moment, she felt exactly how everyone else saw her – the wife of a murderer. It sent something icy trickling down her spine, made her sit straighter, as if to fight it. She wondered how Ben had managed to do it, through the entire investigation – pretend, like she was pretending now.

'Fiona.' Ben breathed her name like a lifeline. She hated that. He had proven, hadn't he, that she was certainly not that. All this time, since his arrest, Ben's one defence had been that he couldn't have done it because he'd loved Nicola. Over and over, he told anyone that would listen how much he loved her. And yes, she knew he was trying to get off a murder charge, but still, how was she supposed to feel about it? That all this time, he'd loved another woman, through their wedding, the birth of their daughters. Didn't Ben for one moment consider how she might have felt? He could have told her he loved her, too, could have told her that he had to say it for the trial. Could have apologised for it, begged her forgiveness. He'd done none of that, she thought bitterly. He'd apologised for the mess in general, but he'd been all denial, the whole time. And he'd never once apologised for loving Nicola, never once told her he loved her just as much. Even if it wasn't the truth, he could have told her – at least then she'd have known he cared enough to lie.

She took a breath to steady herself, inhaling the stale recycled air that smelled like old socks and onion. Felt her spine stiffen with resolve. She owed him nothing, not after what he'd put her through. She came as a courtesy, nothing more. Came because, despite everything, he was still her daughters' father. 'I came to tell you that we're moving,' she said shortly. 'The girls and I.' She was pleased with how crisp her words sounded, how firm.

'Fiona, I . . . What? You're moving?' She felt the weight of his hollow gaze on her.

'To Devon, yes. To be near my parents – you know they moved there when they retired and I . . .'

'But you never got on with your parents.' True, they hadn't had the easiest of relationships. They hadn't approved of her getting married so quickly, for one – though they turned out to be very right about that, didn't they? And despite the fact they hadn't been in her life very much over the last ten years, they were something. She knew they would help with the girls, that they'd be there for her when it came down to it. Which was more than she could say for Ben.

'Well, the girls will love being by the sea, and so will I. We need a fresh start, away from . . . all this.' She spoke briskly, refusing to let emotion creep into her voice. It was so hard when he was looking at her like that, reminding her of the hell he'd put her through these last six months. She tried to focus on the fact that she was leaving. To focus on the promise of the future rather than drowning in the present.

'So you're taking them away. From me.'

'We need a fresh start,' she said again. And how dare he make it sound like it was something *she* was doing to *him*? How dare he insinuate that she was the bad guy in this decision? She pressed her feet hard against the floor to stop herself from either running from the room right now, or else leaning across and hitting him. She hadn't decided which was more appealing.

She could hear the muttered conversations between the other prisoners and their visitors in the silence that followed. She caught the odd word through the babble of voices, words that didn't make sense out of context. She hoped that meant no one else could overhear her, either. It was hard enough having this conversation out in the open, where she was only too aware of the eyes on her, judging her, the way the whole town had been judging her since the beginning of this.

'When?' Ben asked, his voice dull, like he'd already given in. Given up. It was easier, she decided, that there was barely any trace of the man she knew there. No trace of the man who had stayed with her in the hospital room through her twenty-hour labour with Emily, whose face had expressed so much joy when he held his first child. Second child. Not that she'd been one hundred per cent sure of that at the time, not that Ben had shown any fatherly concern towards Sarah ever.

'Next week.' She ignored his jolt. She had to do what was right for her and the girls, not for him. 'It's the Easter holidays for Emily, so an easier move.' He said nothing in the pause that followed. 'Sarah's coming with us, too,' she said, feeling the words tumbling from her, the need to avoid sitting here in silence too much to ignore. 'She seems to think she'll find a new job easily enough, and she wants to be around Lily and Emily since she, well—' The fact that he still had the nerve to hold her gaze at that was unbelievable. She had to admit, she'd been surprised when Sarah had agreed to come with them, given she had a good job here, a flatmate she liked. But she'd assured Fiona that Nika would understand, and Fiona was grateful – it was important that Lily and Emily had a relationship with her, their sister. At least if they wouldn't have a father she could give them that.

'Well,' she continued, 'I just came to tell you that. I thought you should know, and now you do so I'll . . .' She stood, felt the nearest guard trace her movements with his eyes. Still Ben said nothing, just watched her with that dejected gaze. It was unnerving. She was glad, she told herself. She'd heard it all before, the pleas, the excuses.

That didn't stop her feeling just a bit guilty, though, leaving him here like this, this ragdoll version of the man she'd married. She hated that, too. The guilt. She shouldn't have to feel it on top of everything, so she turned it into anger, that he should be making her feel guilty when she was most certainly doing nothing wrong.

The rest of the visitors were still seated, a few couples holding hands across the tables, their relationships clearly not ruined by whatever landed those men in here. Fiona had every intention of walking out and not looking back, of making this the ending it was supposed to be. But couldn't stop herself from turning to him, from asking. 'Did you know? Did you know that Sarah was your daughter?' She hadn't asked him outright before. The defence lawyer had, she knew, because it became a key factor in the court case, the fact that Ben hadn't wanted the secret to come out. But she'd avoided it, just like she'd avoided asking him for the entirety of the marriage. 'Did you know that's what Nicola wanted to tell her?'

'No,' Ben said, meeting her gaze full on. His eyes, Sarah's eyes, seemed too big now that his face was thinner. 'No to both, Fiona. I would have told you if I knew, please believe that.' But how could she? How could she believe anything he told her, after everything?

'I didn't do it, Fee,' he said wearily, like he wasn't really expecting her to believe him. He must have guessed what she was thinking. They still knew each other's tics, after all – that hadn't changed.

'Well, it wasn't an accident,' she snapped. The prosecution had convinced not just the jury of that but her, too.

'Then someone else did it.' The words hung between them. It was the first time he'd said it, said exactly those words – to her, anyway. During the murder investigation, they'd never discussed theories. She'd wondered at the time if it was because he'd suspected her, if there was just the sliver of doubt there for him, as it had been for her. After all, Nicola had been poisoned quite literally in their back garden. She hadn't seriously believed he'd done it, though, not until the evidence was slammed down in front of her. Still, they hadn't speculated together, had retreated into themselves, showing up not so much fractures as clean breaks in their marriage.

They stared at each other for what felt like several long minutes. The room seemed quieter, like it and everyone in it were holding their breath, waiting for her to make a decision. Whether to entertain the possibility, whether to fight for him now where she hadn't before.

She took a breath, tasted the staleness. But before she could say that final goodbye, as if he knew she was about to turn away from him for good, he spoke again. 'Fiona, do you really think I would have been so careful not to poison the girls, but yet let you eat it?' It was something that had come up in the court case, something the prosecution had used to point out Ben's guilt – that he'd been so careful not to poison his daughters, but that he couldn't control who else consumed the poison.

'You love Lily and Emily,' Fiona whispered.

'I love you, too, Fee.' His eyes were imploring on hers. And it was like he knew, like the bastard *knew* that's what she'd been desperate to hear and was using it to make her believe him.

'You loved Nicola more,' she said sharply. When he didn't deny it she felt her heart cave in on itself, even though she'd already known it.

She turned on her heel once again. 'Think about it, Fiona. When did you ever eat round the annex? You were hardly going round there for tea and cake with Nicola.' She glared at him over her shoulder but his eyes stayed steady on hers. 'So for the poison to get into your system, it had to be at our house. And then it would have had to be deliberate – to poison you and not the girls.'

She stared at him disbelievingly. Of course he was saying this. It was the first time she'd been to see him since the conviction, so of course he'd be saying it wasn't him, would be trying to blame it on someone else. 'Maybe you did it deliberately then,' she said coldly.

He laughed, though it was devoid of all humour, not the light, charming laugh she knew. 'Why on earth would I do that? And Fiona,' he said before she could interrupt, 'if you don't believe that I feel anything for you, you've said yourself – I love my daughters. I would never do anything to risk taking their mother away from them.'

Damn it, there were tears in her eyes despite herself. She took one heaving breath, dashed a tear away, and straightened her back. 'Goodbye, Ben,' she said. She'd meant it to come out sharp, final, but it sounded sad instead.

She was breathing heavily, fighting the sobs that threatened to overwhelm her as she got her phone, purse and car keys from the locker she'd had to store her valuables in, walked past the guards with their metal detectors, the sniffer dogs. She couldn't let him get to her. There was nothing to suggest it could be anyone else – no evidence, no other motive. She'd made her decision, was starting to come to terms with it – she wouldn't go back on that now. Couldn't put herself through it all over again.

She had one voicemail and she listened to it as she stepped out into air that, if not fresh, was at least better than inside.

'Hi, Fiona, it's Maddie again here calling from the Daily Mail. *I just wanted to check you'd got my last message . . .'* Fiona gritted her teeth, hung up.

Bloody Maddie. She was sure she was one of the ones who had turned up at the house, waiting on her front doorstep until Sarah came over and got rid of them. They'd been hounding her even before the conviction. The *Daily Mail*, the *Daily Mirror*, the *Sun*. Not to mention the local newspaper. She had no idea how they knew where she lived, how they'd got her number – though she supposed it wouldn't have been too hard to find someone in this town willing to share. She'd made the mistake of answering her phone to the first unknown number, had been so confused to find herself speaking to a journalist that she'd nearly started answering the questions before she'd realised what was happening.

She threw down her phone on the passenger seat once she got to her car, almost relieved that anger had crushed her need to cry. This. This was what Ben didn't understand. This was why she had to take the girls and go, down to the coast where no one knew who they were, where she didn't have to worry if the next doorbell might be another one of them, offering her money to hear 'her side of the story'. She'd been plunged into infamy with the case, the target of gossip everywhere she went. Everyone had an opinion, and just because she'd refused to talk to any of the journalists, it didn't mean they hadn't shared those opinions. She'd been cast as a victim, as an idiot for not noticing, as a good wife for sticking by Ben or a terrible one for not fighting for him. She knew people in town were reading about her, knew they were also making judgments on her whenever she went to the local shop, or to pick Emily up from school.

It wasn't just that she was a wife of a murderer, the mother of his children, but the *romanticism* of the whole thing. The affair, the secret child. The papers had even made the poison itself out to be romantic – belladonna meant, quite literally, beautiful lady.

The lover's choice of poison, a nod to Ben's tragic love for Nicola.

Extract from Court Transcript, dated 05/04/19

Appearances:

BG – Benjamin Thomas Gregory
LJ – Laura Jenkins, prosecution
TB – Thomas Barrett, defence

LJ   I have just a few points to clarify.
Mr Gregory, we've previously established
here that the belladonna poison found
its way into Nicola's system through
her tea. That is, the police forensic
team found evidence of the plant mixed
with tea leaves on the compost heap.
On your compost heap. On the night in
question, you have admitted to giving
Nicola a cup of tea, isn't that right?

BG   Yes, but I didn't know the tea leaves
had been mixed with the poison.

LJ   You have previously said that 'I must
have accidentally put the belladonna
into her tea the night she died'.

BG   That's what I mean – it was an
accident.

LJ   But how is something like that
      accidental?

TB   Your lordship—

JUDGE Miss James, if you could rephrase?

LJ   You are a self-professed experienced
      gardener, Mr Gregory. How would you not
      recognise the belladonna when putting
      it into her tea?

BG   Look, it must have been crushed up
      small enough for me not to notice or
      something. I was just trying to help
      her, to get some fluid into her - and
      I'm not convinced it was even that cup
      of tea that killed her despite what you
      all say.

LJ   Why tea? Why not water, if all you
      wanted was to get fluid into her?

BG   She liked tea.

LJ   Exactly. She liked tea - and you knew
      that, knew she drank it often, knew
      that tea would easily hide the taste of
      the sweet belladonna plant, didn't you?

BG   No, I didn't.

LJ   You didn't know that she liked tea?

Or you didn't know that belladonna was
sweet?

BG   I didn't put the belladonna in the
tea. Of course I knew she liked tea
- everyone likes tea, for God's sake.
And look, the night she died - the tea
you're talking about, she barely drank
any of it. Phil and Fiona can probably back me up on that - it was still
sitting on her bedside table. Besides,
doesn't belladonna take a while to work?
Why would I give it to her and then
immediately go and get Fiona, call the
ambulance? Why wouldn't I wait for it to
take effect? She was already ill when
I went round that night, I've told you
that, told everyone that, over and over,
but none of you will listen to me.

LJ   And how do you know it takes a while
to work, Mr Gregory?

BG   My lawyer and I looked it up, as soon
as I found out I was going on trial.

LJ   You didn't know anything about the
plant beforehand, then? Despite the
fact you performed a Google search on
your phone, specifically looking at the
properties of the belladonna plant?

BG   I didn't search that on my phone.

LJ   I see. And yet, if you didn't, then who did?

BG   I don't know. I leave my phone lying around a lot, anyone could have got to it.

LJ   Who, exactly?

BG   I'm sorry?

LJ   Who do you think has access to your phone?

BG   Well, I don't know. I mean, my wife, I suppose, my daughters . . . People at work. I leave it on my desk, one of them could have picked it up, maybe, needed to use it or something.

LJ   I see. Is your phone password protected?

BG   Well, yeah, it's an iPhone, it has a passcode.

LJ   And who has access to this passcode?

BG   Well, my wife probably knows it.

LJ   Your wife, of course. So do you mean that you think your wife may have been researching the belladonna?

BG   No! No, I'm not saying that, I didn't
       mean that.

LJ   All right, then, apart from your wife,
       would anyone else know your passcode?

BG   I tell people the code all the time -
       if someone asked to borrow it I would
       have just let them. Besides, why would
       I have let the police have my phone, if
       I thought they'd find something on it?

LJ   Well, I suppose that's a question only
       you can answer. Perhaps you thought
       they wouldn't find the search, because
       it was deleted. I have to say, if it
       were an innocent search then I find it
       hard to understand why someone would
       try to delete evidence of it.

BG   Look, I can only tell you over and
       over - I'm sure it must have been
       someone else searching on my phone.
       Fiona. Or Sarah, for instance. She's
       got into gardening, she could have
       wanted to know more about the plants in
       our garden.

LJ   Mr Gregory, you are pleading guilty
       to the charge of manslaughter, yet the
       evidence provided by the medical exam-
       iner suggests that Nicola was being
       poisoned over the course of many weeks,

which suggests a fair degree of pre-meditation to me. Not only that, but there were large quantities of the belladonna-tealeaf compound found in your compost heap – more than just one cup of tea's worth. You were poisoning Nicola over the course of many weeks, mixing the belladonna into her tea every few days, weren't you, Mr Gregory?

BG   No! No, I wasn't. I didn't murder Nicola. I don't care what the evidence says, I didn't. I loved her.

LJ   When did you switch to tea leaves, Mr Gregory?

BG   What? I don't remember.

LJ   About six months ago, that's what your wife said.

BG   Fine, maybe.

LJ   Coincidental timing, to switch to tea leaves just before the poisoning started. It would have been harder to mix the belladonna in with a teabag, wouldn't it?

BG   Exactly! Look, I wasn't the one to make the switch – it wasn't my idea. It was

Nicola's own idea, I think, or maybe
Sarah's, I can't remember. Something
about plastic in teabags, I don't know,
I just went along with it.

LJ   I see. The night she died, Nicola left
a message on her daughter, Sarah's,
phone, saying she had to tell her something 'before it was too late'. Were
you present for that call, Mr Gregory?

BG   No.

LJ   So you didn't hear her leave that
message?

BG   No.

LJ   You didn't worry, perhaps, that Nicola
was finally going to tell Sarah the
truth – something both you and she had
been keeping from her – that she is,
in fact, your biological daughter?

BG   I— No. I didn't hear it.

LJ   You didn't worry, after Nicola told
Sarah this, that your family life could
be ruined? That your wife would leave
you? That your niece – that is to say,
your daughter – would be horrified that
you'd kept this secret from her, all
these years?

274

BG   No.

LJ   So you wouldn't have minded if Nicola
      told Sarah that you were her father?

BG   Look, I didn't even know myself so how
      was I supposed to know Nicola was plan-
      ning on telling Sarah?

Chapter Thirty-Three

'Fee!' Becky, a pretty, blonde nurse from the hospital who was always smiling bounded over to her and gave her a quick, hard hug. 'We thought you'd bailed on us.' She smiled, and though it was clearly a joke Fiona wondered if there was a little bit of truth behind it. Wondered again if she could actually face it, put on the smile, the banter for this when she'd just seen her husband in prison.

'Come join us and we'll get you a drink.' Becky grabbed Fiona's hand and pulled her across the pub to a booth where the rest of them were sitting. Fiona glanced around nervously. It wasn't a pub she knew well, despite the fact it was just round the corner from the hospital. Because she had to drive to and from work, and because she had the girls, she rarely went for a drink after her shift. It was all right in here, she supposed, though it seemed like it was trying to be both a traditional English pub, with antlers on the walls and dim lighting, and a more modern, trendy venue with the bright red leather booths, a chalk board with a list of cocktails, rather than specials. She wasn't really sure it worked. And, in all honesty, she'd rather be outside in a garden on a day like this than cramped up in a too-hot, too-dark room.

She smiled at Becky as they approached the others, and Becky winked at her. She was the one who'd insisted they do this, who'd said it would be good for her. Ever since Ben had been led away by the police, she'd avoided this

– drinking with people, being in any sort of relaxed environment, talking to people at all, really. Though maybe it had started earlier than that, if she was honest with herself. Since the day she'd found out Nicola was poisoned.

Becky ushered Fiona into the booth next to Cynthia from HR, Malcolm, one of the radiology techs, and Kate, another of the nurses. There were a few more people standing and talking across the other side of the booth, glasses half empty already, and they all smiled and made fake cheering noises when she sat down. She tried her best to smile back but it felt brittle on her face, like the slightest unkind word might break it.

'Fiona, so glad you could make it,' said Cynthia. Fiona felt her eyebrows trying to shoot up into her forehead, but managed to keep them where they belonged. But, really, the way Cynthia said it, when it was her own leaving drinks, for God's sake! 'I was just telling Malcolm and Kate that your replacement starts next week – she lives just over in Clifton, her two sons have gone off to university and . . .' Fiona nodded, barely listening, as Cynthia prattled on. She glanced over her shoulder looking for Becky, but she'd already disappeared.

So few of them had come. That was better, she told herself. She hadn't wanted lots of people, hadn't wanted a big send-off – it had been an effort to come out in the first place, so she didn't need the whole hospital here leering at her, judging her. Especially after seeing Ben. She was back there for a second, looking at his pale face, listening to him tell her he loved her. No. She wouldn't let herself feel anything for him. It was too little, too late. God, she needed a drink. She was too hot already, and her stomach felt bloated, despite the fact she'd barely eaten today. A side effect of the HRT she was taking, no doubt.

'Don't you think so, too, Fiona?' Kate sprung at her suddenly, her brown eyes intense on Fiona's face.

Thankfully, Becky chose this moment to reappear, thrusting a glass of white wine into her hand, beads of condensation already forming on the outside of the glass. Fiona took it gratefully.

'Where's mine, Shorty?' Malcolm asked, using the nickname he'd started, based on her surname rather than on the fact she was actually short.

He grinned at her and Becky raised her eyebrows. 'Free wine is only for people I like,' she said, dead straight-faced. Malcolm continued to grin, a little uncertainly, while Becky stared him out. It was only when Malcolm's face dropped that Becky laughed. 'Oh, you know I'm only kidding. But seriously, it's your round, no?' She winked at him.

Fiona took a sip of her wine, felt almost guilty at the relief she felt when the cool sharpness of it slid down her throat. She watched as Malcolm huffed, then manoeuvred himself out of the booth, shaking his head mournfully at Becky. 'Only because you asked, Shorty, not for anyone else.' She felt a pang, watching the two of them, the easy banter between them. She couldn't remember the last time she'd had that with anyone at all, couldn't imagine a time in the future when it wouldn't feel like an effort just to talk to someone let alone make jokes. She supposed that was another reason she was grateful to have Sarah around – Sarah didn't need constant conversation, preferred to be in silence a lot of the time, which suited Fiona just fine.

Becky waved him off, clearly oblivious to the way his gaze stayed trained on her whenever she was in the room. Fiona understood that, the need to soak in some of that light, even more so now. She'd thought she'd had that once, with Ben. Those early years, it had been like no one else was in the room when he was there. Another thing she'd never have again. There were those damn tears, threatening the back of her eyes again. Seeing him today had opened it all up, proven that she was not as good as she thought she was at banking it all inside her. She took another hurried sip of wine, but this time it didn't slide down so easily, getting stuck on the lump in her throat.

Kate slid into Malcolm's space, and leaned across Cynthia to speak to Fiona. 'So how *are* you, Fiona?'

Fiona forced her lips to turn upwards, though she was pretty sure it couldn't pass as a natural smile. 'Oh, I'm fine, you know. As fine as I can be.'

'It must have been awful,' Kate continued, and Fiona, at a loss of what to say, looked at Becky for support, but she was now chatting to a woman Fiona was pretty sure worked in the canteen, though she couldn't be totally sure. It didn't surprise her that Becky knew her – she knew everyone – but it did surprise her that a woman she didn't even know the name of was at her leaving drinks. She wondered if she'd come for the gossip, to report back that she'd been in the same room as semi-famous Fiona Gregory. Fiona chased away the bitterness with a gulp of wine, even as she reminded herself to be careful, that she had to drive home.

'I don't know how I could have survived it,' Kate was saying now, shaking her head in what was clearly supposed to be a sympathetic way, though her eyes gleamed as they traced the new lines on Fiona's face, seeking some slither of gossip no doubt. God, she shouldn't have come, shouldn't have given in to the craving for normalcy.

'Well, you do what you have to, don't you?' Fiona's words were a bit sharper than she'd meant them to be. But what did Kate want her to say? That she was barely surviving it herself, that there were times she wasn't sure if she'd be able to keep going?

'And your girls, how are they doing?' Kate pressed.

'They're fine,' Fiona said shortly. Or as fine as they can be, given their dad had disappeared without a word to them. She glanced again at Becky, hoping for some help, but instead caught the end of what Canteen Woman was saying, pushing back her greying hair as she did so. 'It just goes to show, doesn't it? You can think you know who you sleep next to every night, but then some people just don't, do they?'

Fiona wasn't sure if it was her imagination, or if everyone in the booth had now turned to look at Canteen Woman, considering her words. Then she felt the force of all their eyes on her face, burning her skin, almost accusatory. Like she should have known what Ben was capable of all along. Something ugly slithered in her stomach and she fought the need to throw the rest of her drink in Canteen Woman's face.

'So, tell us where you're moving to, Fee?' said Becky, in an overly bright voice. Fiona didn't miss the glare she shot at Canteen Woman, and was grateful for it.

Fiona swallowed the remainder of her glass of wine and though she was disappointed that it seemed to have run out so quickly, she shook her head when Becky pointed at it to ask if she wanted another one. 'Well, we move to Devon next week,' Fiona said, trying to force her voice to stay normal, not to let on at the twisting inside her. 'I've rented a house right by the sea, which the girls will love, and I've found a lovely school for them.'

She kept talking, her words coming on autopilot, the same thing she told anyone when they asked her about her life. But all the time her mind was working. These people, they didn't understand how she couldn't have seen it in Ben.

They would have read the news, so they knew that he wasn't just guilty of murder, but that he planned it, administered the poison over several months. A psychopath – she'd seen that word bandied about, even though she'd tried to avoid reading the articles. And maybe they were right. Her chest constricted, making it painful to keep up the mindless flow of conversation tumbling from her. Surely she *should* have known, should have seen it over all their years of marriage. She'd left her daughters alone with him, for Christ's sake. Her stomach turned. No. Fiona's tongue stuck to the top of her mouth mid-sentence, her explanation that she'd already applied for a few general admin roles cut short. No. Ben wouldn't have hurt the girls, she was sure of that.

Fiona became aware that everyone was watching her and suddenly wished she'd been paying more attention to what she was saying. Malcolm was there, too – at some point he'd come back with more drinks and she hadn't even noticed.

'Well, that's good,' Becky jumped in, giving Fiona another reason to be grateful for her as a friend. 'You don't need to stick to hospitals, do you? Anywhere would take you for an admin role, for sure.'

Fiona nodded, picked up her wine glass only to remember that it was empty. 'Exactly.'

'And Sarah's coming with you, is she?' Becky carried on.

Fiona frowned a little – she didn't remember telling anyone this, but apparently she had. Just what else didn't she remember saying or doing, in this mindless, empty state she'd been in since Ben had been led away? 'Yeah. She's coming so she can look after Lily and Emily for me, and is going to help with rent, thank God.' She tried for a smile, was relieved to see it returned around the table.

The thought of Sarah made her reach into her handbag, take out her phone. Sure enough there was a message from her – Fiona had texted her as she was leaving the prison to check in. Not telling her where she'd been, of course. She pressed the screen of her phone to the palm of her hand then stood up abruptly. Several sets of heads jerked up to follow her movement. 'I'm really sorry, I've just got to take a call, I'll be back in a minute.' A few nods around the table, and Fiona shuffled out the booth and bolted for the door, quite suddenly unable to take a moment more of this.

The 'garden' was really just a couple of wooden picnic tables out the front of the pub, though they were still full, on this first spell of good weather they were having, despite the fact it was right on the road, traffic whizzing past at regular intervals. Fiona leaned against the white wall of the pub, opened up the message Sarah had sent her. A photo, clearly a selfie, of Sarah and her two girls, Emily beaming into the camera, Lily looking over the top of the phone, clearly having missed the order to 'smile' as she so often did. Fiona felt a tug on her heart, almost painful. Ben's daughters, all three of them. And he'd abandoned all three of them.

Fiona let the hand holding her phone drop to her side, closed her eyes. Wished she could just crawl up into bed and sleep for days, just to have a break from it.

'Fee?' She opened her eyes to see Becky coming out the pub door, the chatter inside briefly booming out across the patio before the door swung shut again.

Fiona smiled weakly. 'Did you come out to check on me?'

Becky shook her head, grinned. 'Nah, I came out for a cig.' She wiggled her pack of cigarettes in the air, sighed dramatically. 'Stupid, isn't it, that I work in a hospital and still smoke, but I figure I'll stop when I'm forty, then I'll still have plenty of years of being healthy to even it out.' She offered the packet to Fiona.

Fiona started to shake her head, then stopped. 'Do you know what? I will have one.' She took one, lit it with Becky's lighter, and breathed in deeply. She hardly ever smoked, couldn't actually remember the last time she had, but she enjoyed the light-headedness it brought, and since she couldn't drink any more and drive safely, it seemed like the perfect solution.

They stood in silence for a moment, blowing out puffs of smoke which twirled together in front of them before fading away. Becky leaned back against the pub wall next to Fiona. 'Want to talk about it?' she asked casually, without looking at Fiona.

Fiona glanced sideways at Becky. It was the first time she'd actually offered outright. She stubbed out her cigarette on the wall beside her, dropped it. 'Not really.'

Becky nodded, put out her own cigarette. 'OK.'

And though she said nothing more, Fiona felt her eyes start their stupid incessant stinging. She screwed them up, daring the tears to come. 'It's also OK if you're angry,' Becky said softly.

Fiona's lip trembled when she spoke next. 'Honestly? I don't know how I feel most of the time. One minute I'm feeling one thing, the next minute it's something else entirely. I don't know how to process it, I guess.'

'That's OK, too.'

Fiona rubbed her hands over her face. 'You would've thought I'd have figured it out by now, all the months I've had.'

Becky raised her eyebrows, then laughed, the sound so surprising that it made Fiona start. 'Yeah, you're right,' said Becky. Fiona stared at her, the answer definitely not what she'd been expecting. 'I'd really have expected you to get over it by now – after a couple of weeks, if I'm honest. I mean, it's not *that* bad, is it?' She grinned and for the first time in what found like forever, Fiona felt a real smile in response, the beginnings of a laugh.

'I've barely cried, do you know that? Through the trial . . . I guess it just didn't feel real, and since then, I've had to keep it together for the kids. It all feels like a really bad dream, you know? Like I'm expecting to wake up or something.' She ran a hand through her hair. 'God, that's such a cliché.'

'Use all the clichés you want, mate.' Becky paused. 'I didn't read the news. I don't read the local papers anyway, and I didn't want to hear it all third hand. I just . . . thought you should know.'

Fiona swallowed the lump. 'Thanks.' She knew what Becky was saying – that she was a blank canvas to talk about it, if she wanted to. But she couldn't face it, even then. So instead she sighed sadly. 'I shouldn't have come to this.'

Becky reached out, squeezed her shoulder. 'I'm sorry if you felt like I was making you. I just thought it might be good for you, you know?'

'You're not the only one. Sarah says I should stay, enjoy myself for once.' She raised her phone, waved it in the air as an explanation.

'She sounds like a godsend, that one.'

'She really is. She keeps surprising me, you know? I thought she'd have run a mile, after she found out everything. Further than that. I thought she would've fled the length of the bloody country and never want to speak to me again, but instead she stayed, and she helped. I'm not sure I deserve her.'

'Well, you do. But she's a strong one, I'll give you that.' Becky crossed one leg over the other, seemed to lean even further into the white pub wall. 'I remember being so impressed with how she dealt with everything when Charlie died. Leukaemia, awful way to go.'

She cocked her head. 'You remember?'

'Yeah, I was there, wasn't I? Not on that ward, but around, and of course I took a special interest.' She glanced over meaningfully at Fiona.

'Right. Sorry, that time is all a bit . . . hazy.' Becky just nodded, like that was to be expected. There was no judgement on her face, but Fiona felt the guilt anyway. The guilt that her husband was the one to send Nicola off to meet Charlie in the afterlife. And the guilt that she hadn't been a better person, that she'd let her own petty jealousy stop her from being a friend to Nicola, to help her with what she was going through. Ben had been there for her, consoling her, sharing her grief – his step-brother, her husband. She'd convinced herself that she was doing the right thing, leaving them to it, but really she'd just been protecting herself.

Fiona cleared her throat, tried to stop her thoughts from spiralling. 'We lost Sarah after that for a few months. I mean, we barely saw her, she became so withdrawn. We were all so worried about her.'

'Can you blame her?' Fiona shook her head, but Becky carried on, her words slurring slightly in a way that suggested she was perhaps a little tipsy. 'I mean, not just dealing with her dad dying in that terrible way, but finding out the way she did . . .'

Fiona frowned. 'Finding out?' It was Becky's turn to frown. Fiona pushed away from the pub wall. 'Becks, what do you mean?'

'I thought you knew,' Becky said slowly. She pushed away from the pub wall, too, opened her cigarettes and lit another one. 'Look,' she said, taking a long pull, 'Cynthia told me and you know what she's like, so this could all be wrong. But like I said, I took a special interest because it was your family and well . . . The way I heard it, Sarah offered to be a bone marrow donor for her dad, and wanted to give blood for his blood transfusions.'

Fiona let out a whoosh of breath in relief. 'Right. I knew that – Ben did the same.'

'Right. But it turned out that Sarah couldn't donate, because her blood type was incompatible with Charlie's.'

'God, that's awful – she didn't tell me. She must have felt so powerless.' No wonder Sarah became obsessed with giving blood after that. She was trying to save other people because she hadn't been able to save her dad.

'Well, yeah, I'm sure she did. But the thing is, the reason she couldn't donate was because her blood type is AB, and Charlie's is O.'

For a moment Fiona felt almost like she was suspended in mid-air, waiting for something to sink in, waiting for when she'd crash back down to the ground. 'But that means . . .' But no, she couldn't finish the sentence out loud. Because she already knew, she didn't need Becky to explain it to her. She knew that, with blood types like that, there was no way that Sarah could have been Charlie's daughter. But . . . But when *Sarah* had been given this information, then surely she would have figured that out too. Figured it out over a year before Fiona had told her, before she claimed to be shocked and appalled at the knowledge.

It meant that Sarah had known, all this time, that Charlie wasn't her father.

Chapter Thirty-Four

'I have to leave.' Fiona whipped past Becky. Her mind was reeling, unable to process this new information, unable to figure out what exactly it meant. Sarah had *known*. All this time she'd known, and she'd *lied* about it . . .

'What?' Becky's voice, though right behind her, sounded distant, like she was on a different plain of existence somehow, one where Sarah hadn't lied to her. 'I thought you said you were staying?'

'I have to get back to the girls,' Fiona said, harsher than was fair – after all, this wasn't Becky's fault. Then she realised something, spun back to Becky. 'Why didn't you tell me this earlier?' she demanded. Becky actually took a step back.

'I told you,' she said slowly, with the air of one trying to calm a rabid dog, 'I thought you already knew.'

'I didn't.' Fiona shook her head, aware that she just might look a tad frantic. 'I thought *I* was the one to tell Sarah, and . . .' She pulled both hands through her hair. '*How* could you not have realised that, Becks? The trial . . . the trial was all about how Sarah had only just found out about Ben – that Ben was trying to stop Sarah finding out, so he . . .' But she swallowed down the rest of the words, for the first time not because she couldn't bear to say them, but because there was a seedling of doubt growing inside her. Ben had said just now that he hadn't known Sarah was his daughter. He was still insisting even now, when there was no point in denying it, when his sentence had already been served.

'I didn't follow the trial in the news, Fee,' Becky said, her calm tone faltering, just a little. 'I just said that, remember?'

Fiona shook her head again, not because she didn't believe Becky but because she couldn't process it all fast enough. The picnic benches swarming with people blurred in front of her and she felt like the pavement was tilting sideways underneath her. She blinked to try and clear it, sure that it wasn't the one glass of wine making her feel like this. This didn't necessarily mean anything, she told herself. Becky had said herself that she'd only heard this second-hand – it might not even be true, might be utter nonsense. She should talk to Sarah, give her the chance to deny it. But then, a little voice piped up at the back of her mind, of course Sarah would deny it, if she'd already kept silent, had lied to a jury during a murder trial. She was hardly going to own up to Fiona now, was she?

Fiona swept away from Becky, leaving her to frantically stub out her cigarette, and barged past people in the pub to get to the booth. Grabbing her handbag and ignoring the various people who tried to say something or other to her, she spun on her heel, muttering a faint goodbye to the nearest person. Malcolm, she thought it was. She didn't care in that moment what they thought of her. They'd clearly already made up their minds about her, had only shown up because of fake friendship, some weird social code, or purely to get a good look at her. This would just be a good story for them – the crazy wife of a murderer, bailing on her own leaving party with a panicked look in her eyes, without so much as a goodbye.

Becky caught up with her just inside the front door and scurried after her as Fiona bolted out of the pub and towards her car, fumbling in her handbag for the keys. 'Fee, what's wrong, what am I missing?' Becky pleaded. 'Why has this made you so upset?'

Fiona only pawed around more anxiously in her handbag. Where were her goddamn keys? 'I don't know,' she mumbled, directing her voice to the depths of her bag. 'I don't *know*, but Sarah told me differently and why? Why would she lie to me?'

She hadn't meant it as a genuine question, didn't expect Becky to answer, but she did anyway. 'You mean why wouldn't Sarah have told you Charlie wasn't her dad when she first found out?' How was Becky this calm, Fiona wondered, when the axis of her own world had just been irrevocably altered? She looked up at Becky numbly, nodded. Becky took a breath, and Fiona smelled faint cigarette smoke. For some reason the smell of it, so normal, seemed to calm her racing heart. Perhaps she was overreacting, her emotions weren't exactly on even footing these days. 'Well, I don't know, but maybe she didn't want to upset anyone, not after everything.'

'But she lied under oath, Becks,' Fiona whispered. 'Why would she do that?'

'Maybe she thought it had gone too far, and she couldn't take it back?' Fiona said nothing, and Becky carried on hurriedly. 'Fee, look, I know you've been through a lot, but I'm sure there's a logical explanation for this, OK?'

'Yeah. Maybe.' She looked down into her handbag, felt tears well up. 'I can't find my keys,' she said pathetically. Becky took her handbag from her gently, reached in and produced her keys after a second. Fiona took them silently, staring at them, like somehow they held the answers. Then she snapped back to herself.

She pulled Becky into a quick, tight hug. 'I'll call you later, OK? I need to figure this out. Tell the others bye.'

'Of course, mate. But, look, do call me, OK?' Becky sounded a little nervous, and Fiona really hoped that was on her behalf, rather than because she was worried the others were right about the fact that she really had gone a little crazy.

Fiona scrambled into her car, taking deep, calming breaths as she started the engine. She had to stop this spiralling, had to think objectively. OK, so Sarah had probably known, all this time. God, she was so stupid! Her obsession with giving blood!

She'd made Fiona and Ben go with her once, about eight months ago, to the Bath donor centre, insisted that they, too, should give blood. And they were hardly going to deny it, not when Charlie had just passed away. It was one of Sarah's better days, Fiona remembered – she'd been more talkative, actually seemed to want to be around people for the first time since Charlie's funeral. And Fiona remembered how Sarah had explained to Ben and Fiona about the different blood types. Fiona had thought, at the time, that she was just trying to explain why she couldn't have given blood to Charlie, had needed to talk about it out loud so that she could lessen the guilt she so clearly felt. She'd known, before the nurse had even told them, hadn't she? Had known that Ben's blood type was B, had talked about how Nicola's was type A. Nicola, who hadn't been invited along, for some reason. Fiona remembered the whole day so damn clearly because that was when she'd known with absolute certainty that Sarah was Ben's daughter, had stopped being able to deny what their similar looks, what the timing of the affair had meant. She'd had to go for coffee with the two of them in Bath afterwards, had to watch the two of them sitting next to each other, and wonder how no one had ever noticed before then.

She realised she was currently accelerating straight towards a red light. She took her foot off the pedal. Told herself to stop it. She was overreacting. All this meant was that Sarah had lied about not knowing Ben was her biological father. It didn't prove anything else, didn't necessarily change anything. Because the important thing was that *Ben* hadn't known that Sarah knew – of that she was sure, or as sure as she could be of anything right now. Which meant that he still had a motive for killing Nicola, that hadn't changed. Sarah knowing about Ben didn't change the fact that Ben could have been angry with Nicola for not resuming the affair, or could have wanted to kill her to stop her telling Sarah everything.

The light changed to green and the car jerked forward in first. But what Ben had said about the poison being in her system . . . She felt something cold trickle along the insides of her forearms. He was right – she hadn't ever eaten around the annex, really, had avoided going there as much as possible. She hadn't thought anything of it at the time, too caught up in the hell of the trial, but what Ben had suggested – it made sense. It made more sense that someone deliberately snuck traces of the poison into her food or drink – hers and not Lily or Emily's – than it did for her to have accidentally ingested it at the annex.

She looked at the car clock. Thirty minutes. Never had the journey home felt quite so long.

Could the jury, the detectives have been wrong? Was there a chance that Ben really *was* innocent? Maybe they should have hired a better lawyer. One not quite as inexperienced. She didn't know now why they'd gone for him, just that his enthusiasm had seemed like a good idea at the time. And, if she was honest, she hadn't been paying enough attention. She hadn't truly believed Ben was innocent, hadn't believed he'd deserved the best lawyer available. But what if Ben really had just believed the lawyer when he said that the best thing to do was to plead manslaughter? What if he'd been so panicked about it all, that he'd thought he'd had no choice? And there she'd been, letting her doubts get the better of her so that she stopped seeing things clearly, stopped trying to help.

The tea leaves. She remembered the court case – wasn't there something about the tea leaves? She'd been barely in the room while Ben was being cross-examined, had shown up only because the lawyer told her to. But they'd said that it was easier to poison Nicola because of the tea leaves, hadn't they? And it was Sarah, *Sarah* who had suggested they'd made the switch, wasn't it?

Come on, she urged the car as it made it up to 80 mph.

Was she seriously considering that Sarah had killed her own mother? Sarah, who had been such a rock for her through all this, who had sat with her own children, played with them, looked after them. Sarah, who had been so angry with Ben, had sat through his trial glaring at him, so pure in her anger towards him. Sarah, who had loved her father, beyond all else, who hadn't spoken to her mother for months after his death, had been eaten away by guilt and rage at first, for not being able to save Charlie.

No. No, surely not. She didn't have any evidence to suggest that could be true, and the detectives – the detectives had interviewed her, along with the rest of them. Surely they would have noticed if something was up. Even if . . . even if Sarah had become more interested in the garden since her dad died. Had been the perfect student, keen to learn as much as possible about all the different plants.

No. There had to be a logical explanation for this, for why Sarah would lie, would pretend she hadn't known.

Maybe she had thought that if she'd said anything, it would have lessened the chance of Ben being convicted – and if Sarah had thought that Ben was the one who killed her mother then she wouldn't have wanted that, would have done anything to make sure he went to prison. She was a determined girl, after all, and was known to stick her heels in. Yes, Fiona could see Sarah thinking like that.

She tried to push the car faster but it groaned at her. She had to get home, had to.

But to do what? To confront Sarah?

No. She was going to go home and have a calm, reasonable conversation with her niece, with Lily and Emily's sister. That was all. There was a logical explanation for this, just like Becky said. There had to be.

Extract from Court Transcript, dated 07/04/19

Appearances:
SG - Sarah Elizabeth Gregory
LJ - Laura Jenkins, prosecution
TB - Thomas Barrett, defence

LJ   Ms Gregory, you didn't know until recently that Benjamin is your biological father, is that right?

SG   Yes, that's correct. I only found out when Fiona told me a few months ago. I still can't really believe it. I can't believe they never told me, all these years. It's . . . well. I was still coming to terms with the fact that . . . this . . . had happened to my mother, that I'm now an orphan and now it turns out I'm, well, not, I suppose.

LJ   I wonder - do you know if Ben knew that he was your father?

SG   I've since spoken to him and yes, he knew, whatever he is saying in court. He knew and he never said anything.

LJ   Why do you think that is?

SG   Well, I don't know. He said it's
       because my mum didn't want to tell me,
       and he was respecting her wishes. I
       didn't want to ask him more. I didn't
       want to talk to him at all, after what
       he's done. But . . .

LJ   But?

SG   But I don't think it can be true. My
       dad . . . my real dad, it would have
       broken his heart to find this out,
       just like it's broken mine, but after
       he . . . after he died, then my mum
       didn't have a reason to keep it a
       secret anymore. Ben did, though - he
       didn't know Fiona knew, Fiona never
       told him that she'd figured it out.

LJ   So you think Ben was the one who
       wanted to keep it a secret?

SG   Yes. I think he didn't want my mother
       to tell me, but she tried to anyway.
       And then, God, and then the bastard
       killed her. God, I'm sorry, I don't—

LJ   That's OK, take your time. So, Ms
       Gregory, just for clarification - you
       say that your mother tried to tell you
       about it. Am I right in saying that

you think the voicemail your mother
left on your phone the night she died
- when she told you she had to tell
you something - was about the relationship between her and Ben?

TB Your lordship, my friend here seems to
be suggesting that the witness knows
exactly what the voicemail in question pertains to, which obviously can't
possibly be the case.

JUDGE Yes, Miss James, could we—

SG Yes. To be clear, I think that my
mother was leaving me that message
because she wanted to tell me that Ben
was really my father. And I think Ben
overheard that.

JUDGE Ms Gregory, if I could ask you to
stick to answering direct questions,
please.

SG I'm sorry. I just . . . I want to
be very clear on this - I think the
police have the right person here. I
think Ben was the one who killed my
mother. Whether that's because he was
resentful about her not wanting to
start the affair again, or whether he
wanted to shut her up, to stop me from
finding out the truth - I don't know.

But I know one thing – Ben tore my
family apart, he took everything that
matters most from me. He deserves to
rot in jail for what he did.

Chapter Thirty-Five

Fiona let herself into the house as quietly as she could, barely daring to breathe as the front door clicked shut behind her. Nonsense. This was utter nonsense, creeping into her own home. She was being ridiculous. But telling herself that didn't stop her heart from beating faster than was comfortable, didn't stop the adrenaline that was coursing through her, making each movement feel jittery.

The house was silent and she felt something hot shoot through her, immediately imagining the worst. She sprinted to the kitchen, barely daring to think. Then let out an enormous breath. They were there, playing in the garden. Lily and Emily laughing as Sarah chased them, pretending to be the monster. She was at her most exuberant, Sarah, when she played with the girls. The gate to her and Ben's special part of the garden, which she hadn't been able to go into since he'd been arrested, was open. Her fingers went into a little spasm at her side but she didn't move to open the back door, didn't let herself dwell too much on that. Not yet.

Instead she went upstairs, her breathing coming too quickly. But Sarah wouldn't hurt the girls. No. She'd had plenty of chances – if she'd wanted to, she would have done it already. Fiona was just being ridiculous, paranoid. Having your sister-in-law murdered by your husband would do that to you. She'd rushed home with no real plan and now, in the bright light, surrounded by all her possessions, that felt stupid.

She let herself into the spare room which was currently acting as Sarah's second room, for when she wasn't staying overnight at her own flat. Fiona glanced around, twisting her hands nervously in front of her. This may only be Sarah's part-home, but she'd made it her own – flowers on the windowsill, a jewellery box on her bedside table. And photos. Photos in frames dotted around the room, all of Sarah and her dad. A few of her flatmate. But none of Nicola. She'd noticed that before, in a vague sort of way, but it had never worried her. She'd thought the pain must be too fresh for Sarah, or that maybe she had photos of her mum at her own flat, away from Fiona. After all, Sarah wouldn't want to remind Fiona of what her husband had done, would she?

But now, it felt sinister. All these photos of Charlie, none of Nicola, like Sarah was pretending she'd never even had a mother.

Fiona walked round, looking at each photo individually. She'd never thought of Sarah as capable of killing her mother. Why would she – she had no motive. But did the fact that she'd known Ben was her father give her one? Sarah had loved her dad, more than anything, it had been almost unbearable to watch her when he was ill – trying to find a way to save him, refusing to give up with the fierce determination that was so characteristic. Her grief at losing him was terrible – no one had been able to get through to her, to help her. Especially not Nicola.

Fiona tried to imagine how Sarah would have felt, finding out about her biological father that way. Admittedly, even if she had been his biological daughter, she still might not have been a match, but Fiona could imagine Sarah's take on it, fuelled by grief. Could imagine thinking that the only reason she was unable to help Charlie was because of a lie her mother had told her for her whole life. She must have been angry, for sure. Might have even hated Nicola in that moment for not telling her. And she'd seen Sarah when she decided something was wrong, seen how unmoveable she could be on it. She judged people harshly at times, Fiona knew that, yet she'd never thought it was anything worse than having slightly too high standards.

No. It was unthinkable. Unthinkable that a daughter could kill her mother like that.

And yet . . .

Fiona allowed herself to consider it. All the evidence against Ben, and Ben's insistence, throughout the whole trial, that he didn't understand any of it. The book on poisonous plants – Sarah could have put it there at any point, couldn't she? And the day Ben was arrested . . . Sarah had brought them books that day, had insisted on putting them on the bookshelf. Ben's phone – she could have easily borrowed it. Hadn't Ben told her that Sarah had used his phone to ring the doctor, had told them all that the doctor said it was nothing to worry about? And the gardening . . . Sarah had wanted to learn, had needed the distraction. Fiona frowned as she thought about the deadly nightshade. Hadn't Sarah liked those plants, suggested they might look good in the garden? Or was that just Fiona's hazy mind, trying to make it all fit together?

One thing was for sure, though – Sarah had had just as much access to Nicola's food and drink as Ben had. She'd been hanging around the house earlier on the day she died – could she have slipped something into Nicola's tea then? She wasn't there at the time of death, but that could just be because she'd made sure *not* to be, so as to make herself less likely to be a suspect.

And she'd been ever so sure that Nicola had been murdered, even before the police had said anything. Why?

Had she been so sure because *she* was the one who killed her? Because she wanted not just her mother, but also Ben, to pay?

She walked back downstairs in a daze. Surely not, surely this couldn't be happening.

This time, when she went into the kitchen, she opened the back door, stepped out into the garden. The light was fading now, night-time shadows creeping into the garden, obscuring patches of it even from her, who knew it so well. It was once her saviour, this garden, a place for her to take a break from whatever was bothering her. The flowers used to hum to her, comforting her. But now the purple and white clematis, the pink hebes, the green of the berberis just before it flowered – all of them taunted her as they began their lives once more. All of them seemed to look at her knowingly, as if to say they'd known what was happening, what one of their sisters was being used for, and she should have known, too.

Lily and Emily noticed her first and ran over to her in excitement for a fleeting hug, only to dart back to Sarah again, intent on their game. Sarah pushed her hair away from her slightly flushed face. 'You're back early,' she said with a smile. She rested one hand on Emily's shoulder, the picture of a doting older sister, playing with her younger siblings before bedtime. But it was wrong. Fiona felt that, her body reacting instinctively. She needed to get the girls away from her.

The smile dropped off Sarah's face. 'What's wrong?'

'Nothing.' Fiona forced a bright smile, hoped her face didn't betray her. 'Nothing, sorry. It's just – isn't it nearly bedtime?' She raised her eyebrows at her daughters so she didn't have to keep looking at Sarah, who was now cocking her head, like she knew something wasn't right.

'Sarah said we could stay up,' said Emily with a wicked grin, knowing full well she was playing the adults off against one another.

Sarah flashed Fiona a grin. 'Sorry – guilty.'

'We were helping in the garden,' said Lily earnestly.

'Were you?' It was an effort to keep her voice normal, to force the reaction Lily was expecting. 'That's good, my darling. And were you having fun?' Lily nodded vigorously.

'Sorry, I can get them to bed now, if you want?' Sarah asked, ignoring Emily, who was tugging on her arm. Fiona's skin began to tingle, watching them.

'No,' Fiona said on a whooshing breath. 'It's OK, finish up the game or whatever – they can have a couple of minutes, then I'll put them to bed.' She didn't want to make a scene, needed time to think, to process.

'I'll get the watering can!' Emily announced, and set off down the garden to where it was discarded under one of the pear trees. Lily, of course, followed.

Fiona cleared her throat once the two of them were out of immediate earshot. 'I – I went to Nicola and Charlie's graves today.' Her voice was little more than a whisper.

Sarah raised her eyebrows. 'Oh?' Was it what she expected to see, or did Sarah's expression harden, just a bit?

'I took some fresh flowers there,' Fiona said slowly, watching Sarah intently. 'Thought it would be nice as we're leaving, you know.'

Sarah flicked her long hair back behind her shoulder. 'Yes, I've been meaning to do that, actually. I haven't taken flowers to Mum's grave in too long.'

Fiona felt a jolt run though her. 'There were some old white lilies there, though,' she said, trying to stay casual.

'Yeah. I took them a while back. Like I said, I need to get up there more often, but you know how it is . . .'

'I do indeed,' Fiona said softly. Sarah shrugged, smiling a little, and turned towards where Lily and Emily were now calling her name. 'But didn't Nicola hate white flowers? I thought she said they reminded her of death, or illness or something.'

Sarah glanced over her shoulder at Fiona. 'Oh, did she? I didn't know that.' She said it so casually, but it couldn't be right – she had to have known.

Every nerve in Fiona's body tingled with warning as Sarah walked over to Lily and Emily. The girls shot off, no doubt still intent on their game, checking behind them to see if Sarah was following. They shot right through the gate to the wild side of the garden, Sarah now jogging behind. Fiona followed numbly, but burst into a run when she saw where Emily had stopped.

'What are you doing?' she shouted, ready to pounce on Sarah, to tear her daughters away from her. Sarah looked back at Fiona, seeming genuinely alarmed.

'We're helping,' Emily said proudly, picking up a discarded plastic spade from the ground, one that was part of a beach set.

'It's dangerous,' Lily said, nodding, collecting her own yellow spade from beneath a mound of dirt.

'Sarah said we don't need it anymore,' Emily finished.

All Fiona could do was stare, the world ringing around her, her daughters' mindless chatter lost in the abyss between them, as Emily and Lily dug their plastic spades into the ground around the belladonna. As Sarah picked up her own spade, shoved her foot on it and made the final blow, tearing the roots away from the earth. The tall plant fell with a gentle thud on the ground next to Sarah.

And Sarah looked across at Fiona, over the heads of her two half-sisters, and smiled.

Acknowledgements

Any credit I deserve for writing this book should be equally split with my amazingly talented editor and friend, Katie Brown, without whom this book would quite literally not exist. She has been a force of nature throughout the whole process, from that very first evening drinking far too much wine, through patiently helping me reshape the book into a far, far better beast, and continuing to be incredibly supportive after the fact. This book is as much her achievement as it is mine, and I'm very grateful to her for helping me to become a published author. Katie, you are a Queen.

Becky Short also deserves credit/blame for this book becoming a reality – it was her suggestion of afterwork drinks one evening that led to the conversation that would eventually become *Bad Seed* – she is proof that drinking is never a bad idea and this is another reason I'll be forever thankful to have her as a friend.

Enormous thanks and love to Anna Davis and the CBC cohort of 2015 – Ella Dove, Catherine Jarvine, Sean Lusk, Ben Walker, Jo Cunningham, Lynsey Urquhart, Sarah Shannon, Charlotte Northedge, Robert Holtom, Bill Macmillan, Victoria Halliday, Ahsan Akbar, Georgina Parfitt and Paris Christofferson. You are all amazing and supportive, got excited about this book without knowing anything about it and have always refused to let me downplay it. I can't wait to celebrate the other thirteen publishing deals one day.

Huge thanks to Erin Kelly, whose invaluable feedback on a completely different novel gave me the advice and encouragement I needed to continue writing, as well as making me a better writer in the process. Not only that, but a week's summer school with Erin made me come away motivated to continue writing, despite the rejections, and to keep improving. Thank you.

They say not to judge a book by its cover but I really hope everyone does – thanks to enormously talented Emma Rogers for creating an absolutely gorgeous package – you are a legend and I have no doubt more people will pick up this book because of you.

I know first-hand that it takes a whole team of people to publish a book. Thanks to Kate Moreton for championing the book and putting up with my rambling emails, as well as Lucy Cameron, Lucinda McNeile, Amber Bates, Anne Goddard and Claire Keep – thanks for all your work behind the scenes.

Research is such an important part of any book – thanks to Elle Selby for putting up with my potentially idiotic questions about how the police force works and for answering with patience and enthusiasm.

So many friends have helped me along the way, convincing me not to give up on writing, no matter how long it takes. Special thanks to Vix Franks, Rosie Shelmerdine, Laura Webster, Naomi Mantin, Emily Stock for at some stage reading one or many previous incarnations of novels as well as Lucy Hunt for utting up with forced novel brainstorming sessions while we were housemates.

Thanks to two amazing bosses – Alison Barrow and Georgina Moore – legends of the publishing industry but also hugely encouraging of my ambition to be an author from the word go.

And finally, it might a cliché to mention family, but thanks to my sisters, Sophie, Jenny and Sally for being great (and for offering to buy the book once it's published), and especially to my wonderful father, Ian Hunter, who has lent me money to go on writing courses despite his better judgement, dealt with the hysterics of yet another rejection, and generally put up with me saying I was going to be an author for the last nine years, despite there being no concrete proof of that whatsoever – until now.

Credits

Trapeze would like to thank everyone at Orion who worked on the publication of *Bad Seed*.

Editor
Katie Brown

Copy-editor
Jon Appleton

Proofreader
Loma Halden

Editorial Management
Lucinda McNeile
Charlie Panayiotou
Jane Hughes
Alice Davis
Claire Boyle
Jeannelle Brew

Audio
Paul Stark
Amber Bates

Contracts
Anne Goddard
Paul Bulos
Jake Alderson

Design
Lucie Stericker
Joanna Ridley
Nick May
Clare Sivell
Helen Ewing
Emma Rogers

Finance
Jennifer Muchan
Jasdip Nandra
Afeera Ahmed
Elizabeth Beaumont
Sue Baker
Victor Falola

Marketing
Tom Noble
Lucy Cameron

Production
Claire Keep
Fiona McIntosh

Publicity
Kate Moreton

Sales
Jen Wilson
Victoria Laws
Esther Waters
Frances Doyle
Ben Goddard
Georgina Cutler
Jack Hallam
Ellie Kyrke-Smith
Inês Figuiera
Barbara Ronan
Andrew Hally
Dominic Smith
Deborah Deyong
Lauren Buck
Maggy Park
Linda McGregor
Sinead White
Jemimah James
Rachel Jones
Jack Dennison

Nigel Andrews
Ian Williamson
Julia Benson
Declan Kyle
Robert Mackenzie
Sinead White
Imogen Clarke
Megan Smith
Charlotte Clay
Rebecca Cobbold

Operations
Jo Jacobs
Sharon Willis
Lisa Pryde
Lucy Brem

Rights
Susan Howe
Richard King
Krystyna Kujawinska
Jessica Purdue
Louise Henderson